UNRAVELING AN ENIGMA

BOOK TWO IN THE ENIGMA SERIES

SHANDI BOYES

COPYRIGHT

Cover: SSB Covers and Design
Photographer: Lindee Robinson Photography
Models: David Turner & Alyse Madej

Some photo edits were made to the photograph.
Join my Facebook page for updates on the books I'm
working on.
www.facebook.com/authorshandi

I Married a Mob Boss *

Second Shot *

The Way We Are

The Way We Were

Sugar and Spice *

Lady In Waiting

Man in Queue

Couple on Hold

Enigma: The Wedding

Silent Vigilante

Hushed Guardian

Quiet Protector

Enigma: An Isaac Retelling

Twisted Lies *

Bound Series

Chains

Links

Bound

Restrain

The Misfits *

Nanny Dispute *

Russian Mob Chronicles

Nikolai: A Mafia Prince Romance

Nikolai: Taking Back What's Mine

Nikolai: What's Left of Me

Nikolai: Mine to Protect

Asher: My Russian Revenge *

Nikolai: Through the Devil's Eyes

Trey *

The Italian Cartel

Dimitri

Roxanne

Reign

Mafia Ties (Novella)

Maddox

Demi

Ox

Rocco *

Clover *

Smith *

RomCom Standalones

Just Playin' *

Ain't Happenin' *

The Drop Zone *

Very Unlikely *

False Start *

Short Stories - Newsletter Downloads

Christmas Trio *

Falling For A Stranger *

One Night Only Series

Hotshot Boss *

Hotshot Neighbor *

The Bobrov Bratva Series

Wicked Intentions *

Sinful Intentions *

Devious Intentions *

Deadly Intentions *

Coming Soon

Nanny Dispute *

Protecting Nicole (December 26) *

WANT TO STAY IN TOUCH?

Facebook: facebook.com/authorshandi

Instagram: instagram.com/authorshandi

Email: authorshandi@gmail.com

Reader's Group: bit.ly/ShandiBookBabes

Website: authorshandi.com

Newsletter: https://www.subscribepage.com/AuthorShandi

DEDICATION

All the fans of Isaac and Izzy.
Thank you for your messages of support.
I hope you enjoy Unraveling an Enigma.

1

ISAAC

"How much longer do they expect me to wait?"

I glare into the police officer's dark eyes that are gawking at me with a hint of infatuation. He's so young, he looks fresh out of the academy. Even his uniform still has the crinkles from where it was folded after manufacturing.

"They either charge me or let me go." I turn my gaze to the camera hanging in the corner of the room. "My patience is stretched thin."

Although I've been remanded at the Ravenshoe Police Department for the past two hours, I've yet to be informed of the fabricated charges they're attempting to pin on me. Other than being handed a two-page report on my rights while in custody, I haven't had any contact with the agents who arrested me—including Isabelle.

After throwing down the documents the rookie officer handed me onto the desk I'm sitting behind, I run my hand over my head. It freezes halfway when the agent who read me my rights enters the room. When he tilts his head to the side, his smirk arrogant, I ball my hands, fighting not to wipe the pretentious look off his face with my fists. This isn't a game. It's never been a game to me.

His arrogance falters when my gray eyes land on his. He clears his throat with an annoying cough that echoes in the silence teeming between us, no doubt to ensure fear isn't heard in his voice. He doesn't need to speak for me to know he's scared. His whole stance gives it away. His slumped shoulders, twitching thighs, and the skittish gleam in his eyes are all I need to see to know he's scared. Rightfully so, he should be.

"I can remand you for two days without charge if I so wish." I'm impressed when his words only come out with the smallest quiver. "So, I suggest you get comfortable, Mr. Holt." This time, his voice gains an edge of arrogance.

When I stand, his eyes follow me. I'm not big. I'm average height for a guy, just over six feet tall, and I'm not bulked with muscles like my fighters, but it isn't my size that has men quaking in their boots. It's my reputation. A reputation that took me years to build, and one I plan to keep no matter how ruthless it makes me seem. This isn't just my business, it is my life—it's what I live for. I fought my way to where I am, and I'll fight to keep it. Nothing has diverted my attention from my goals and aspirations the past five years. Nothing at all, until I saw her.

This will sound conceited, but I've grown accustomed to the vicious ploys women use to get my attention. The spilled drinks, the damsel in distress. Hell, I've even been offered money from wealthy business associates just for the chance to occupy my bed. However, Isabelle was by far the most elaborate ruse I've ever come across. I'll give it to her, she performed well. She played me like a fucking fiddle.

The instant my eyes landed on her sprawled at my feet, I knew she'd be my eternal weakness. For years, I've never looked at women without comparing their qualities to Ophelia's. That didn't happen when I appraised Isabelle's striking features. I only saw her—her big, beautiful chocolate eyes, her pouty cupid's bow lip, and the most seductive body I'd ever seen.

If she hadn't been on her period, I would have claimed her in that washroom thirty thousand feet in the air. Alas, it seemed more than womanly issues were between us. I'm usually more vigilant with the people I permit into my life. Exercising control has ensured my empire's success the past seven years, but one look into Isabelle's eyes had me forgoing all lucid thoughts. She had me acting as if I were a college boy enjoying the thrill of the chase.

I had never been that way before—not even with Ophelia. It truly shocked me, so much so, for the six weeks following Isabelle's sleepover at my apartment, I kept my focus solely on my empire. My ploy was working. Isabelle only slipped into my thoughts three to four times a day instead of the standard eight. I had everything under control—until she kissed me.

Our kiss was unlike anything I had ever experienced. It catapulted my obsession with her to a never-before-reached level. From then on, every move I made was strategically planned to get her into my bed. The cupcakes order, her apartment, even Cormack's long weekend away—that was all me, an intricate ruse to make Isabelle mine. My bed. My house. My rules. *Mine.*

When my ruse worked, I thought I had won the ultimate prize. I had Isabelle. She was mine—then it all came tumbling down. Only now, after being arrested by her, do I realize my assumptions were terribly inaccurate. I don't know Isabelle at all. She's practically a stranger.

Or she'll soon become one.

2

ISABELLE

"Jeez, do you think there's enough oxygen in the room to sustain both of those personalities?"

I stop pacing in the observation chamber attached to the interrogation room to stray my frightened eyes to Brandon. His brows are drawn together so tightly, a 'V' is in the middle of his forehead. When he notices my confused gaze, he nudges his head to a once-frosted window. It's no longer frosted. It's clear enough to unearth the heart-stuttering image of Isaac and Alex undertaking a sweat-producing stare-down. They're being kept apart by the stainless-steel table Isaac has been sitting behind the past two hours.

Isaac's handsome face is scoured with anger, but his impressive stature still bounces off him in invisible waves. Alex's stance is just as rigid as Isaac's. His blue eyes are narrowed, and his twitching top lip is noticeable from a distance.

When Brandon fiddles with some knobs on the sidewall, Isaac's profound voice rumbles into the observation room, sparking an excited shiver to zap down my spine. "You have ten minutes to issue your findings before I walk out of this room and head straight to my lawyer to commence my own proceedings."

"You won't be walking out that door in years, let alone minutes."

Queasiness hits my stomach, my body incapable of ignoring the viciousness in Alex's tone. I'm the only one bothered by his comment. Isaac smirks, unaffected by the underlying threat in his tone.

After retaking his seat, Isaac taps the face of the platinum Rolex circling his wrist. "Tick tock."

Alex's nostrils flare as the spasm in his lip moves to his jaw. "I strongly suggest you take my advice and call a lawyer, Mr. Holt."

Isaac scrubs his jaw, highlighting its magnificent cut. "I was once told only people with something to hide need a lawyer."

When his eyes flick to his right, air hitches halfway to my lungs. He appears to be staring right at me. "I thought this was a two-way mirror?"

"It is." Brandon sounds as shocked as me.

Through trembling thighs, I move to the furthest corner of the room. My pulse triples when Isaac's commanding gray eyes track me. Even the tense circumstances can't stop me from smiling. I love that he can sense my presence as strongly as I detect his. It proves what I've always known—we were made for one another.

"That's freaky." Brandon's massively dilated eyes bounce between Isaac and me. "What's the deal with you two—"

Before his interrogative question can escape his lips, we're interrupted by Alex. He storms into the room with his hands clenched into tight balls. The twitch of his top lip is more noticeable now he's standing before me. I swallow bleakly, eradicating the lump in my throat when his knee-quaking eyes snap up from the polished concrete floor. "Brandon, I need that envelope—"

"Here." Brandon shoves the yellow envelope he's been clutching the past hour into his chest.

As he yanks out the envelope's contents, the anger on Alex's face switches to conniving. He smiles a full-toothed grin, appearing to have the world at his feet. After appraising each photo, he locks his eyes with mine. They have a gleam behind them, one I don't know how to explain. Winking, he jerks his chin to the door he stormed through only seconds ago. "Follow me."

I touch my chest. "Me?"

He doesn't reply. He just strides out of the room even quicker than he arrived. I shadow him, my steps reluctant and shaky. When he stops outside the closed interrogation room door, I shake my head, advising him I can't go in there. His request won't just cause a conflict of interest, my heart also won't survive the carnage.

Ignoring my silent pledge, Alex swings open the door. "Remain quiet and follow my lead."

"You have two minutes remaining, so you better make this quick—"

Isaac stops goading Alex when he notices me entering the room on his heel. The amused twinkle in his eyes morphs to irate as his jaw gains a quiver. I can barely contain my breaths when he suddenly stands. He stares down at me with his pulse beeping in his neck and his hands shoved into his pockets. Although his dominance can't be denied, the man standing across from me isn't the man who made love to me this morning. He's the strikingly handsome shell of Isaac Holt, but he isn't the Isaac I fell in love with.

This is the first time I've seen him since his arrest. For the past two hours, I've been endeavoring to pry information from the agents surrounding me. It did me no good. They're just as baffled by his arrest as me. None of them had any useful information. I shouldn't be surprised. I've been a part of Alex's team the past six months, and I've yet to discover one shred of information that corroborates Isaac is the man his FBI file portrays him to be. Nothing he's done the past six months warrants his arrest. If anything, he should be commended. He does more good for the residents of Ravenshoe than bad.

My thoughts are interrupted by Alex's deep timbre. "Sit down." He glares at Isaac, his stance strengthening as he fights to show Isaac he isn't intimidated by him.

He isn't fooling anyone.

After shifting his head to the side, Isaac inhales a giant whiff through his nostrils. "Can you smell that?" His voice is so rugged, it hits every one of my hot buttons. "That's the smell of fear, baby."

He strays his eyes back to Alex before doing another undignified sniff. When the most wickedly evil smile hardens his features, my panties become moist. There must be something wrong with me. Isaac is clearly angry, but instead of my body shuddering in fear, it's quaking with excitement.

"The only person who should be afraid is you, Mr. Holt." Alex slides the envelope Brandon handed him earlier across the table. "Especially when you discover what I have hiding up my sleeve."

Isaac's eyes drop to the envelope. He peers at it for a mere second before devoting his attention back to Alex. "Your ten minutes are up."

When he commences placing on his suit jacket, Alex stares at him in shock, flabbergasted by his calm demeanor. Once he has the three buttons secured, his eyes lift to mine. His gaze is captivating, yet fear-provoking. I'm not scared. I'm just petrified by what he says next. "It was a pleasure meeting you, Isabelle." It's so formal like today was our first and *only* meeting.

The undeniable connection teeming between Isaac and me doesn't render Alex speechless like me. "Aren't you the least bit curious as to what evidence I have on you?"

Isaac's lips crimp before he shakes his head. "You don't have any evidence on me as I always ensure my hands are thoroughly cleaned."

Even though Alex only groans for a nanosecond, it's long enough for Isaac to hear. He smiles, the twist of his lips cruel. When he heads for the door I'm standing next to, instinctively, my hand shoots out to seize his wrist. I have no clue what I'm planning to say. I just know I can't let him go without saying something.

Before a syllable can escape my lips, I'm interrupted by Alex. "I strongly suggest you don't leave town, Mr. Holt."

Anger beams out of Isaac, however, it has nothing on the hurt in his tone when he replies, "This is my town. If anyone is leaving, it won't be me."

With that, he exits the interrogation room, not once glancing back at me.

3

ISABELLE

Goosebumps form on my neck when a frigid breeze blasts through my jacket. After adjusting my satchel, I continue weaving through the dense foot traffic. Although the torrential downpour has thinned the usually jam-packed sidewalks, there are still a lot of people scampering by. Most, unlike me, packed an umbrella when rain was forecast this morning. Since my morning was spent in an Isaac Holt lust phase, the weather was the last thing on my mind when I left my apartment.

Mere hours ago, Hugo advised me to wait under the awning of my building if it was raining. So much has happened since then. It honestly feels as if weeks have passed, not hours. When Isaac left without any formal charges being pressed, Alex was furious. He was the maddest I'd ever seen him. Although his anger was off-putting, nothing could leash my curiosity on discovering what was in the envelope. Alex was convinced he had a credible reason to arrest Isaac, and the evidence he had was sitting mere inches from me. The temptation was too great. I had to sneak a peek.

The envelope was barely in my hot little hand for a second before Alex snatched it from my grasp, then stormed out of the interrogation room. With tension high, I spent the afternoon hiding in the supply closet. None of my fellow agents uttered a word to me, but their questioning looks were enough to have me laying low.

Although my career should have been at the forefront of my mind, it wasn't. Isaac was. I tried his cell numerous times the past two hours. All attempts to reach him were thwarted. My calls went straight to voicemail, and my text messages were unanswered.

Apparently delusional, I waited under the awning for Hugo for thirty minutes this evening before the fog in my head cleared. I'd become so accustomed to him collecting me every night, it became the norm, so it took longer than I'd care to admit for me to register that he'd no longer be picking me up.

By the time I walk into my apartment building, I'm soaking wet from the tips of my hair to my nearly snap-frozen toes. I'm beyond freezing, but it's nothing compared to the iciness surrounding my heart. In some ways, the downpour was a godsend. The people rushing past me to enjoy their weekend were unaware not all the dampness on my cheeks was rain. I held back my tears for as long as I could, but now that they're flowing, I'll have no chance in hell of reeling them back in.

A fresh batch of tears stings my eyes when I stagger through the front door of my apartment. A man with an aura like Isaac permeates the air, clinging to the environment hours after he's left. I can still smell him throughout my apartment.

My hurried strides to the bathroom stop when I spot the rumpled sheets on my bed. Only twelve hours ago, I was in that bed telling Isaac I loved him. I do love him. I love him more than words will ever explain. That's why I have to make this right. He needs to know I didn't do anything wrong, and that I'll support him through this.

I rush into the bathroom to take one of the quickest showers I've ever had. When the scorching hot water hits my toes, they burn from the sudden change in temperature. Once I'm donning a fresh set of clothes and dry shoes, I sprint out of my apartment, grabbing my umbrella from the entryway closet on the way by. Because it's a Friday night, it takes a lot longer than usual to wrangle a cab.

By the time the taxi pulls into the driveway at Isaac's private residence, it's a little after nine o'clock.

"Thank you." I hand the driver my credit card to pay the exorbitant fare.

Once he drives away, I jab my shaky finger into the intercom button on the wrought iron security box. Several long, tedious minutes pass with my call remaining unanswered. Assuming Isaac isn't home, I head back to the road while yanking my cell out of my pocket. If I'd been thinking straight, I would've asked the cab driver to wait. Alas, my mind is nothing but a blurred mess of confusion tonight.

ANOTHER TWENTY MINUTES pass before headlights beam down the eerily black, isolated road. While sheltering my eyes from the blinding light, I pace toward the vehicle that has come to a stop at the entrance of the driveway. My quick strides halt when I realize it's Isaac's black Mercedes-Benz town car, not the taxi I was expecting.

Seconds feel like minutes when the driver's side window slowly glides down. My normal heart rhythm returns when Hugo's apprehensive eyes peek past the tint. "It's not a good time, Izzy."

"I know, but I need to see him." My voice is barely a whisper since it's full of shame. "I have to explain—"

"You have a lot of explaining to do, but believe me, now is *not* the time."

I take a step back, shocked. This is the first time Hugo has been anything but friendly. Although his angry tone stabs my heart with fresh wounds, nothing can leash my campaign. "Please, Hugo. I'll get down on my hands and knees if I have to."

I'll do anything to see Isaac again, to articulate my side of the story. Once Isaac realizes I was defending him, he might be open to the possibility of forgiving me. "I never meant to hurt him. That was never my intention. I love him, Hugo."

Hugo exhales harshly while scrubbing the scruff on his chin. After taking in my watering, pleading eyes, he punches the security code into the black box with force. My heart drums my ribcage more with every creak the gate makes as it slowly opens.

Once the gate is opened, Hugo leans over to open the front

passenger door. With my heart in my throat, I slide into his car without a peep oozing from my lips. The driveway leading to Isaac's private property has always been impressive, but it feels so much longer when awkward tension is firing in the air. Although Hugo doesn't say anything, the unease bouncing off him is disgusting. It stifles the air of oxygen, making not just my insides a mucky mess but my skin as well.

When we come to a stop outside the front stairs, I curl my hand around the door latch. I'm just about to fling open my door when Hugo hits the central locking button, trapping me in the car. With furrowed brows, my eyes stray to him. Now is not the time for jokes.

I realize I have the situation all wrong when he asks, "Are you carrying a weapon?"

"No." I shake my head. "I'd never... I don't... I'm not here officially."

I'd never come to Isaac's house on work-related matters. I'm only here for personal reasons.

"I was asking for safety reasons, Izzy." Hugo's voice is raspy and jam-packed with emotion. "I've never seen Isaac like this before. I honestly don't know how he'll react when he sees you."

I grit my teeth, battling not to sob. I hate that they did this to him—*I did this to him.*

I'm still lost as to everything that is happening, so I can imagine how bewildered Isaac is. It feels like I'm trapped in a horrible nightmare. I'd give anything to wake up and start this day anew. My rendition of Groundhog Day would be perfect right now.

After reading the truth from my eyes, Hugo unlocks the doors. I suck in a big breath to calm the nerves fluttering in my stomach before clambering out of the car and climbing the stairs of Isaac's residence.

My eyes snap to Hugo when we break through the large glass door. Torn cushions, ripped paintings, upended furniture, and broken ornaments cover nearly every surface from the entryway and living room. "What happened?"

Hugo joins me at the side of the trashed living room. "The two hours they had Isaac in the interrogation room, they did an in-depth search of his property." He shakes his head, his cheeks reddening. "No room was left untouched."

The photographs that once adorned Isaac's mantel are scattered on the floor along with shattered glass, the frames broken from being handled so roughly. The insides of the sofa cushions have been yanked out, leaving white fluff strewn over the beautiful woolen rug Isaac made love to me on. Not even his expensive white leather sofas were spared. They have knife gashes down the middle of them, reducing them to trash instead of the priceless antiques they once were.

Noticing the direction of my gaze, Hugo murmurs, "You never know what someone might be hiding inside a couch."

I pace out of the living room when a light switching on down the hallway attracts my attention. My heart beats triple-time when I walk the hallway Isaac has carried me down many times the past month. Every step I take adds to the queasiness swirling in my stomach. The beautiful paintings that once graced the walls have been removed. Some are untouched. Others are so severely damaged, they're beyond repair.

When I round the corner, I halt, my heart squeezing. Isaac is in his office. He's still wearing the suit he was arrested in, but he's removed his jacket, vest, and tie, and his crisp blue business shirt is rolled up to his elbows. I can only see the glass of whiskey in his hand since he's facing the window that overlooks the manicured gardens below. His stature still commands attention, but his slumped shoulders and low-hanging head exposes his defeat.

After rolling my shoulders, I enter his office, stepping over first-edition books and months of paperwork scattered across the floor. I'm barely halfway across the room when Isaac senses my presence. As he shifts on his feet to face me, the anxious expression on his face morphs to fury. He's blackened with rage.

Before I can comprehend what's happening, he storms my way. My first thought is to flee, but as quickly as that idea transpired, it vanishes. Running won't fix anything. I made a mistake, and I'm big enough to admit that.

Hugo places himself between Isaac and me. "Give her a chance to explain."

My heart launches into my throat when Isaac shoves him aside. He sails across the room as if he is weightless, landing on his backside with an almighty thump. I scamper backward, only stopping when I'm pinned between Isaac's imposing frame and the bookshelves lining his office. Although my body is shuddering with anxiety, excitement is still coursing through my veins. My inner vixen doesn't care how angry Isaac is. All she cares about is his closeness.

When Hugo leaps back onto his feet, I signal for him to

stand down. I created this mess, so I need to fix it. Hugo stops his aggressive charge, but he watches us closely with his fists clenching open and closed. Isaac won't hurt me, but I don't see that being the same for anyone who dares to come between us.

Isaac's hot, heavy breaths blast my overheated cheeks with more warmth as he glares down at me in disdain. He must have consumed a substantial amount of alcohol since he left the Ravenshoe PD because not only is his breath riddled with whiskey, alcohol is seeping from his pores, suffocating his alluring scent.

I swallow, hoping a bit of moisture will help free my words from my mouth. It does—somewhat. "I didn't tell them anything—"

"You're lying."

"No." I shake my head, nearly sending tears toppling down my cheeks. "I never shared anything about you. I'll defend you before I ever prosecute you."

Isaac chuckles, a scary, menacing laugh. "You'll defend me?" When I nod, he throws his hand around his barely recognizable office. "Is this defending me?"

"This wasn't me. I was at the police department with you the entire time. I never left your side. I didn't even know they'd been granted a search warrant."

"Stop lying, Isabelle." His roar startles me so much, my jump nearly spills the moisture pooling in my eyes. "Don't you dare cry. You have *no* right to cry."

I bite the inside of my cheek, fighting to keep my tears at bay. Isaac hates when I cry, and he doesn't need more hurt added to the already bursting-at-the-seams pain in his beautiful eyes.

Confident I have everything under control, Isaac continues to interrogate me. "No one knows this place exists except Hugo and you." His narrowed gaze flicks to Hugo, who's watching our exchange with cautious, wide eyes. "It isn't even registered in my name because I wanted to ensure something like this would never happen. So, either you or Hugo told the authorities about it. Hugo has been with me for years. You've only been in the picture the past six months—around the same time my empire was placed under the spotlight."

"It wasn't me." My knees feel like they're going to fall out from beneath me when he glares at me, but it doesn't stop me saying, "Maybe the surveillance team followed you here one day, or..." I stop mid-sentence, incapable of finding a reasonable explanation as to how the authorities learned about his private residence. "I don't know who it was, but it wasn't me."

Isaac smirks a wickedly evil grin. It doesn't make my knees pull together. If anything, it has the opposite effect. I'm more unnerved now than I was when I had my gun pressed against his chest.

When he steps back, I gulp down a big breath, grateful I can fill my lungs with air again. It's forced back out in a hurry when he slings his eyes to Hugo and says, "You're fired."

What? "Isaac, no. I'm not saying it was Hugo. I'm just saying it wasn't me."

My pulse quickens from the sheer closeness of his handsome face when he turns back to face me. "You've declared it wasn't you, so either Hugo told them I lived here, or the surveillance team followed him here. Unless you're willing to recant your confession, Hugo is fired."

When my lips twitch, Hugo shakes his head, advising me not to fall into Isaac's trap. Although I hate lying, I can't let Hugo take the blame for this. With everything going on, Isaac needs someone like Hugo in his corner.

Before I lose the nerve, I murmur, "It was me."

My eyes stray to the ground, needing to look at anything but Isaac. If he sees my eyes, he'll know I'm lying. They're the gateway to my soul.

"Look at me, Isabelle." The anger beaming out of him fans the hairs stuck to my temples when I keep my eyes planted on a pile of crumpled papers to the left of his desk. He's furious I'm ignoring him, but not as much as I'm angry at myself when he sneers, "Get out of my house before I show you just how unlawful I can be."

He pulls away so viciously, hot air blasts my already over-heated face. He strides to a bar on our right to refill his glass with whiskey. Once it sloshes over the rim, he returns to his original position by the window. I watch him in silence, begging for him to look back at me just once. He does no such thing. He's so angry he can't stand the sight of me. When an arm unexpectedly curls around my shoulders, I jump out of my skin. "Sorry."

Hugo spins me around before guiding me down the hallway we walked only minutes ago. It breaks my heart walking away from Isaac, but I'm not sure what else I can do. Today has been such a clusterfuck of emotions, I'm surprised I'm still standing.

Halfway down the hall, glass being smashed sounds out of Isaac's office. I stop dead in my tracks, a cold chill running down my spine. When I attempt to turn around, Hugo maintains his firm clutch on my shoulders. "He needs time, Izzy. You both need time."

By the time we reach Isaac's town car, shock has truly set in. My heart sits heavy in my stomach as everything around me blurs. During our drive back to Ravenshoe, I keep my gaze planted on the gloomy sky. There's not a single star in heaven tonight—even it can feel the darkness wreaking havoc with my stomach.

After pulling on the curb at the front of my apartment building, Hugo drifts his eyes to me. They're full of apprehension and remorse. "You shouldn't have lied."

"Who said I did?"

He huffs. "Come on, don't treat me like an idiot. I know you lied." His tone is a cross between angry and confused. "I just don't understand why. Isaac will never forgive you if he thinks you deceived him."

Tears burn my eyes. "I did deceive him. I may not have told the Bureau about his house, but I did deceive him. I've been lying to him for months."

Not allowing Hugo to deliver one of the many replies I see in his eyes, I scramble out of his car, then dash for my building as quickly as my quivering legs will take me.

4

ISAAC

s I bend down to gather my shattered whiskey glass from the floor, my mind drifts back to my exchange with Isabelle. I'll admit I handled the situation poorly, but I've been pushed to my absolute limits today. I'm also drunk, so the brunt of my fury was handed to a woman not deserving of all my anger. It is excusable, though. My home, my private residence, the one thing that's solely for me, has been trashed beyond recognition.

Artwork I collected over the years is damaged beyond repair, antique furniture was hacked with box cutters, and priceless ornaments are chipped and broken, but even more concerning than that is the damage they did to items with a high sentimental value. I can't replace those things. They're irreplaceable. They didn't need to conduct their search the way they did. Whoever did this wanted my attention. They have it now. I won't stop until I find out who did this as I refuse to be blindsided for the second time.

When I was arrested this morning, I felt Isabelle's presence before I saw her. That's not uncommon. She has that effect on every red-blooded man she meets. Time stands still when she enters the room. She doesn't walk, she floats like an angel. Just one glance into her rich eyes makes my cock hard as stone. I'm talking from experience when I say it only takes a mere second to grow infatuated with her. That's how thought-provoking she is.

When I sensed her presence this morning, I spun to face her, prepared to launch into a campaign about her not needing to panic, and that everything would be okay, so you could imagine my surprise when I noticed she was wearing a bullet-proof vest and had a Bureau-issued revolver in her hands.

I've known for months she was hiding something. I just had no clue it was something so mammoth. The woman who invades my every waking thought is an undercover FBI Agent—an elaborate ruse to pry me for information. People are always gunning for me. I learned early on in my career about tall poppy syndrome. If you're already wealthy, say like Cormack, with old family money, it's okay your success is expected, but if you build your wealth from pennies as I did, you must be doing it unjustly and illegally. There's no middle ground.

People often assume my wealth was gained from fraudulent, underhanded activities. It wasn't. Don't get me wrong, I'm not saying I am a saint. Like many red-blooded Americans, I've dabbled in some illegal activities. Enough to warrant an FBI investigation? I don't think so. Obviously, my reputation has even superseded me.

When I say I fought my way to where I am, I'm not being facetious. Bare knuckles and a dirty concrete floor gave me the capital to start my empire.

For months, my college roommate, Cormack McGregor, pestered me to go out with him on the weekends. He was the definition of a popular school jock. He wasn't just well-liked because of his cocky personality and playboy reputation but because his family was obscenely rich. They didn't just have decent-paying jobs, they were so wealthy, Cormack wouldn't have to work a day in his life if he didn't want to.

I was attending college on a scholarship, so a majority of my time was spent with my head in a book to ensure I maintained the grades needed to keep it. Regrettably, Cormack didn't understand the word 'no.' After pleading relentlessly for an hour, I agreed to put my business paper on hold for another night.

Inquisitiveness made itself known with my gut when an hour after me agreeing, Cormack pulled his BMW into the driveway of a derelict building on the outskirts of a town forty miles from our college. Cormack noticed my grim expression, but he did nothing to settle it. He just smiled a beaming, full-toothed grin before making his way into the dusty building. I trailed closely behind.

We walked into a dingy space that appeared to be a college gym in its heyday. The walls hadn't seen a coat of paint in years, the windows were covered with cobwebs, and the floor was brown, appearing as if it hadn't seen a mop in over a century.

The further we walked, the greater the smell of sweat became. I unearthed the reason for the scent when we broke through the hundreds of people huddled in a circle in the middle of the warehouse. Two well-built men were fighting toe to toe. One had blood running from a split above his left brow. The other had a variety of bruises scattered across his torso. Both were covered in soot.

The crowd sighed in sync when the guy with the split eye was hit with a grueling right-swung fist. He plummeted to the floor, his sickening crunch occurring a mere second before an African-American man in his early twenties checked him for a pulse. Although he was breathing, he was knocked out, so the plain-clothed referee declared the fight over by technical knockout.

My interest piqued when he handed a wad of cash to the winner. He shared a portion of his prize money with a middle-aged man at the side of the makeshift ring before giving a smaller cut to the referee. Once they dragged the unconscious man out of eyesight, a new, less-battered fighter took his place. He was massive, easily five to six inches taller than me, and his bicep was bigger than my head. His veins were either laced with steroids, or he worked out for hours on end.

My eyes strayed to the referee when he snatched a microphone off a portable speaker on his right. "All right, gentleman, who's it going to be?" He scanned the crowd, eyeing off men as big as the one standing mid-ring. "Is anyone brave enough?"

The room fell into silence. It was both uncomfortable and amusing.

"What does he want?"

Cormack's attention diverted from a pretty blonde cozying up to his side. "He's looking for a contender to fight Bruno." He nudged his head to the brute in the ring. "People are reluctant to fight him because he's undefeated."

"How much is the buy-in?"

A condescending grin formed on his face. "For who?"

"Me," I answered without pause.

Cormack laughed so loud, he gained the attention of the MC/referee. "Do we have a challenger?"

Cormack stopped shaking his head when I said, "Yes."

The MC cupped his mic with his hand before stepping closer to me. "Who's your fighter?"

I gave him a playful wink, loving the unease in his tone. "Me."

"Seriously?"

Broadly smirking, I nod. "What's the buy-in?"

"Two G," the MC replied.

I cursed under my breath. If I had known where Cormack was taking me, I would have gone prepared, but I didn't carry that sort of cash around, but I knew someone who did.

I lifted my eyes to Cormack, who was watching me curiously. "Buy me in, and I'll give you a cut of the profit."

His brows pulled together as he glared at me in disbelief. "Are you fucking kidding me?" His tone was dead serious like he was petrified about my well-being. "He'll kill you."

"He has to catch me first." I smirked like the arrogant prick I was. "Trust me. I know what I'm doing."

He took several minutes pondering my request before he reluctantly yanked his wallet from his jeans. "I don't care about the money, but if you die—"

"Won't happen."

My eyes darted down to my clothes. I'd never fought in jeans before, but I didn't have anything else to change into, so they had to do. After pulling off my shoes and socks, I handed them to Cormack.

He cocked a brow before thrusting my shoes into the chest of the blonde attached to his side.

Her huff of annoyance changed to a gasp when I removed my shirt. With flaming cheeks, her bugged-eyes glided down my body. I winked at her shocked face before shadowing the MC into the ring. Tae kwon do, boxing, mixed martial arts, karate. You name it, I had done it. After being weak and sick the first five years of my life, I became obsessed with anything that required strength and conditioning.

My body showed my dedication.

Halfway back to Cormack's car, he leaped into the air. "You crazy son of a bitch!"

I smirked; smugness was all over my face. "I told you to trust me."

The fight had gone as I had predicted. Bruno was all brute and no brains. He was exhausted after only a handful of swings of his chunky arms. That's when I moved in. Two left and right combinations, then a swift kick to his temple, and he was kissing the pavement. I didn't break into a sweat, and not one of Bruno's hits landed on me.

Cormack slid into the driver's seat of his car before drifting his eyes to mine. "Do you have any plans next Friday night?"

When his curious gaze floated over my face, I arched a brow, unimpressed by his prying glance.

He smiled at my snappy reaction. "We have to play this." He flattened my hair, then fiddled with the collar of my shirt. After squinting his eyes, he murmured, "Yes." His rummage through his glove compartment produced a pair of thick-rimmed glasses and an ugly peaked beanie. "Perfect."

He laughed when I put on the items as requested. All I needed was some knee-high socks, and the dorky, school nerd look would be perfected.

"Now, we've got the perfect ruse."

FOR THE NEXT SIX MONTHS, we jibbed the underground fight scene at any college within a three-hundred-mile radius of ours. I would arrive separately, dressed down in the dorky clothes Cormack supplied, acting innocent and unaware. Only once Cormack negotiated a fight did I reveal my true self.

With my bank balance the highest it had ever been, I quit my barista job at the local coffee shop so that I could concentrate on my new Friday-night schedule. Most circuits had a two to three grand buy-in, but a few men got cocky. They increased the purse, believing they were playing me. I walked away with four grand those nights.

I met Col Petretti's son, Dimitri, on the way out of one fight that netted me a little over three grand. "How long do you think your con will last?" He strolled our way, his strut cocky. "You're almost out of contestants in this circuit.

I smirked before continuing to Cormack's car. I had been approached by several wannabe managers the past few months, but since I wasn't interested in what they were selling, I kept walking. Our days were numbered—I had fought at nearly every college I could—but I already gave a share of my profits to Cormack, so I wasn't willing to part with more of my money.

My eagerness to get away slowed when Dimitri said, "I can guarantee you five grand a fight." His voice was void of any emotion. He appeared to have the world at his feet. It was only his eyes that gave away his deceit. They were empty and soulless. "Fight for my father, and he'll pay you five thousand dollars a fight."

When I peered at Cormack, he notched up his shoulder, leaving the decision up to me. It wasn't his life on the line every fight, so he always left that side of the business to me.

"Where are the fights located?"

"Hopeton." Dimitri stepped closer, his attitude too arrogant for my liking. "Just near your hometown."

My brow arched. He had done his research on me, making me realize my ruse may end sooner than initially perceived.

"How often are the fights scheduled?" Five thousand dollars a fight was impressive, but not if I only fought once a month.

When Dimitri shrugged, my lips hard-lined. "Not interested—"

"What if I guarantee you five thousand a week, even if you don't fight."

My heart whacked out a funky tune. My future goals and aspirations would greatly benefit from five thousand dollars a week. Any deliberations ceased when Dimitri said, "Five thousand dollars a week, and my father becomes your owner."

My jaw ticked. "My owner?"

Dimitri smiled and nodded, like the idea of me being owned would impress me. It didn't.

"Nobody owns me."

"Everyone is owned." Dimitri's voice was haunted and shallow.

I stepped closer to him—so close, I could smell his fear. "Nobody owns me."

Dimitri's eyes flashed to the side when car doors being opened broke through the silence teeming between us. Two large men in expensive suits stepped out of a black Escalade. One of the men, whose attention was fixated on me, pulled back his suit jacket to show he was carrying a semi-automatic weapon.

"As I said, everyone is owned." Dimitri signaled for the men to stand down before he joined them. Just before he slid into the back of the Escalade, he drifted his eyes back to me. "I'll be in contact."

When his taillights blurred into a sea of many, I shifted my focus to Cormack. "Who the fuck was that?"

He shrugged because back then, we didn't have a clue who we were dealing with.

5

———

ISABELLE

I press my palms on the vanity sink before raising my eyes to the mirror. Disheveled—that's the only word I can use to describe myself. My hair is oily and unkept since I haven't washed or brushed it in over forty-eight hours, and my skin is pale, which amplifies the dark rings under my eyes. I look horrific. Rightfully so. I spent my weekend wrapped up in my bedsheets, but I barely slept a wink. My sheets are the closest thing to Isaac I have, so I haven't let them out of my sight.

Some good came from my lack of sleep, though. A small portion of the confusion in my mind lifted. Alex must not have unearthed anything incriminating during his invasive search of Isaac's home, or he would have never let Isaac leave during questioning. It's immensely satisfying knowing the Bureau doesn't have enough evidence to issue an arrest warrant on Isaac, but I'm still confused as to why he was arrested to begin with. Alex would have needed something substantial for the judge to agree to a search warrant, but for the life of me, I can't work out what it is.

I do know one thing. No matter what it is, I'm sure it's a misunderstanding. Isaac isn't the man his FBI file portrays. He's kind, honest, and has the biggest heart. I'm so confident in my assumption, even with him giving clear signs he wants nothing to do with me, I'll continue defending him. I'll fight for justice right alongside him, not stopping until his name is clear of controversy.

After a steaming hot shower, and a good thirty minutes striving to remove the disheveled look from my face, I walk out of my apartment. It's a crisp, dreary morning. The rain brought in a cool change, and my wool jacket and beanie-covered head make it easy to ignore. The smell of rain and fresh-cut grass filters in my nostrils when I exit the rotating glass doors of my building. Birds are chirping in the distance, and the constant honk of impatient motorists announce morning commuter traffic is at full capacity.

Since the rain has cleared, the sidewalks are more popular than they were Friday night. In true modern times, most travelers conduct their journeys with a cell phone attached to their hands. It's rare to see anyone without an electronic device these days. It's nice to keep in contact, but since they rarely look up from their phones, I'm constantly elbowed or barged.

Not wanting to get trampled, I move to the furthest edge of the sidewalk. Traffic is dense, but my odds of being hit by a car would be significantly less than the number of elbows I've already been subjected to this morning.

Two blocks down, the beat of my heart increases to a steady pace. A dark blue sedan is tailing me. I wouldn't have noticed if its speed wasn't matching mine. Commuter traffic is thick, but it's not heavy enough they need to drive at a walking pace.

While adjusting my satchel, I inconspicuously peer over my shoulder. The sedan's dark tint is already a hindrance, much less the sun beaming off the windshield. I can't see any of the driver's features. When the light ahead of me changes to red, I sprint across the intersection, breaking away from the shadow following me. He can't follow me since there are three cars between us.

By the time I reach Harlow's bakery, I'm covered with a sheen of sweat and suddenly regretting my thick coat. After closing the bakery's front door, I lean my back against it, close my eyes, then suck in several big breaths to settle my flipping heart.

Once I've regathered my composure, I pop my eyes back open. The nerves I've just expelled return full force when I'm subjected to Harlow's furious wrath. Her arms are crossed in front of her chest, and her hazel eyes, which have tears, are glaring at me. Her lips twitch like she's about to speak, but no words seep from her mouth. It isn't that she can't talk. She just doesn't want our showdown witnessed by the handful of customers enjoying the breakfast items her bakery supplies every morning.

With a shake of her head, she spins on her heels to enter the kitchen at the back of the bakery. I take off after her, smiling a greeting to Renee, one of her workers, on my way past. My brisk pace slows when I notice Harlow's clenched fists. She's angry, but it has nothing on the disappointment in her eyes. They reveal what her anger centers around. She knows my secret.

"Legally, I couldn't tell anyone..." My words trail off when she huffs. She's pissed I'm giving her the same old excuse as everyone else, and she has a right to be. She deserves better than that. "I'm still me." I step into the firing zone. "I'm the same person you became friends with. I just don't do the job I said I did, but nothing else about me is different."

A disbelieving chuckle rumbles in her chest. "And your relationship with Isaac? Was that you? Or Izzy, the FBI agent, diving under the sheets for the good of society?"

Ouch. That's a sting my bruised ego did, but I deserve her anger. I did lie to her. "I understand that you're angry—"

"I'm not angry, Izzy. I'm pissed off. You lied... for months!"

"Nothing I told you was a lie." I move closer to her, wanting her to look into my eyes, so she knows I'm telling the truth. "Anything I ever said or did when I was with you, was me, Izzy, your friend. I was *never* an agent when I was with you."

"Some friend." Her glare cuts through me like a knife. "Not only are you suffering the consequences of your actions, but others are as well."

I step back, confused. What is she talking about?

My heart breaks when a tear splashes onto her cheek. "Harlow..."

She holds her finger into the air, begging for a minute. If I didn't feel responsible for her tears, I'd leave her alone as requested, but since she's my friend, and I care for her, I step closer to her instead.

When I curl my arms around her quivering shoulders, she attempts to shrug out of my embrace. I hold on tight, refusing to relinquish her from my grip. "I'm sorry. I should have been honest. I would have if I could."

The reason for her heartbreaking sobs come to light when she murmurs, "Cormack hasn't returned any of my calls this morning."

"Oh, Harlow, I'm so sorry."

Her hand sweeps across her wet cheeks. "He probably thinks I knew all along you were working with the FBI."

"I'll explain everything to him. I'll make this right, I promise."

I have to make this right. Harlow loves Cormack. She told me precisely that only days ago. I wish I had put more thought into the ripple effect my deceit would create. Alas, when I'm in Isaac's world, I forever wear rose-colored glasses.

My eyes float up from the floor when Harlow murmurs, "Cormack has a reason to be suspicious. I did conspire to set you up with Isaac." She blows her nose before her purge fess begins. "I met him a few weeks before we went out to celebrate your birthday. He ordered cupcakes for a meeting he was holding. With Fallon quitting the night before, I delivered his order instead of having them couriered. It wasn't the norm, but the instant I saw him..." She stops talking, her face expressing what her mouth can't. She fell in love with him on sight, just like I did with Isaac.

"As I was leaving, I ran into Isaac. He interrupted us..." Her heated cheeks have me wondering what Isaac walked in on. "After some not-so-fun to and fro, I discovered Cormack and

Isaac were good friends. Cormack was hesitant, but I convinced him we should conspire to get you two together."

She sucks in a big breath before continuing, "I didn't book a table at that restaurant the night we went out for your birthday because I knew Cormack already had one booked. He and Isaac did the same routine every week. I saw the way Isaac looked at you but thought you were being stubborn. I had no clue what I was pushing you toward. I'm sorry."

"It's okay. It's not your fault. I should have been honest from the get-go."

She nods, agreeing with me. "Please tell me you weren't with Isaac solely for the FBI." She glances into my eyes, hers once again welling with tears. "Because if you were, not only will Cormack never forgive me, I won't forgive myself."

Her devastated tone kills me, but nothing can alter the facts. "I love Isaac, Harlow, more than I could ever explain, so you can be assured I was never with him for the bureau."

She nods for the second time, once again believing me.

If only Isaac could be as easily convinced.

By the time I leave the bakery, things aren't back to normal between Harlow and me, but they're better than they were when I arrived. I'll do everything in my power to ensure Cormack understands that Harlow is innocent in this situation. I don't care if Cormack never speaks to me again. He can despise me for the rest of his life, but he needs to take his anger out on me, not Harlow.

A vehicle parked across the street from the bakery halts my quick exit. A blue sedan is parked two spaces up. Although I can't confidently declare it's the same vehicle that was tailing me earlier, my intuition is warning me to remain cautious.

With my body facing the shop frontage, I commence walking down the street. I don't even get four steps away before the sedan begins following me. When I increase my speed to a jog, it also increases its speed.

Against my better judgment, I freeze before turning to face the vehicle that's come to a stop three car lengths behind me. If they're going to blatantly follow me, I want them to be aware I know of their pursuit. When I step closer to my pursuer, it heads in the opposite direction. It reverses down the street, its tires squealing from the heavy compression of the accelerator.

My heart feels seconds from escaping my chest cavity, but instead of it pounding in fear, it's thumping with adrenaline. I'm sick and tired of being pushed around. It's time for me to give as good as I'm getting.

6

ISABELLE

Numerous pairs of eyes track me when I enter my office building. Ignoring the tension ridding the air of oxygen, I deliver the morning coffees as I have every day since joining the team six months ago. Since Alex isn't in his office, I leave his on his desk.

Brandon is the only agent who acknowledges me during my deliveries. He's quiet, but his eyes are missing the judgment every other agent had while glaring at me. Once my deliveries are over, I store my satchel in the bottom drawer of my desk, then fire up my computer. While it starts the slow process of downloading the malware required for my job, I hang my coat on the rack next to the front entry door.

When I spin back around, I come close to losing my footing. A female agent I haven't met previously is standing within an inch of me. "Sorry I didn't see you there."

"That's fine. I'm sure your daftness can be excused after the tense week you've had." Her eyes are friendly, even though her tone is anything but. "Isabelle Brahn, I assume?"

"Yes." I accept the hand she's holding out in offering.

"Theresa Veneto. I'm from the Internal Affairs Division of the FBI."

Her handshake is robust, nearly as sturdy as her lips, which are set in a straight line. She's attractive—if you can look past the harshness of her punitive glare. If I had to guess her age, I'd say early to mid-thirties. Her long blonde hair frames her oval face, and her eyes are blue.

"How can I help you, Ms. Veneto?"

It takes me yanking my hand out of her clutch to free it from her rigid grip, and even then, she seems reluctant to let me go. I stuff my hands into my pockets, uneased by her odd-ball behavior. When her humored eyes float around my office, I follow the direction of her gaze. Every agent in the direct vicinity of us is watching our exchange, including Alex, who's standing next to Brandon's now-empty desk.

"Perhaps we should take this somewhere private?"

When she gestures for me to follow her, I do, albeit hesitantly. She guides me to the dimly lit conference room where Brandon and I discovered Isaac's connection with Col Petretti. My already wobbly strides increase their shake when I notice a male agent in the room. He's seated behind a camera tripod on the table that once held the files I've been scanning the past several weeks. They're not the only thing missing. My uncle's moldy storage boxes have also been removed.

When I enter the room, the male agent assesses my body in a creepy, skin-crawling way. "I understand Isaac's interest."

Either missing her partner's statement or happy to ignore it, Theresa requests for me to sit in the chair across from the video camera. Just as I plop down, a knock rattles the window behind my head. Relief washes over me when I see Brandon on the other side.

"As the union representative for this division, I need five minutes to talk to Ms. Brahn before her interview commences." Brandon's tone conveys he's not seeking permission. He's telling them this is what is happening.

Theresa huffs, annoyed. "Five minutes."

The male agent places on his suit jacket, his belly so round, the buttons nearly burst during fastening. When the glass door of the conference room closes with them on the other side, I drift my eyes to Brandon.

"Wha—"

"Be quiet, Izzy."

"I—"

"Shut up, Isabelle."

I freeze, stunned. This is the first time I've heard him curse. When he jerks his chin up, I look in the direction he nudged. There's a security camera mounted in the corner of the room. It's flashing red, indicating we're being watched.

"What the hell," I murmur to myself when the blinking light ceases a few seconds later.

Before I can ask what is happening, Brandon locks his panicked eyes with mine. "I strongly advise you to plead the fifth—"

"I don't have anything to hide."

My relationship with Isaac may be construed as immoral, but nothing I've done the past month was criminal.

"Please don't be stupid. They're here to charge you with conspiracy in aiding and abetting a criminal by supplying him with official government documents. If you don't plead the fifth, you're looking at over twenty years in jail."

"Why?" I mutter, my one word breathless. "I've never given Is—"

"Shut up!" Brandon's growl vibrates right through my chest. "I can't guarantee they don't have ears in here." After pressing his sweat-slicked palms to the white melamine tabletop, his gaze seeks mine. "Plead the fifth, then I'll do everything in my power to help you through this." Even though his tone is stern, his request still comes out as a plea.

I still feel it's the wrong thing to do, but I nod. Brandon has gone out of his way to help me. He wouldn't do that unless he believes it's imperative.

"I'll stay with you during your interview, but no matter what they say or do, continuously plead the fifth."

My stomach churns so much, I feel like I'm about to be sick, but I still nod—somewhat. It's more a halfhearted agreement than a determined one.

Not long later, Agent Theresa and her partner re-enter the room. "Your five minutes are up." She nudges her head to the door, giving Brandon his marching orders.

"Isabelle has requested a union representative be present during her interview."

Theresa's jaw ticks as her eyes drop to mine. "Is that correct,

Isabelle?" She sneers my name like it left a nasty taste in her mouth.

I nod. "Yes, that's correct. "

When she closes the door with more force than needed, the room plunges into an awkward silence. She dumps a spare chair next to Brandon's thigh before taking a seat in the one opposite me. It's not hard to work out who plays good cop and bad cop in her partnership. Theresa's face is as hard as stone, whereas her partner looks seconds from laughing.

His smile sags when Theresa ribs him with her elbow. After coughing to clear his throat of laughter, he leans over to switch on the camera. The instant it flashes its familiar red light, Theresa breaks into the bad cop script every agent is taught during training. It's just not the standard set of questions I was anticipating. "Are you in a relationship with Isaac Holt?"

"I plead the fifth."

Theresa's manicured brow bows as her face strains with confusion. She wiggles her ear, certain she heard me wrong. "Sorry, what did you say?"

"I plead the fifth amendment."

With an evil grin, she tries another tactic. "Are you in a *sexual* relationship with Isaac Holt?"

I swallow harshly, praying my voice doesn't stutter when I reply, "I plead the fifth."

"Have you had physical contact with Isaac Holt since your placement commenced in this division of the FBI?"

"I plead the fifth." My reply comes out sterner than I'm anticipating. It can't be helped. Theresa's tone could only be murkier if she dumped her words in the Hudson before articulating them.

Theresa flicks her humored gaze to Brandon. "She's clever. A rookie agent knowing to plead the fifth. Who would have thought?" After returning her eyes to me, she snarls, "Are you planning to answer any of my questions, Ms. Brahn, or will you continue pleading the fifth amendment?"

Her partner chuckles when I declare, "I plead the fifth." Blood races through my body, my annoyance at an all-time high. "I choose not to answer your questions on the consideration that I may be unwillingly incriminating myself."

Brandon may have suggested I plead the fifth, but I'm not as stupid as she's making me out to be. I did learn some tricks during my time at the academy.

A scrape bellows around the room when Theresa stands from her chair. After running her hands down her starched-to-within-an-inch-of-its-life blouse, she snags a manila folder from a black leather briefcase open on the desk. "You read a law book during your training... *impressive.*" She taps the folder on the desk three times, her smirk condescending. "So, you're aware prostitution is illegal?"

"I'm well aware of that."

Brandon squeezes my thigh, wordlessly cautioning me to stay on script.

Theresa isn't worried about his silent warning. She's confident she has her case in the bag. "Just because he didn't leave money on your bedside table when he was finished, doesn't make it any less of a crime."

She places down a sheet of paper in front of me. It's the

lease I signed for my apartment months ago. I'm a little lost as to where our conversation is heading—until she adds a second paper to the mix. As clear as day, written in the owner section of the report is Mr. Isaac Holt.

"I *pay* rent for my apartment in full every month." Ignoring Brandon's painful squeeze that will most likely leave a bruise, I raise my eyes to Theresa. "The owner's details were *not* disclosed when my application was processed.

"I thought you might say that, so I dug a little deeper." She hands me a list of addresses with monthly figures on the side. "The same two-bedroom apartments in your building rent for over three thousand dollars a month—you pay twelve hundred." Her composure drips with cockiness. "That's not even half. Do you get a friends-with-benefits rate?"

It's the fight of my life not to tell her exactly what I think of her and her inappropriate suggestions. I would if I weren't worried she'd use it to railroad me even more than she already is.

"I plead the fifth."

She continues with her interrogation as if I never said anything. "Then, there's this." She slides another piece of paper across the desk. "A charter for a private jet booked under Isaac Holt's name. How romantic; most men don't take their mistresses on holidays with them."

Brandon snatches the flight manifest out of my hand. "Isabelle's name isn't even on the manifest. That's explicit conjecture. Everything you've presented thus far is speculation." His legal knowledge is impressive. "Isaac Holt owns over half of Ravenshoe, so it would be virtually impossible for

Isabelle to rent anything in this town that didn't belong or have an association with him." He stands, knocking over his seat in the process. "This interview is over. If you speak to Isabelle again without a lawyer present, I won't hesitate to contact my father, who in turn, will have a word with your superior officer."

With a sharp yank on my arm, I'm removed from my seat. Brandon guides me out of the room, his steps so furious, I have to jog to maintain his rapid pace. His angry strides don't stop until we arrive in the supply closet that's been my office the past month.

He drags his fingers through his hair, giving it an appealing sexed-up look. "You didn't have a clue about any of that, did you?"

I shake my head. "I plead the fifth."

He mutters something under his breath that sounds similar to "Jesus Christ, Isabelle." His voice is clearer when he warns, "You need to be vigilant about anything you say or do over the next few days."

When I nod, he steps closer to me. "Is Isaac Holt Mr. Unattainable?"

He stares at me with unease, begging for me to deny his accusation.

His pleas are left unanswered when I nod.

"Jesus, Isabelle." He drags his hand over his head, flattening his new do. "How long?"

I hesitate. He just cautioned me to remain quiet, but now he wants all the details. "Officially, a little over a month. But I met him before I knew he was being investigated."

When Brandon gives me a look as if he's not buying my story, I explain, "I'm petrified of flying." My fear is so nerve-wracking, my knees knock even while explaining my concern. "I was working up the courage to enter the boarding area at the airport when my push off the railing had me crashing into Isaac." I smile when the memories of that day filter through my mind. "Isaac took care of me. He iced the bump on my head before offering up a pain reliever for my throbbing head. I didn't think I'd see him again, so you can imagine my surprise when I was seated next to him for my flight to Ravenshoe. If that wasn't already shocking, it was a business-class seat."

I'm still shocked about that day. What would the odds be out of the millions of people traveling that day, we'd be seated together?

"You flew business class?" When I nod, Brandon's lips crimp. "Who paid for your flight?"

I give him my best *duh* face. "The Bureau."

He knows this. When you're assigned a team, travel expenses are included.

"Did you request for your ticket to be upgraded to business class?"

I shake my head at Brandon's question. I don't have the means to upgrade my ticket now, much less back then.

Brandon's chest expands so much, the buttons on his dress shirt nearly pop. "Did Isaac have any way of knowing you were on his flight?"

I almost shake my head until the memories of that day trickle through my mind. "Isaac collected my belongings, so he may have seen the boarding pass I had printed earlier that day, but it would have only been for the quickest second..."

My words stop when the supply closet door swings open. When Alex enters the already stuffed room, its minute size shrinks even more. He bounces his eyes between Brandon and me before they finally come to rest on Brandon. "It's after eleven, and the report I requested first thing this morning is still not finalized, yet you have time for a chit-chat with Isabelle in the supply closet. Perhaps I need to increase your workload?"

Brandon remains quiet, but he doesn't need to speak to express his anger. It's visible on his usually expressionless face. Happy he has Brandon on tenterhooks, Alex shifts his focus to me. "I need to see you in my office." He stalks to the door, only stopping to ensure I'm following him. "Now, Isabelle."

Nodding, I drift my eyes to Brandon, praying today won't be the last time I associate with him on a professional level.

7

———

ISABELLE

*M*y heart smashes against my ribs when Alex lowers the privacy blind in his office. The glass wall I've never seen shadowed frosts, plunging the room into an eerie gray coloring. After switching on an antique lamp, Alex gestures for me to sit in the chair opposite his well-organized desk. Once I'm seated, he sits in a leather chair, then props his elbows on his keyboard. Although his gaze is stern, there's something behind them that has the vein in my neck working overtime.

"Because of your unwillingness to cooperate with their investigation, IA is recommending you go on unpaid leave until they finalize their inquiries."

The room spins around me. This is worse than first perceived.

"Although I don't agree with their scrutiny, I believe it'll be best for all involved if you take a step back." His deep timbre softens to a whisper. "Running an investigation like ours is hard enough. We don't need IA breathing down our necks."

Guilt makes itself known with my gut. The last thing I wanted to do was shroud his department with controversy. That's why I fought my feelings for Isaac for so long, I didn't want this to be the outcome, but now that I'm in love with him, I can't give him up. The only thing I'd change if given a redo of the last three months would be to tell Isaac the truth from the beginning, then maybe I wouldn't be left defending my honor on my own.

"Once IA's investigation is found unwarranted, I'll accept you back into my team, Isabelle, but until then, you need to gather your belongings and leave the office immediately."

With a fake smile plastered on my face, I nod before standing to my feet and heading for the door. Once I have the stainless-steel handle grasped in my hand, I crank my neck back to Alex. "Isaac isn't the man you think he is."

I exit his office, denying him the opportunity to reply. Several eyes follow my brisk track to my desk. Other than my satchel, phone, and FBI-issued revolver, I don't have any other personal belongings, so I'm ready to leave in mere seconds.

As I place my gun into my satchel, the heat of a gaze captures my attention. Theresa is gawking at me from across the room. A smirk is stretched across her face, hiding her vicious snarl, and her arms are crossed in front of her chest. Her condescending stature reveals what I already know—the instant I leave this office, gossip about my dismissal will spread like wildfire.

I stop returning Theresa's glare when a deep voice says, "I'll walk you out."

My eyes stray to Brandon, who has his backside propped against my desk. "I appreciate the offer, but I don't want you thrown under the bus with me."

He makes a *pfft* noise. "I don't care what they think. You're my friend, Izzy, and until proven guilty, which will *never* happen, I'll have your back."

I bump him with my hip, pretending his words don't have me on the verge of tears. "Thanks, Brandon."

When we exit the brick-and-mortar building I use to call my office, I squint. When you sit behind a desk all day, you forget how bright the midday sun is. Since winter is approaching, my cheeks are more than appreciative of the warmth.

With a sigh, I sling my arms around Brandon's neck. "Thanks for your help."

His hug is warmer than the sun, only dampened by his whispered warning, "Fly under the radar, Izzy. Once I have any information, I'll bring it straight to you."

"I will, and thank you again."

As I inch back, a smirk tugs at my lips. Not even the brisk weather has reduced the hue on his cheeks. He's such a sweetheart, and although I'm sure he's regretting siding with me, I'll be eternally grateful he is a part of my life.

"See you around?"

He returns my earlier hip bump. "You'll be back here filing before you know it."

"Don't forget the coffees. God forbid Alex would have to fetch his own cup."

Brandon's laugh makes what I'm about to do ten times easier. With a wave, I mosey down the sidewalk. I don't turn back around, but I know his eyes remain on me until I turn the corner. I can feel it deep in my bones.

I stand on the corner of First Avenue and Welsh Boulevard, a little perplexed on what to do. It's only 11:20 a.m., so it's too early for lunch, but I'm lost on how else to occupy my time. Just as I consider going to Harlow's for brunch, a brilliant idea pops into my head.

Stepping onto the curb, I flag down a taxi. Because of the early hour, I secure a ride rather quickly. I scamper into the back seat, removing my coat in the process. The driver has the heat up so high, the cab is super muggy.

"Destiny Records in Hopeton, please."

After securing my belt, I raise my eyes, noticing the cab hasn't pulled away from the curb yet. When my eyes collide with the driver's in the rearview mirror, he eyes me with caution. "Hopeton is an hour's journey from here."

My eyes bulge. I've lived in Ravenshoe for six months, but a lack of free time meant I've never ventured far. I had no clue about the distances between towns.

"How much will the fare be?" Nerves jangle on my vocal cords. Alex said I'm on leave without pay, so I need to be cautious with my spending until IA finalizes their investigation.

The driver twists his lips. "Approximately one-fifty each way."

"Each way?"

When he nods, I hand him a few bills from the limited number in my purse before sliding out of his cab, taking my coat with me. I just lost my job. I can't afford hundreds of dollars in cab fares. A bus ticket, on the other hand, I'm sure I can scratch up the fare.

I'm standing at the bus stop, checking the times of the buses departing to Hopeton when a rumbling voice asks, "Where are you going, Izzy?"

Hugo's grinning face comes into sight when I slant my head to the side. "I'm trying to fix some errors I made."

A bus leaves for Hopeton every hour. With the stops in between, it'll take me a little over two hours to get there, but I have to do this. I hate that Harlow and Cormack's blossoming relationship is suffering because of me.

When Hugo jerks up his chin in understanding, I drift my eyes over the shiny red muscle car he's sitting in. Two black stripes roll down each side of its candy apple red paint. Its tires are as wide as they are tall, and the healthy purr of its engine is encouraging as many admiring glances as its owner. Upon noticing my appreciative gawp, Hugo revs his engine, startling a baby waiting to board the bus with his mother.

"A little different from your usual ride."

"This is my baby." Hugo's tone hints at the fascination he has with his car. "A fully rebuilt 1969 Chevelle."

I smile at the pride beaming out of him. *Boys and their toys.*

"Get in; I'll give you a lift."

"I'm going to Hope—"

Hugo cocks his brow. "I know where you're going. Get in."

"Are you sure you don't mind?"

His brow arches even higher.

"Okay, thanks."

Grinning, I dash around his gleaming muscle car and jump into the passenger seat. After tossing my jacket and satchel into the back seat, I peer at Hugo's profile. He's dressed differently today. His black suit and white dress shirt have been switched for dark denim jeans and a long-sleeve shirt. He has the sleeves pulled, showcasing a vast collection of tattoos I didn't know he had.

"Day off?"

A chuckle bubbles in his chest. "Something like that."

His gaze strays from the road to me. I'm wearing my standard office attire, which consists of black skinny-leg trousers and a long-sleeve silk blouse. "How about you? I didn't see you leave the office this early the six months I was tailing you."

Although I should be peeved at his admission he was watching me for so long, I've got more pressing matters to deal with. "I've been suspended without pay."

Disappointment is relayed in my tone. Even if IA's investigation comes back with no factual findings, my personnel record will be forever smeared by this controversy. Sexually cavorting with a target was never recommended during my training. My career won't come back from this. I'm just praying my personal life won't be as badly affected.

My eyes snap to Hugo when he says, "I want to say I'm surprised by your suspension, but I'm not. If you want to live a double life, you need to be more cautious." I dance my eyes between his, waiting for him to elaborate on his response. Mercifully, he doesn't keep me waiting for long. "My sister's file was sealed so tightly, not even Isaac's detective friend, Ryan, could gain access to it, but you, a supposed secretary in legal aid, found out what happened to her."

Oh.

My pupils dilate even more when he says, "That was your *second* mistake. The first was the morning you followed Isaac when he was attending a meeting with Delilah Winterbottom. You didn't check your surroundings for potential conflicts before making the call. I heard everything you said."

"So, you've known all along that I'm an agent?"

A smile furls Hugo's lips high before he nods.

"Then why didn't you say anything to Isaac? Why didn't you rat me out?"

He shrugs like it's no big deal. "Because I knew once you learned who he really was, you'd also protect him."

"Also? So you're protecting Isaac... you're his bodyguard?"

He screws up his face. "Isaac doesn't need a bodyguard. I more protect those he cares about."

Loving his honesty, I test the waters. "Who are you protecting them from?"

He coughs to clear his throat. "Col Petretti."

My hands ball into fists. "Why does Col have a vendetta against Isaac? Isaac may be capable of many great things, but not even he can be held accountable for a traffic accident."

My attitude gets nipped in the bud when Hugo discloses, "Col doesn't blame Isaac for Ophelia's death; only Isaac believes that. Col believes he's a snitch."

Confusion slips over my face. "Why would he think Isaac is a snitch?"

"The plea bargain Roberto Petretti got after running my

sister was only given after he agreed to supply the DA evidence on his father's shady deals. Since Col wasn't linked to any illegal activities, only his business associates were caught in the net of Roberto's confession. When they served time behind bars, Col's business immensely suffered, but since Col would never believe his son ratted him out, he blamed Isaac." He flexes and unflexes his fingers on the steering wheel. "Roberto already made my family suffer. I won't let his family hurt another."

My heart breaks for Hugo. Even though he masks his pain well, he carries the loss of his sister and nephew in his eyes. When I curl my hand over his balled one on his thigh, his eyes drift to mine. "Don't give up on Isaac, Izzy. He looks at you like my best mate looked at my sister. As Jorgie would say, you can't fight fate."

"I'll try." I don't want to give up on Isaac. I just don't like my chances of regaining his trust. It's so easy to break, but it takes more than a lifetime to repair. Doing anything to stop the tears burning my eyes from falling, I ask, "How can you protect Isaac if you're always shadowing me?"

When Hugo laughs, the grief straining his face slackens. "As I said earlier, Isaac doesn't need protecting. He's more than capable of looking after himself. If you don't believe me, ask Col's right-hand man. He learned a hard lesson on what happens when you threaten someone Isaac loves."

My heart nearly bursts from his statement. If I heard him correctly, he's implying that Isaac is in love with me. If that's true, there may still be hope for me yet.

For the rest of our trip, Hugo remains quiet. I don't mind. It gives me a chance to work through the panic his confession elucidated. Half of me is excited he thinks Isaac is in love with me, whereas the other half is petrified I'll never get the possibility of discovering the truth from Isaac myself.

When Hugo pulls into the parking lot at the back of Destiny Records, I swing my eyes to him. "Thanks for the ride..." My praise halts halfway when he throws off his seat belt and curls out of his car.

I join him on the sidewalk before eyeing him with suspicion. He smiles at my quirked brow before honking my nose. "Have you met Peta, Cormack's receptionist?"

I shake my head.

"When you do, you'll understand my eagerness."

He winks before strutting through the automatic glass door at the front of Destiny Records. When I follow him, no more words are needed. Peta is beautiful, in a sexy, schoolteacher type of way. Her tight, high-waisted skirt paired with dangerously high stilettos makes it appear as if her legs never end. She reminds me of a young Halle Berry. Even their skin tone and facial structure are a perfect match.

I mill around in the foyer when Hugo makes his way to Peta's desk. I'll let him work his magic since Peta doesn't have eyes for anyone else in the room the instant she spots him. She bats her lashes as her nude lips gnaw on a ballpoint pen.

After a few minutes of chit-chat, Hugo returns to my side. He rubs his hands together while smiling a blinding grin. "Cormack is finishing up an important appointment, then the next twenty minutes of his schedule is free."

A ghost of a smile sneaks onto my lips. Although I'm

pleased with Hugo's negotiating skills, not all my smile centers around that. His gaze never left Peta during his comment.

"Why don't you ask her out?"

With a grimace, he shrugs. If he's planning to reply with words, he loses the chance when Isaac strides out of Cormack's office. His demeanor is so commanding, I'm not the only set of eyes watching his every move. He's so breathtakingly beautiful, my eyes hurt while assessing his perfect face and body, so I can't blame others for enjoying the view as well.

After shaking Cormack's hand, Isaac shifts on his feet to face Hugo and me. His outward appearance doesn't give any indication he has spotted us, but I can feel the heat of his gaze raking my body—it bristles every fine hair on my body and has my knees touching.

When his attention shifts to Hugo, his jaw gains a new tick. There's more tension in the room now than there was Friday night when Hugo placed himself between us.

As he makes his way to the front door, no words are spoken between us, but I'm hopeful my eyes will relay how much I miss him and that I'm sorry for hurting him.

Once he's no longer in sight, my watering eyes lift to Hugo. "You're not on a day off, are you?"

He grins. "Nope. I set a new record by getting fired twice in one night."

8

ISABELLE

A smile curves my lips when I read Harlow's message.

After returning her message saying I only did what I should have done months ago, I show Hugo our joint success. Cormack was more than willing to listen to my pleas for forgiveness. I don't know if it was brutal honesty that got him over the line, or Hugo telling him over a dozen men are lining up to take his place in Harlow's life if he weren't up to the task.

From the recognition that dawned across Cormack's face, I'd say it was the latter. Harlow is beautiful. She has a strong work ethic and an even stronger heart. If Cormack waited too long, another man would snatch her away from him without a single regret.

"At least someone listened to my advice."

I wait for Hugo to pull his car into the front of my building before asking, "What happened between you and Isaac that got you fired?"

His teeth shine in the sun when he smiles. "I told him to pull his head out of his ass."

"Seriously?" When he nods, I slap his bicep. "How the hell are you still breathing?"

His chuckle bounces around the interior of his car. "You can't punish someone for being honest. He didn't give you a chance to explain yourself. He should have."

His blind faith is shocking, but oh so needed after the shit few days I've had. "Why do you trust me so much, Hugo?"

He shuts down his engine before tilting his torso my way. "If you wanted to pin anything on Isaac, you had plenty of chances before you guys became official." He licks his dry lips. "I might have also given you a handful of tests."

"What kind of tests?" I'm more curious than angry.

My throat grows scratchy when he says, "The envelopes in Isaac's apartment, they weren't real. I planted them to see if you'd take them." He works his jaw side to side. "I also tapped your phone to see if you reached out to anyone after Isaac met with Henry Gottle at the McGregor residence."

I glare at him, furious he invaded my privacy, but also grateful he always has Isaac's best interests at the forefront of his mind.

I take back every nice thought I've ever had about him when he mutters, "Also, there was the whole club 57 incident—"

"You said you turned off the cameras!"

He gags—loudly. "Believe me, I turned them off long before anything raunchy happened. I prefer participating in sexual activities, not watching them like some sicko behind a computer monitor, but thanks for your faith, Izzy."

I try to hide my smile, but the smallest one curves my mouth. You couldn't hear the pure disgust in his voice. He's mortified just at the idea of watching Isaac and me get naughty.

Hugo tries to do a better job of explaining himself. "Isaac went in brutal, but you didn't even blink at his aggression." He smiles a cheeky grin. "Well, you did, but it was more that girly flutter-your-eyelashes-excessively type of blink that makes guys wonder if you have something stuck in your eye."

"Kind of like the look Peta was hitting you with earlier?"

He gives me a playful wink. "Something like that." He waits for my eyes to stop rolling before adding, "After I told Isaac to pull his head out of his ass, I said the same thing to him that I said to Cormack. Isaac didn't handle it as well as Cormack did. Even intoxicated, his right hook is hard as fuck."

"He hit you?"

Hugo's shoulder touches his ear. "He wasn't aiming to kill. He was just pissed. I'd have been more concerned if he didn't react to my taunt. You should have been, too."

Honestly, I'm torn on the whole situation. Did Isaac respond because he was jealous, or did he just not appreciate Hugo telling him what to do? I know without a shadow of a doubt that Isaac hates being strong-armed, so perhaps it had more to do with that than jealousy?

With my head not held as high as it was moments ago, I

lock my eyes with Hugo. "Do you want to come up? I could use a drink or four, and I'd love some company."

I'm also enjoying Hugo's frankness. He's sharing information left, right, and center today, so anything I can do to extend that, I will. Even after investigating Isaac for six months, and dating him for one, I'm still only just scratching the surface of his enigmatic personality.

"Are you ready for the repercussion that may bring?"

I stare at Hugo, confused by his statement.

"First, Isaac saw us together at Destiny Records. Now, he'll see me walking into your apartment."

"You think he'll react?"

"I'm not assuming anything, Izzy; he *will* react. It just may not be in a way either of us are prepared for. He's naturally dominant, but when it comes to you, he's beyond saving. I'll come up if you want me to, but you need to make sure that's a step you want to take."

I take a moment to contemplate. I want Isaac to interact with me, but not because he's coerced to. I want him to talk to me because he wants to, not because he's banging his chest in an alpha male turf war.

I return my gaze to Hugo, who's watching me intently. "Thanks for the lift."

He dips his chin, only just hiding his smile. "If you need anything, you have my number."

"Thanks, Hugo." I press a kiss to his cheek before curling out of his car. My backside is halfway out when a question I should have asked at the beginning formulates in my head. "Do you know why Isaac was arrested?"

He shakes his head. "I figured if anyone would know, it'd be you."

"I'm as clueless as the rest of us."

With a shrug, I exit his car and make my way to my building. Hugo waits until I'm in the lobby before pulling his car away from the curb. His engine is so loud, I can hear it even when he's halfway down the block. While exiting the elevator on my floor, I ruffle through my handbag hunting for my keys. When I lift my gaze, a squeal erupts from my lips. Agent Theresa Veneto startles me from stepping out of the nook in the entryway of my apartment.

I skirt past her and walk to my door. "I'm not talking to you without a lawyer present."

Fiddling with my keys, I fight them into the lock. My hands are jittering so badly, I can't get the darn key into the small hole.

"I'm not here on official business." Theresa's whole composure is pretentious and mocking. "I'm here to talk to you, woman to woman."

Ignoring her no-doubt lie, I jam my keys into the lock, sighing when the lock mechanism clicks in the uncomfortable silence of my hallway.

"Isaac Holt isn't who you think he is."

My slitted eyes snap to hers. "No, he isn't who *you* think he is." I turn to face her, standing eye to eye. "Isaac's file leads you to believe he's a terrible man, but when you look past the highly fabricated documents, you'll see he isn't close to that."

She grins an evilly mocking smile. "I heard you were stupid, but I didn't realize you were also naïve. You're swimming way out of your depth, little girl."

I plaster my best fake smile onto my face, striving to portray that her words didn't bruise my ego. They did, but I'd rather she didn't know that. After returning her mocking stare, I walk through my apartment door, closing it behind me.

"Isaac attacked his last girlfriend's brother so horrifically, he spent weeks in the hospital, recovering from the multiple injuries he sustained."

That halts my swift movements. The pulse beeping through my body is nearly deafening when it clusters in my ears. I had to hear her wrong—surely. Isaac isn't a violent man. He's just misunderstood. Isn't he?

Sensing that my reluctance is slipping, Theresa pushes open my door, then steps inside my domain. Her lips twitch, preparing to talk, but I beat her. "CJ was in a traffic accident with his sister, Ophelia."

As her lips crimp, she shakes her head. "CJ's injuries were not sustained in a traffic accident. Isaac inflicted them."

"I don't believe you." I'm not lying. Our exchange earlier today reveals she's out for blood, meaning she'll do or say anything to get her target. I'm not falling into her trap.

She smirks again. It's a mocking, condescending smile like the one she gave me earlier today in the conference room. "I thought you might say that." She digs a yellow envelope out of her handbag, then hands it to me. "As I said earlier, I'm here warning you, woman to woman. What I'm about to show you must stay between us. This isn't an official visit."

After swallowing to soothe my dry throat, I nod. She's not

the only one willing to lie if it gives her the upper hand. My hand trembles when I pull out the paper inside the envelope. I'm not concerned Theresa has anything incriminating on either Isaac or me, but it's from spotting the date and time on the bottom right-hand corner of the photo inside. It's dated an hour before Ophelia's traffic accident.

I suck in a deep breath to get over my shock before studying the photo with the eyes of an agent. Isaac's sweat-drenched body is in the middle of a boxing ring. He's fighting a gentleman of similar age, or perhaps a few years older than him. It looks like a brutal battle, although most of the damage has been endured by Isaac's competitor, who happens to look oddly familiar to CJ Petretti.

Although things look damning, I'm not willing to pass judgment until I know all the facts. "The Bureau is aware Isaac was a participant in an underground fighting ring years ago. This doesn't make him a terrible man. Fighting is a professional sport."

"No, it doesn't make him terrible, but what about this?"

She hands me a second photo. It's similar to the first one, but it's zoomed out, showing the spectators surrounding the ring—the most imperative, Ophelia. She's standing at the side with tear-stained cheeks and wide eyes. The devastation on her face twists my insides. She's much braver than me as there's no way I could watch my boyfriend fight my brother.

Before I can work through half my confusion, Theresa snatches the photo from my grasp, returns it to the envelope, then snags her cell phone from her handbag. Her fingers fly over her phone screen for three heart-thrashing seconds before she twists it around to face me. There's a video displayed. It shows Ophelia being held back by a large brute of a man. She's crying.

"Please, Isaac, stop." She somehow manages to get away from the man holding her hostage, her escape conceding with her climbing through the ropes. "Please, Isaac, don't do it. I'm begging you."

My hand shoots up to cover my mouth when the screen flicks to Isaac in just enough time to witness him complete a gruesome roundhouse kick to CJ's left temple. CJ crashes to the ground with an almighty thud, his eyes closed, his body lifeless. Tears well in my eyes when Ophelia screams a bloodcurdling cry before she rushes to her brother sprawled lifeless on the dirty mat where she tries in vain to wake him up.

When the video freezes at her staring down at her lifeless-looking brother, I push Theresa's phone away from me. "That doesn't show the full version of events that happened that day."

The evidence looks horrid, and my heart is pained for what Ophelia went through, but you need both sides of a story before forming an opinion. Theresa's video doesn't give me that. It's as one-sided as she was during my interrogation earlier today.

Theresa glares at me like I'm an imbecile. "I may not know the full story, Isabelle, but neither do you. You *think* you know the real Isaac Holt, but you don't know him at all..."

Her words fall short when I slam my door into her face while murmuring, "That's why he's an enigma. He's supposed to be misunderstood."

9

———————

ISAAC

My breaths are jagged, my body is slick with sweat, and my heart is pounding against my chest. The perspiration and panted breaths are from the intense workout I'm currently undertaking at an old, derelict warehouse I own on the outskirts of town. The last statement, my pounding heart, is from seeing Isabelle again.

Today is the first time I've laid eyes on her since my less-than-stellar reaction to her arrival at my home Friday night, but she's the reason I'm working out in freezing temperatures in only a pair of running shorts. I'm aimlessly trying to replace the sexual energy coursing through my body with adrenaline because even knowing her secret didn't dampen the fire that raged inside me when I saw her. It will never be doused. It's irrepressible. My hands itched to fondle, probe, and explore her seductive body when I saw her in the foyer of Destiny

Records. Her beautiful chocolate eyes were burning through to my soul, begging for forgiveness.

It took all my strength to walk away from her. Every step I took was taken with trepidation. With all the women I've bedded the last six years, the chase grew weary, my interests waned within days, if not hours. That never happened with Isabelle. It never grew old. The more I had her, the more I craved her. Her beautiful cupid's bow lip on mine, her hands touching and exploring me with as much interest as I studied her. I couldn't get enough. I never yearned for anything or anyone when Isabelle was in my arms. Now, I have to find a way to move on—to live without her.

Just knowing I'll never taste her again has me swinging my fists harder at the bag hanging precariously from a steel beam by a large chain. Blisters started forming on my knuckles over an hour ago, but my swings haven't dampened. When I entered the warehouse, I threw on a new pair of gloves. I could have forgone the hassle and worn my run-down pair hanging over the fraying ropes of the boxing ring, but I needed a distraction, and I wanted to feel the pain that comes from breaking in brand new gloves. If I feel pain on the outside, it may lessen the ache I'm feeling on the inside.

Another thirty minutes pass before my focus shifts from punishing the bag. My distraction is caused by a cell phone shrilling through the abandoned warehouse. It isn't my sleek, modern phone stopping the swing of my fists. It is the one that only rings during an emergency.

After grabbing a white towel dangling from the chain above the sagging bag, I swipe it over my head to absorb the sweat running down my face while heading for my gym bag lying unzipped on the dirty concrete floor. My burner cell hasn't rung since the morning I got arrested. The last call I took on that phone was in Isabelle's apartment. She was sitting straddled on my lap, nibbling on my earlobe. I was so immersed in her, I didn't consider the repercussions of continuing my conversation in front of her. Call me a fool, but even only knowing her for six months and being in a relationship for a month, I trusted her. I trusted her from the moment I saw her.

I was a fucking idiot.

"Yes," I bark into the phone, my gloomy mood heard in my voice.

"The price has gone up to one point five million dollars."

My grip on my phone tightens. "I told you I didn't care about the price. I want it done, so get it fucking done."

My caller breathes heavily down the phone. "All right. I should have an answer by the end of the week."

Not bothering to reply, I snap down the screen of my phone. A ragged breath escapes my lips when my eyes wander around the warehouse. My muscles are deliriously exhausted, which has dampened the fire roaring through my veins, giving the effect I was striving for when I arrived hours ago, but something is still off. I don't feel myself.

Being betrayed does that to a guy.

When I dump my unregistered cell back into my gym bag, I notice I only have an hour before my reservation with Cormack, meaning I'll have to shower in the locker rooms instead of driving back to my apartment. I could go home, but I haven't been back there since it was trashed by the bureau.

Catherine organized a cleaning crew to come in the following day, and all the furniture and broken items have been replaced, but I can't bring myself to go back there. It was my private oasis, my home, but now it feels like an empty shell.

After stripping off my shorts, I step into the steaming hot shower. The scorching water pumping out of the mildew-coated showerhead kneads and massages my weary muscles. Closing my eyes, I flatten my palms on the dirty, mold-covered tiles before lowering my head into the stream of water. The pressure gives relief to the headache that's been plaguing me for the past three days.

I generally survive on approximately four to six hours of sleep a night, but even that amount has eluded me the past few nights. My hands instinctively dart out to pull Isabelle toward me, then when my hands come up empty, the complexity of the situation dawns on me, and my endeavor for additional sleep is lost.

Climbing out of the shower, I dry myself with a white gym towel I have in my bag. Its material is so stiff, it scratches my skin when I run it over my body. It reminds me how Isabelle's nails raked my back when she's in ecstasy, or how she clawed at my thighs while sucking my cock.

Ignoring the erection I'm now sporting, I place on the suit I was wearing when I arrived, but forgo my vest, tie, and jacket. My body is still overheated from the intense workout, so I don't want to be constrained by a tie. I also don't want more uncomfortableness added to the choking feeling that's been clutching my throat since my arrest.

After snagging my bag off the ground, I make my way to my

car, where I make the usually forty-five-minute trip to Raven-shoe in under thirty.

The restaurant hostess's lips curve into a lusty grin when she notices me heading her way. "Good evening, Mr. Holt."

"April."

I continue on my quest, not bothering to wait for her to usher me to the booth Cormack and I frequented every week for the past five years. Our routine only faltered because Isabelle was in the picture. Although I was more than happy to make things official, I couldn't risk taking her out in public for fear Col would see us together.

This restaurant charges exorbitant prices for the most minuscule portions of food, but the whiskey is top-shelf, and its cigars are unsurpassed. I wouldn't expect anything less from its owner. Our tradition of eating here started a few months after I earned my first million dollars. I invested every cent I made fighting heavily into stocks. Some weeks, I made seven thousand dollars fighting, but I lived as if I were a poor student who didn't have a penny to my name. I kept my grades up, so my scholarship remained valid and ate ramen noodles and canned spaghetti for supper like every other student around me. No one, except Cormack, knew my bank account was growing at a rapid pace.

With how turbulent the stock market was, it took a little longer than I would have liked for my bank account to show its first million-dollar balance, but once it was there for all to see, the achievement was incalculable, and we had reason to celebrate.

When Cormack and I first burst through the doors of this

very restaurant, we were only young. I was just shy of my twentieth birthday, and Cormack was only twenty-one. We dressed in what we thought was respectable clothing, both wearing long-sleeve dress shirts and black trousers. We even rustled up two ties from the clothing Cormack grabbed in haste when he left his family estate with the intention never to return.

The restaurant manager took one look at us, then attempted to have us thrown out. I say attempt as I didn't take his rejection sitting down. After scuffling with two security guards, and leaving one with a broken nose, I told the manager that I intended to buy the restaurant and fire his ass on the very first day I owned it.

I did precisely that eleven months later.

My hunger for success was embedded in me from a very young age. When I was four, I was diagnosed with an aggressive form of Hodgkin's Lymphoma. My only chance of survival weighed on extensive chemotherapy combined with a stem cell transplant. My parents were tested, and neither was found to be a genetic match, which isn't unusual. Most genetic matches only occur in siblings, and those odds sit at only one in four. Luckily for me, Nick was a perfect match. That may have had something to do with the fact he was conceived in a test tube to save my life.

With a high dosage of chemotherapy and the stem cells from Nick's umbilical cord when he was delivered eight weeks early, I survived, and my fighting spirit was unleashed.

People say childhood memories are configured from stories you were told while growing up. Mine aren't. I remember I felt invincible when Nick's stem cells were transplanted. I knew at that precise moment I was going to live, and I promised myself to live my life to the fullest. I also assured my baby brother that one day I'd repay him for giving me the gift of life. Every day I actively pursue that promise.

Nick is apprehensive to accept my generosity. His reluctance is spawned from watching our mother be a mooch a majority of his life. My parents were already separated before Nick joined our family. He glued them together for a couple more years, but like all glue, it eventually dried, and their marriage failed. My mother wanted possessions. My father wanted love. It's very rare to achieve both.

After sliding into the booth Cormack is already seated at, I greet him with a jerk of my chin before signaling for the waiter to bring us our whiskey and cigars.

"Izz—"

I cut off Cormack's comment with a stern glare. "Can I at least get a glass of whiskey before you mention her name?"

Cormack is my one and only true friend. Most people I associate with are acquaintances, business companions, or staff, but I class him as my friend—a very dear friend—but even he's treading a fine line by mentioning *her* name to me. After I was arrested, I banned Isabelle's name from being mentioned. Not once has my demand been met.

Cormack chuckles, not the slightest bit fazed by my infuriating glance. "You might want to ask them to leave the bottle as I plan on mentioning *her* name more than once."

10

ISAAC

"Hey, boss, I'm surprised you're still here." Tina prances into my office before propping her backside onto my desk. "You haven't stayed back this late for weeks."

She's not lying. Before Isabelle, my nights were spent in my office, watching the sales roll in. Thousands of transactions are made each night in my clubs, yet not one patron bats an eyelid at the inflated prices I charge. They're willing to pay for the privilege of drinking in an establishment as sophisticated as mine. The Dungeon is my greatest business achievement thus far. It's an over-eighteen dance club that grew to the number one dance club this side of the country within two months of opening. It was designed with sex and sensuality in mind. That old saying will never die. Sex does sell, and I use it in my business adventures at every given opportunity.

Although I'm proud of how well it's doing, my onsite presence has been severely lacking the past month. Since Isabelle worked days, and I typically work nights, my usually unyielding focus shifted from my business goals to a more personal endeavor. My desire to spend time with Isabelle often had me leaving the office before my clubs reached capacity. I have a dedicated team, so my businesses never lagged the past month, but even if they did, I valued my time with Isabelle enough, I would have taken a hit.

I stop scrolling through reports when the heat of a gaze captures my attention. Tina is gawking at me, her lashes excessively fluttering. "Did you need something?"

My tone comes out clipped. I'm not in the right frame of mind to deal with her inexorable attempts to get back between my sheets. Tina in the bedroom was precisely how I had anticipated. Her look and personality match her sexual prowess to perfection— she's both feisty and wild. With her small height and petite frame, she can bend more ways than an Olympic gymnast. She was the first girl in a long time who could keep up with my intensity in the bedroom, but I pride myself on my ability to read people, and what was relayed through her eyes was enough to have me running for the hills.

Before Isabelle, I had no intention of securing a long-term relationship. My goals were solely dedicated to my empire. I didn't think anything would deter my goals. Isabelle did. She flipped the coin on everything and had me believing I could love again. If I were smart, I would have walked away from her the instant she crashed into me at the airport. Alas, she was more cunning than her humble eyes give her credit for.

My thoughts return to the present when Tina crosses her

legs in front of herself. Her tiny denim shorts ride up high on her thigh, exposing inches upon inches of creamy skin. As she rakes her teeth over her red-painted lip, her infatuated eyes peer down at me. "An FBI agent is requesting to see you. Travis has her holed up at the front entrance."

I'd be lying if I said my first thought didn't go to Isabelle. It's only been three days since she was beneath me, but it feels like months. My sexual drive has always been excessive, but with Isabelle, it was tenfold, reaching levels even I didn't know existed.

Tina's overly-manicured brow shoots up into her hairline. "Did you want me to let her in or tell her you've left for the day?"

Although no other words spill from her lips, her eyes beg me to request for Isabelle to leave. I kept quiet on my relationship, but Tina is very perceptive, so she knows something is more askew with my private life than I'm letting on.

"Boss—?"

"Give me five minutes, then let her in."

Tina huffs before sauntering toward the door. Even pissed, her hips swing provocatively with every step she takes. Once she's back into the main area of the club, I close my laptop screen then head for the inbuilt bar at the side of my office. I need to distract my hands from touching Isabelle. When she's in my vicinity, not even deceit can quell my desire to have her beneath me.

My back molars grind together when I discover my bottle of Teeling 30-Year-Old Single Malt Irish Whiskey is empty. "Nick," I grumble under my breath.

My little brother Nick, whom I love dearly, would happily polish off a three-thousand-dollar bottle of whiskey without seeking permission. I can't blame him. He would have needed a stiff drink after dealing with the psychotic lady who accosted him in my nightclub earlier in the week.

I've only just selected a second bottle when a female voice filters into my office. "This is more impressive than the last office I saw you in."

My grip on the crystal decanter I'm holding firms so tightly, the glass nearly shatters. I shift my gaze to the other side of the room, the pulse in my jaw unmissable when they land on a set of eyes I'd give anything not to see again.

"I should have put two and two together. Corruption and the FBI generally go hand in hand."

Theresa's lips furl. "I see your sense of humor hasn't improved any."

When she takes a step closer to me, my gaze floats over her body. There's no doubt her outer shell is attractive, but her rotten insides make her hideously ugly, not even the most captivating face could have you looking past them.

If you haven't worked this out yet, Theresa and I have met previously. Our meetings were held in my apartment or 'fuck pad' as Isabelle refers to it. Once I grew tired of our prearranged gatherings, I cut ties with Theresa. She didn't take my decision too well. She's one of many women the past five years who has staged ostentatious ruses to coerce me into interacting with them. Although her attempts were vigorous and undermining, they weren't intricate enough to get past my astuteness.

Isabelle is the only one who has played me for a fool.

Theresa endeavors to conceal her excitement at my glance of her body, but the pink hue on her cheek and the unbridled desire of lust reflecting in her eyes, unearths her deceit. She's hopeful for a trip down memory lane. I'd give up everything I have before that would *ever* happen.

"Humor was never my strong point, but you already know that isn't my finest quality." Call me conceited, but I'm aware my strongest assets are displayed in the office and between the sheets.

"You're still not lacking any cockiness."

When I take a step closer to her, her pupils dilate. "You and I both know if I wanted to fuck you on my desk, I could."

The pulse in her neck increases as her heavy-hooded gaze flicks to the desk I'm standing next to. When her tongue darts out to replenish her dry lips, I know I have her exactly where I want her.

"But we also know that'll *never* happen."

The vein in her neck is still thrumming, but now, it's more from anger than desire.

"So, either tell me why you're wasting my time or get the fuck out of my office."

Not waiting for her to reply, I undo the button on my jacket, then take a seat in my leather chair. She remains quiet, but I don't need to see her to know she's still in the room. If her overly floral perfume isn't enough of a hint, her ragged breaths are a sure-fire indication.

I stop pretending to read a business proposal when Theresa

questions, "Are you familiar with a lady named Isabelle Brahn?"

Slowly, my eyes lift from the document I'm now clasping so firmly it has a crinkle down the middle. Theresa is glaring at me, her face blemished with not only disdain but jealousy as well. I smirk egotistically, unwilling to play the game she's had us playing the past four years.

"Never heard of her before."

Although my outward appearance doesn't allude to my piqued interest, on the inside, I'm immensely intrigued. Usually, official government visits center around my empire, not my personal life.

Theresa splays her hand across her cocked hip, exposing a revolver holstered on her waist. "That's interesting." Her tone is as mocking as her smirk, "As Ms. Brahn seems to know you very well."

"Everyone in this town knows who I am," I reply, not attempting to take a nibble out of the bait she's throwing out.

"Oh, that's right. I forgot about your infamous reputation. Maybe seeing a photo of Ms. Brahn might jog your memory?" She places a photo onto my desk. "I understand it could be hard for you to recall the faces of the *many* women you've slept with."

The smallest grin tugs my lips high. The photo Theresa presented is of Isabelle on the beach, wearing the microscopic black string bikini that almost had me falling to my knees when I first saw her in it. Nearly every inch of her beautiful curves is on display. My hands twitch in sync with my cock just from drinking in her seductiveness through a photo.

After tightening my jaw, I scrutinize the picture with more detail, while striving to keep my eyes off Isabelle's provocative frame. Anytime I'm presented with something official, I pay careful attention to every minute detail because it's usually what you're not looking at that should receive the most attention. Like the smallest guy in the group will most likely have the hardest punch, the quietest are usually the most ruthless. And obviously, the most beautiful women are the most scheming.

Ignoring the surge of blood pumping through my body, I scan the background of the photo. It was taken during our long weekend at the McGregor residence. Not only is the jetty and wooden boat shed in the background, so is Colby. Just from that minor detail, I unearth more knowledge about the FBI's investigation into me than what Hunter, my head of security, has informed me.

After every detail of the photo is memorized, I return my eyes to Theresa. "There's no way I'd ever forget a woman who looks like this." She exhales harshly as her eyes thin. Loving her annoyance, I add more salt to her wounds. "Perhaps you could do me a favor and pass my number on to Isabelle."

"I'm sure you can locate her number in her tenant application."

Theresa snatches Isabelle's photo from my hand. Through slitted eyes, she shoves it into the black handbag hanging from her now-slumped shoulders. I devote my attention back to the document I was perusing before she interrupted me, struggling not to chuckle at her obnoxious reaction. Only once my office door being slammed shut sounds through my ears do I raise my burner phone to my ear.

"Boss."

"Anything?" I ask curtly.

I hear a ruffle like someone is shaking their head. "Not a peep."

I run my index finger over my brow. "Good. Keep a close eye on her."

After disconnecting my call, I dial another number.

"Boss."

"I need you to get me everything you can on a Ms. Theresa Veneto."

"On it—"

"Hunter?"

"Yeah," he replies over the sound of his hand scrubbing his thick beard.

"I need it today."

11

ISABELLE

"*D*on't scream, it's me."

My surprised eyes snap open as my heart constricts. I don't need to roll over to know Isaac is slipping between the sheets of my bed. His delicious scent is filtering through my nostrils, sparking my senses. When he splays his hand across my stomach to pull me back, moisture burns my eyes. His cock is hot and heavy against my back, and his suit has been removed, leaving him in nothing but boxer shorts.

"Isabelle..." Isaac growls in warning when I attempt to roll onto my opposite hip. I want to express how sorry I am for everything that has happened. I want to explain why I lied to him. I'll even shamelessly beg for forgiveness if required.

"No talking, not yet." His teeth sink into my shoulder blade before his tongue lashes the puncture mark. "I need to taste you first, to have you underneath me. It's been too long. I can't wait any longer."

Every nerve in my body tingles with anticipation. It's only been four days since we last tangoed, but it feels more like a lifetime. It's hard to explain, but this is us—we show our affection through sexual contact. Our love, our desires, our needs, they're reflected in the most intimate ways. So, with that in mind, I'll forgo pleading for clemency and express my regret in a sexual nature.

Goosebumps pebble my skin when Isaac's hand skims under my black silk camisole to cup my engorged breast. His talented fingers soon have my nipples erect and paying careful attention to every tweak he does. Excitement blasts through me, making me sticky and hot. I love how talented he is. He always ensures I'm thoroughly satisfied before he'll ever consider the possibility of getting himself off.

When he rolls over to pin me to the mattress, my breathing stills. His cock is thick against my damp panties, and the sheer closeness of his handsome face has my heart gaining an extra beat. Even in the moonlight, his entrancing features can't be concealed. With his razor-sharp jaw, plump, full lips, and striking eyes, he's a true masterpiece crafted to perfection.

He assesses my face as robustly as I just appraised his. Although his gaze is lidded, I can see his hurt reflecting back. My deceit hurt him. His eyes are circled with dark rims, and the scruff on his chin is the thickest I've seen it.

"Isaac—"

Before my apology can spill from my lips, his perfectly structured mouth seals over mine. He nips on my bottom lip before his tongue soothes the sting his teeth made, then he wrangles it with mine. It's a soul-stealing kiss that is warm, inviting, and demanding. It represents the man I'm in love with to a T.

"These are my lips, Isabelle, only mine," he mutters in his sexy, raspy voice.

"Always." My heart bursts with love from the dominance in his tone. "They'll never be anyone else's."

I adjust the tilt of my hips so I can rub against the girth teasing my clit. I barely get in two grinds when he inches back, removing his erection from my buzzing clit. "Not yet."

He drags his lips down my chin and along my neck. The prickles of his unshaven chin add even more excitement to our heartfelt reunion. My legs scissor when he places a hot trail of kisses down my body. Little bites, soothing licks, and the roughness of his five o'clock shadow have me teetering toward the brink of ecstasy in no time. His stamina has always impressed me, but tonight it's at a whole new level. He can control himself for hours if needed, ensuring he always gives a stellar performance in the bedroom.

Even after a month, his dedication never wavered. I was always satisfied to the point of exhaustion before he attempted to chase his own climax. Even during the dreaded red week of my cycle, he took care of me. I felt like a teenager when he brought me to climax without removing my panties, but it was incredible. I shouldn't have been surprised. He's an incredibly gifted man, both in and out of the bedroom.

Isaac's teasing kisses stop at the waist of my black silk panties. He lifts his lust-ridden gaze to my face, appraising my body on the way by. As he smirks a deliciously wicked smile, he shreds my panties off my body. I gasp at his domineering gesture, loving the switch of dynamics between us. I'm an independent, strong woman, but I'm more than happy to relinquish my power to Isaac. He'd never use it against me. If anything, he uses it to make me stronger. I've never felt stronger than when I'm beneath him.

The scent of my arousal filters in the air when Isaac stares at my bare mound, memorizing every detail as if it's the first time he's seen me naked. My knees curve inward when he snaps his eyes shut to inhale a large whiff of air through his nostrils. "You smell so fucking good."

When his eyes pop back open, they're even more captivating than usual. They show his hunger. His every need. His desire. And they're all pointing at me. My teeth gnaw my bottom lip when he rests his backside on the balls of his feet so he can take in the entire picture.

His needy voice rumbles through my body, clustering in my aching pussy when he says, "Place your feet flat on the bed, then bend your knees. Spread open wide for me, Isabelle, I want to see all of you."

Even though my cheeks heat from his bold request, it isn't from embarrassment, it's from desire. There isn't an inch of me he hasn't inspected the past month, and the fact he still craves me as rampantly as I do him spurs on my need to please him. So, after shifting my legs up high on the bed, I do as requested without a peep trickling from my lips.

He runs his index finger down the seam of my wet pussy before slapping my clit with the back of his hand. "So pretty and pink." He presses his thumb on the throbbing node before returning his eyes to mine. "Your eyes are never to leave mine, Isabelle. Do you understand?"

Unable to speak through my dry, parched mouth, I nod. I love watching him worship me, so I'd never do anything to taint that.

His dark, intense eyes remain arrested on mine as his head narrows toward my pussy. My body is thrumming with so much excitement, I'm afraid I may soon convulse. One touch, one lick, and I'll be freefalling, toppling into orgasmic bliss.

Just as his tongue spears into my pussy, my back lurches off the bed. It isn't in euphoria. It's from Isaac disappearing before my very eyes. My bewilderment intensifies when my hand shoots to between my legs. I'm still wearing my black satin panties, and although my camisole top is drenched with sweat, it's still very much in place.

Oh my god, was it all a dream? It couldn't have been; it felt so real.

I flop back onto my pillow with a groan, striving to get the excitement scorching my veins under control. My skin is coated with sweat, and my breaths are ragged. I swear on my uncle's grave, Isaac was just here. With my inner vixen screaming obscenities at the top of her lungs, I drag my spare pillow over my face to muffle her cries. Even she thought it was real. It probably doesn't help that I can smell Isaac's alluring scent in the air. It's infused there, refusing to leave even after bucket loads of tears begged it to go away.

After rubbing my weary eyes, I turn them to the alarm clock that usually sits on my bedside table. It takes a few moments for me to recall why the clock isn't in its usual position. Isaac yanked it out of the wall when we made love. It shattered into pieces when he flung it against my bedroom door.

"I don't care if I have to fuck you for twelve hours straight, you're not leaving this bed until I hear those words come out of your mouth in person," he said that morning.

God, I miss him. His smell, his touch, but more than anything, his allure.

With any chance of going back to sleep lost, I yank back my pale blue bedspread, then flop my legs over the bed. From my new position, I can see the screen of my cell phone, which is sitting in its charging pod.

"Five o'clock," I mutter in disgrace. "I haven't been awake this early in years."

After stretching to loosen up my strumming muscles, I scamper out of bed and pad into my walk-in closet to change my camisole and panties to ones less drenched. In my half-asleep state, I trip over running shoes left discarded on my closet floor. I haven't been jogging in weeks. It wasn't just Alex's demanding work schedule that had my exercise regime lagging, it was Isaac's sexual workouts. There were days I turned up to work feeling like I'd run a marathon. That's how impressive Isaac's sexual prowess is.

I could probably use a little bit of exercise. I haven't been to the grocery store in over a month, so I've been living off stale Frosted Flakes and the emergency stash of Snickers in my freezer. It's not ideal, meaning in only four short days, I'm already struggling to fit into my jeans. Furthermore, a run could help get me out of the funk I'm in.

After throwing on a pair of running shorts, a shirt, and a

thin jacket, I tie on my shoes then exit my apartment. A brisk wind cuts through me like a knife when I break through the revolving door of my building. The sun hasn't begun to rise yet, so the morning is still shrouded in an eerie grayness. The only light supplied is by the moon or the occasional street light scattered along the street.

While putting in my earbuds, I catch the curious gaze of a security officer loitering in the lobby of my building. Upon closer glance, I realize he's the gentleman who returned the elevator to the ground floor at Isaac's request after our disastrous date with Tatiana and Ryan. He watches me curiously when I take off down the near-isolated street with a wave. There are a handful of cars on the road, apparently early morning commuters heading to work, but the sidewalks are devoid of the foot traffic I'm usually hit with each morning.

A grunt spills from my lips when Kings of Leon's hit song "Sex on Fire" pumps through my earbuds. I'm aiming to run out my sexual frustration on a crisp fall morning, and what's the first song I hear? The one that instantly makes my mind drift to Isaac any time I listen to it.

Shrugging off Karma's firm bite of my backside, I continue down the street. It's been a few weeks since I've been on a run, but it's like riding a bike, you never forget how to do it. Before I know it, familiar strides increase the flow of blood through my body. In no time at all, my shirt is damp with sweat, and my heart rate has accelerated to a steady, pounding rhythm. Running is nearly as good as dancing when I need a boost of adrenaline. Both activities are exhausting, but my body thrums with adrenaline hours after. It's similar to how my body reacts after having sexual contact with the incredibly alluring Mr. Isaac Holt.

"Jesus, Isabelle, you're supposed to be running out your sexual frustration, not increasing it," I reprimand to myself.

Annoyed, I brave the grueling St. Thomas Street hill. It's the steepest and longest hill in town. By the time I make it to the peak, my brain is too busy demanding my lungs to breathe, and it can't think about the many other ways I've become breathless the past month.

Raising my arms above my head, I fight in vain to replenish my lungs with the crisp morning air. My hair is drenched from the roots to the tips. Even my socks are soaked through. While removing my jacket to relieve my overheated body, I yank out my earbuds. Birds chirping in the distance are barely heard over the heavy flow of traffic. When I glance around at my surroundings, it dawns on me that I've been running a lot longer than I realized. If the steady stream of traffic is anything to go by, it would be close to seven o'clock. That means I've been running for over an hour and a half. No wonder my muscles are screaming.

On the pleas of my aching joints, I stroll back down St. Thomas Street. It's a nice morning, and I've got nowhere important to be, so I may as well take my time.

My leisurely pace slackens even more when I turn down the street my building is on. There's a dark blue sedan parked half a block down. Although it could be a coincidence, my intuition is warning me not to be gullible.

After swallowing the lump in my throat, I continue my journey, pricking my ears so I can hear if the stationary vehicle commences following me. When an engine roars to life, I twirl back around. Relief passes through me when a white Range Rover pulls out from behind the suspicious vehicle. My relieved sigh turns into a squeal when my abrupt turn around has me crashing into a well-defined chest. My nose stings as moisture clusters in my eyes.

"Shit, Izzy, are you okay?"

Lifting my tear-welling eyes, I'm met with the concerned gaze of Hugo. "I think your pec broke my nose," I murmur through the hand that shot up to soothe my throbbing nose.

When his chest heaves with laughter, I glare at him. He can laugh. He didn't run into the equivalent of a brick wall.

After mouthing a silent apology, he removes my hand from my nose so that he can inspect it. "I don't think it's broken." He pinches the bridge, ensuring everything is in place. "But a nasty bump is forming. We should put some ice on it." After peering at someone behind my shoulder, he jerks his head to my building. "Come on, let's get it taken care of."

Suspicion makes itself known with my gut when he guides me into the elevator car of my building without needing to show ID. Although he's with me, the security officers of my building are usually more stringent.

"Why were you outside my building so early?" Even with my nose plugged, suspicion still runs rife in my voice.

Hugo coughs before selecting my floor on the elevator panel. "I live here."

My eyes snap to his. "What? For how long?"

"Since I started working for Isaac." He notches up his

shoulder like it's no big deal. It is. It's huge. "Isaac doesn't just own your apartment, Izzy, he owns the whole building."

Oh.

As the elevator ascends to my floor, I contemplate how I can ask Hugo something without sounding like I'm interrogating him.

When I fail to find a way, I try straight-up honesty. "Can I ask you something?"

Hugo nods, approving my request without pause for consideration.

"How much rent do you pay for your apartment?"

Smiling, his blue eyes drop to mine. "The same amount as you."

I nearly fist pump the air. I knew Theresa was full of crap.

My inner monologue trails off when Hugo adds on, "Nothing."

When my eyes rocket back to his, he winks at the astonished look on my face.

"I'll have you know, I pay rent for my apartment every month. It may not be quite the same amount as other tenants, but it's debited out of my account on the first of every month, thank you very much."

My last four words are full of sass, but they do little to stop amusement from slipping over Hugo's face. Annoyed at his wrong assumption I'm living rent-free, when the elevator arrives at my floor, I storm out. Hugo shadows me, but not a word oozes from his lips. After kicking off my running shoes, I rush into my bedroom to yank my iPhone from its charging pod.

Hugo's eyes float down to mine when I re-enter the living room. "I'll prove it."

I log into my bank app, ignoring my surprise at discovering I have more money in my account than expected, then complete a search for the past three months by adding the agreed rent amount into the search criteria. My heart stops beating when my search comes up empty. It's not showing any payments to Colt Enterprises, let alone my measly twelve hundred a month.

I stop glaring at my phone, willing for it to back me up when Hugo says, "You may have filled out a direct debit request, but that doesn't mean Isaac's real estate agent filed your paperwork."

12

ISABELLE

While clutching a piece of paper tightly in my fist, my fretful eyes dart up and down the street. Even in my furious mood, I can't risk the surveillance team, or even worse, Theresa seeing me entering Isaac's nightclub. Not only would my suspension most likely be extended, but I'd also risk being arrested.

Confident no one is watching, I slip into the back entrance of Isaac's nightclub. It's only a little after ten in the morning, so there are no patrons inside the club yet, which is surprising. Even during the daytime, his nightclubs have several dozen patrons milling around.

I bounce my curious eyes around surroundings I've taken in more via surveillance than in person. The Dungeon is an elegant-looking club that screams sex and seduction since Isaac's allure is embedded in it. No wonder why patrons don't bat an eyelid at being charged double for drinks. Even I'd pay the exorbitant fee to dance in a nightclub as elaborate as this one.

My heart beats out a funky tune when my eyes lock in on a mirrored window in the far corner of the room. I'm reasonably sure that's Isaac's office. After exhaling my nerves with a big breath, I pace for the door at the side of the mirror.

My quick strides halt when a petite lady with a pixie haircut darts in front of me. She spreads her tiny hands on her even smaller waist before narrowing her eyes. "Isaac doesn't want to see you." She toughens her stance by rolling her shoulders and snarling her top lip. "Ever again."

"Then Isaac will need to tell me that."

I try not to let irritation be heard in my tone. I fail. Just the petite brunette's eyes reveal her interests in Isaac aren't business-related, much less her immediate dislike of me. Although I'd usually be more than happy to put her in her place, I'm not in the mood to deal with her right now. I have much more pressing matters to handle.

When I attempt to skirt past the fairy-looking lady, she blocks my path. I glare at her before stepping to the left. She returns my glare before stepping right.

"Please move." I'm shocked I can render up any politeness. I'm at my absolute last nerve.

She all but pokes me in the chest when she gives me a stern finger point. "You may have gotten your hooks into Isaac outside of these walls, but it won't happen in my club."

"*Your* club?" I cross my arms in front of my chest, my hackles raised. "Please excuse me if I'm wrong, but I'm reasonably sure your name isn't written above the door." My squinted eyes stray to the proprietor's name displayed at the entrance of the nightclub. "Oh, nope, that's right, it still shows *only* Isaac Holt's name above the door."

The pixie's stern composure doesn't flinch at my bitchy remark. She stands her ground, not once lessening the scowl marring her pretty face. "I was here years before you arrived, and I'll be here years after you leave."

I tilt closer to the pixie fairy. Because she's so short, I have to bend my knees to glance into her eyes. "As nothing more than a paid employee."

The pulse in my neck twangs when the rumbling voice of Isaac echoes through the room. "Do you want me to get some mud, or are you two happy to continue wrestling without it?"

He's leaning against the doorframe of his office. The darkness of his gray suit matches his eyes to perfection, and even with an angry scowl straining his handsome face, my heart still skips a beat.

When he notices my avid assessment of his body, his perfectly etched brow arches high, but before he can articulate either disdain or pleasure to my prolonged gawp, the fairy lady snaps, "I was telling Isabelle what you told me earlier. How you have *no* interest in seeing her ever again."

I stare at Isaac, begging for him to refute her hurtful comment. He does no such thing. He just adds to the bruise my ego just got.

"What do you want, Isabelle?" His tone is harsh, but my body still tingles from my name rolling off his tongue.

"I need to talk to you..." My words trail off when the lady standing beside me huffs dramatically. "In private."

Isaac takes several heart-clenching seconds contemplating my request. Once he decides, his eyes drift to the pixie lady standing next to me. When she sees his answer before he can voice it, she crosses her arms in front of her scarcely-covered chest and drops her jaw.

Even though she's aware of his response, Isaac spells it out for her. "Tell Roger I'm leaving five minutes later than expected."

I try to hide my smile, but the smallest smirk curves on my lips. I can't help it. Victory has never tasted so sweet. After a final glare, Tina storms toward the bar, murmuring incoherently under her breath the entire way. Isaac tracks her angry march before returning his grim gaze to me. My pulse quickens when he jerks up his chin, requesting for me to follow him. When he spins on his heels and strides into his office, I do precisely that, my knees knocking with every step I take.

As I enter the opulent space, I absorb the lavish furnishing and manly features. This is only the second time I've been here. The first time, I was too irate about the gigantic love bite Isaac left on my neck to fully take it in. Now, I'd give anything for him to mark me again.

Halfway through my scan, I stumble onto Isaac standing near a glass bar. He's pouring himself a generous helping of whiskey. "Don't you think it's a little early to be drinking?"

His clutch on the bottle he's clasping firms before he glares at me. His gaze sears me motionless, but not in a bad way. It has me heating up everywhere as blistering as the anger I felt when he didn't defend me to Tina.

"Have you slept with Tina?"

I'm reasonably sure I know the answer to my highly inappropriate question, especially considering the circumstances of my visit, but my inessential need to know everything gnawed at my insides until I had no choice but to blurt it out.

Isaac throws down a generous serve of whiskey in one hit. Heat creeps across my cheeks when his face doesn't allude to the sharp bitterness sliding down his throat. After returning his glass to the countertop, he pivots to face me. My breathing halts at how taut his beautiful face is. His eyes are slit, and his lips are furled, but he's still the most handsome man I've ever seen.

"What do you want, Isabelle?" he repeats, even harsher this time.

When his gaze darts down to the paper I'm clutching, it dawns on me why I came to his office. I'm not being facetious when I say my inhibitions are thrown out the window when I'm in his presence. My level-headedness, my composure, and apparently my brain, disappear the instant my eyes land on him.

"I came to give you this." I step closer to him, my thighs shaking. "It isn't as much as you receive from your other tenants, but it's all I can afford."

When his eyes shoot down to the bank check I'm clutching, his jaw spasms. I'm only arriving at his club now as I had to wait for the bank to open so they could draw the check. Although Theresa disclosed the tenants in Isaac's building pay more than double what I pay, I cannot afford the full amount. Instead, I had the check drawn up for the initially agreed twelve hundred dollars a month that was negotiated when I signed the lease. Considering I've been living in his apartment rent-free the past twelve weeks, the check is a little under four thousand dollars.

When Isaac makes no attempt to accept the check, I place it on his bulky wooden desk. "I also called your real estate agent to advise that I'll be vacating your property by the end of the month."

It isn't that I don't appreciate what he did for me—I truly do—I just can't continue living there at the reduced rate. If I did, it would make the Internal Affairs Department's investigation into me appear more legitimate. It will appear as if I gave Isaac private information in exchange for free housing. If I could afford the full monthly rent for an apartment that size, I would, but since I can't, I have no choice but to move out.

My throat works hard to swallow when a thick stench of awkwardness plagues the air surrounding us. Although it's dense, it isn't abundant enough to mask the savage surge of electricity bolting between us. It's so strong, I can hear it crackling and hissing in the air, almost drowning out what Isaac says next, "Is that all?"

Unable to speak for fear my voice will crack, I nod.

"Okay. Good. Goodbye, Isabelle."

I smile to hide the sting of his blunt dismissal. "Goodbye."

Spinning on my heels, I make a beeline for the door. I need to escape before my threatening tears spill over. Just before I exit, paper being ripped overtakes my pulse shrilling in my ears. Sharply, I crank my neck back in just enough time to witness Isaac tearing up the check I just had drawn.

"What are you doing?" I storm back to him to snatch a portion of the now-ruined check out of his hand. "That's a bank check, they've already taken the money out of my account, so whether you cash it or not, the money is already gone; I can't draw you another one."

"I don't want your fucking money, Isabelle!"

I take a step back, shocked at his words, but it won't stop me saying, "I didn't ask to be placed on your payroll either, but I wasn't given a choice, was I?"

He arches his brow. "My payroll?"

"Yeah, your payroll. What did the agent from the IA call me... oh, that's right, a paid mistress aka your prostitute."

My teeth clench when an arrogant smirk stretches across his face. "That's what you are, isn't it? Whether the money was coming from the Bureau or me, you were paid to sleep with me."

I slap him so hard across the face, my hand sets on fire, and his head rockets to the side. Slowly, almost robotically, he returns it front and center. His jaw is twitching profusely, and a dark cloud has formed in his already furious eyes. I nearly stumble out an apology before realizing I have nothing to be sorry for. He insulted me, not the other way around.

"I'm sorry I lied to you. I'm sorry for not telling you about my job at the very beginning, but don't you dare degrade what we had by saying I was paid to do it. You know as well as I do that I *never* slept with you for my job." My tear-filled eyes stare into his, pleading for him to believe my statement. "I love you, Isaac. Whether you choose to believe me or not is up to you, but if you ever find it in your heart to forgive me, be assured I'll be waiting for you. You just need to realize you're fighting a battle bigger than us both."

No longer having the ability to hold up the flood gates in my eyes, I dart out of his office as quickly as my trembling legs will take me. I slam the door shut before leaning my back against it. As I gulp in quick breaths, I beg my tears time and time again not to spill. Unlike Friday, the sun is shining brightly, so I'll have no way of concealing my devastation from those around me.

I stop reaching for the invisible knife Isaac just stabbed into my heart when a snarky voice whines, "I tried to warn you."

Tina braces her back on the bar before unleashing her most brutal assault—her victorious smirk. Enjoying the spectacle of me on the verge of tears, she crosses her arms over her chest before getting her legs in on the show. The indecent length of her shorts when she crosses them assures they'd never be classified as clothing. The panties I wear during the red week of my cycle have more material than her shorts.

I want to snap back at her wordless taunt, but I'm honestly too tired. Instead, I hurry for the back entrance of the club, ignoring Tina's snarky chuckle at my mad dash. "Make sure the door doesn't hit you on the ass on the way out."

With a grunt, I push open the heavy door. My eyes squint as they struggle to adjust from the darkness of Isaac's club to the blinding mid-morning sun. It's so bright, I have to shelter my eyes to see where I'm walking. Eager to return to my apartment to wallow in self-pity in private, my strides are urgent and fast.

When I reach the corner of Welsh and Trover Street, my quick pace slackens. Megan Shroud is a mere foot in front of me. With everything going on, I completely forgot about her and her freakish obsession with Isaac's brother, Nick.

At first glance, she appears as if she's any other woman going about her day-to-day routine. The only reason she's attracting my attention, and that of those surrounding her, is the yellow sundress she's wearing. Although the mid-morning sun has a nice amount of warmth to it, the breeze blowing up the hem of her dress is as cold as ice. I'm chilly wearing jeans and a thin cashmere sweater, so she must be freezing.

Ignoring the nerves fluttering in my stomach, I drift my eyes over the people milling around the bus stop, seeking the agents Alex assigned to Megan's case Thursday morning. My first guess would be the lady sitting at the café across the street. She appears to be reading the paper, but her eyes aren't shifting in a left to right pattern. Uncle Tobias said that error is usually the first thing a target spots when they're under surveillance.

"Even if your gaze never leaves your target, you must shift your eyes accordingly," he used to preach.

God, I miss him.

Once I'm standing shoulder to shoulder with Megan, I glance down at the paper she's grasping in her delicate, yet strong hand. Because her clutch is so firm, I can't see what's printed on the document, but a logo of an interstate bus company is visible in the top right-hand corner.

Unaware of my watchful glance, Megan bounces heel to toe. Her light brown hair hangs freely down her back, framing her makeup-free face. Her nude lips are curved into a smile, and her hazel eyes are sparkling in the sun. Even in her dapper mood, her body can't hide its panic. Her arms are covered with goosebumps, and the tips of her toes are blue, although her expression does not indicate her body's discomfort.

A dull ache stabs my chest. Is anyone looking out for her? She's clearly unhinged.

My worry is pushed aside when the squeak of brakes shrieks through my ears. It's closely followed by the polluted smoke you'd expect from a large coach. A white bus with 'New York City' displayed in LED lights in the window stops in front of Megan and me. Believing I'm waiting for the bus, Megan gestures for me to enter before her.

"Ah... I still need to buy a ticket." I bite on the inside of my cheek, hating that my words come out with a quiver. I shouldn't be so hard on myself. At least I thought of something. I'm not usually quick-witted.

Megan's grin exposes a chip in her front tooth. "The ticket office is through those doors." She points behind me, her voice so weak she sounds like a child instead of an adult.

I stray my eyes in the direction she's pointing. A large circular logo for Bellevue Buses is displayed on the front door. The frontage sign states they specialize in traveling interstate in comfort and safety.

Uneased, I return my eyes to Megan. "Thank you."

I desperately want to ask her where she's going, but she steps onto the bus before I can. When she hands her ticket to the overweight gentleman sitting in the driver's seat, he eyes her attire in confusion. Even in his heated bus, he's wearing a long-sleeve shirt and a knitted vest.

When the lady 'reading' the newspaper crosses the street to shadow Megan onto the bus, I dip my chin in greeting. She fills a vacant spot three places down from Megan before she recommences reading.

I wait until the bus is nothing more than a blip on the horizon before yanking my phone out of my pocket and dialing a memorized number.

"Miss me already?" Brandon jests a short time later.

The cool wind chills my teeth when I smile. "I do... but I also need a favor."

"Another one."

His chuckles settle the nerves in my stomach. I hate asking for favors.

"Megan Shroud was just seen leaving on a bus to New York. Can you please check if she purchased a one-way or a return ticket?"

"Yeah, hold on." Fingers hitting keys of his keyboard sounds down the line, along with his heavy breaths. "It's a one-way ticket."

Relief washes over me. Hopefully, this is a sign Megan finally got the hint that Nick isn't interested in her, but just in case, I add a little more sauce to my favor. "Can you add Megan's name to the travel database? I want to know if she purchases a return ticket."

Brandon remains quiet, but papers are ruffling.

"Brandon?"

I hear his cheeks rising. "Oh yeah, sorry, I was nodding."

"Thanks, Brandon."

He exhales sharply. "Anytime, Izzy."

While placing my phone back into my pocket, a delicious smell streams into my nose. It smells distinctively like the scrumptious pies Harlow serves every day. Other than the message I got from her after I left Cormack's office, I haven't heard a peep from her. Before I stuffed everything up, we texted each other numerous times a day before finalizing our day with a call each night. I want to say her lack of contact is because she's busy, but it's more likely that she, along with everyone else, is still angry at me.

Determined not to make another huge mistake, I make my way to Harlow's bakery. Because it's only mid-morning, the bakery is pretty deserted. When the bell above the door chimes, Harlow stops replenishing the cake fridge. Several heart-clenching seconds pass with her staring at me in shock. The silence is awkward. Usually, when we're together, no one can get in a word between us.

"I've missed you, Harlow." My voice shakes with emotions. We've only been friends for six months, but she is, without a doubt, my very best friend. "Please let me fix this. I'll do anything to make things right between us."

The tears I'm fighting to keep at bay spring down my cheeks when she dashes around the counter to wrap me up in a fierce hug. "I've missed you, too."

We cuddle for several minutes, only breaking when the bell above the door chimes for the second time. In sync, our eyes drift to the other side of the room. Renee is standing at the door, balancing a stack of bakery boxes on her slim waist.

Her brows fetter when she takes in our wet cheeks and glistening eyes. "Go sit, then I'll bring coffee. You both look as if you could use a caffeine IV." Guilt washes over her face, but it doesn't stop her from saying. "Whoever invented the term 'ugly crying' was referring to this when they fabricated it."

I laugh, adoring her sass. She reminds me of a younger,

more rebellious version of Harlow. Although her comment was made in jest, it holds credit. I know I look like shit, but Harlow also appears tired and withdrawn. Dark rings dull her eyes, and her smile isn't as bright as usual. After looping my arm around Harlow's elbow, I drag her toward our table. We assemble at the same table every time we get together here. It's the table Isaac was seated at the first time I laid eyes on him in his home turf. Every time I sit here, the smell of whole grain and rye toasted cheese sandwich conquers up memories. Today is no different. Not even our brutal run-in can weaken them.

Harlow remains quiet while Renee wrangles up two mugs of coffee and a gigantic slice of pumpkin pie. "You can't have coffee without pie." After rubbing my shoulder, she makes herself scarce.

I don't have the heart to tell her I hate anything associated with pumpkin. Pumpkin is disgusting. Even with a whole heap of sugar and a super sweet pastry, I refuse to eat it, but even if she presented me a chocolate pie with a pile of whipped cream, I still wouldn't eat it. My stomach is too twisted up about the anxious expression on Harlow's beautiful face to handle food.

I curl my hand over Harlow's clenched fist. "Do you want me to talk to Cormack again?"

I was hoping Cormack had taken Hugo's advice and patched things up with Harlow, but from the expression on her face, I'm going to assume he hasn't.

The pressure on my chest weakens when Harlow smiles. "No, we're good, but thank you for offering." Her smile enlarges to a full-size grin. "The makeup sex was great, so I should probably thank you."

Our giggles are more noticeable since the bakery is near empty. After blowing on my coffee to cool down its scorching heat, I take a swig. "So, what's with the odd expression on your face? You look..." I stop talking, giving my eyes time to study the look marring her face. "... scared?"

Harlow is as shocked by my admission as I am. She's a tough cookie. She handled the Tatiana incident with dignified composure and handles irate customers daily. I don't think I've ever seen her rattled.

Hold on, yes, I have. She was skittish when we first arrived at the McGregor residence. Before I can ask if the incidents are linked, Harlow confirms it. "Did you know Clara is now living in Ravenshoe?"

Ignoring the tension in my belly, I shake my head. "But I didn't have a clue where she lived."

After swallowing a mouthful of sweetened black coffee, Harlow's eyes meet mine. "She was residing in New York but moved to Ravenshoe permanently the weekend following our trip to the McGregor residence. She's living in a fancy building on Hyde Place."

My heart stops beating. It could be a coincidence, but Isaac's *fuck pad* is in Hyde Place. Before I can work through my confusion, Harlow continues, "Do you remember me begging you not to leave me alone when you first woke up from your famous wine and Xanax blackout concoction?"

I jerk up my chin. "Yep. I just recalled that it was the first time I'd seen you rattled."

Harlow rolls her eyes. "That was because of Clara. She doesn't like me very much."

"Is she creating trouble between you and Cormack?"

Her lips thin. "I can't one hundred percent testify to that, but I'm reasonably sure she's narking in his ear at every available opportunity." Her eyes lift and lock with mine. "The billionaire and the baker isn't a story she wants plotted out."

I make a *pfft* noise with my lips. "Then she's an idiot. Thousands of readers would gobble up a story like that. She just doesn't understand modern-day fairy tales." Leaning over the table, I re-clutch Harlow's hand in mine. "Give as good as you're getting, Harlow."

She arches her brow. "That goes for the both of us, Kettle."

"Yes, it does," I agree with a nod. "And from here on out, I'm going to do precisely that."

13

ISAAC

"That doesn't look like the face of a traitor."

I close my laptop screen, which is displaying an image of Isabelle leaning against my office door. In the photo, her teeth have caught her bottom lip, and her eyes are snapped shut as she battles not to let tears spill down her ashen face. The hurt projected in her beautiful chocolate eyes when I insulted her cut through me like a knife, so I've been torturing myself the past hour by watching the surveillance video of the incident over and over again. It only made me more confused. If she were paid to sleep with me, why did she react to my taunt?

"What Hugo told you is true, Isaac. If you wait too long—"

My vicious glare halts any further relationship advice Hunter is planning to give. "If you still want to be employed by the end of the day, keep your thoughts to yourself."

Hunter, my head of security, pops his shoulder onto the

doorjamb of my office. As he authenticates my threat, he scrubs his hand over the scraggly beard covering his jawline. His dark blond hair is pulled back into a low-riding man bun, and his tattoo collection is barely concealed by the checked shirt he's wearing rolled up at the sleeves. He has what could be termed a rough-and-rugged appearance.

When I interviewed him for a position within my empire, I initially judged him on his outer facade instead of his impressive security capabilities. He soon proved his worth when he hacked into my supposedly unhackable security system to siphon my bank account of two million dollars. He was so brazen, he did it in front of me. I fired my head of security the day he joined my team. That was a little over four years ago.

"Was that Isabelle?"

Hunter pushes off the wall to stride into my office, his hurried pace slackening when my narrowed eyes land on him. "Yes, but if the search you completed on her had been more thorough, you'd be aware of that."

Hunter dares to smirk. "I stand by my search—"

"Then, obviously, I need a new head of security."

"When you find the guy who hid her information so deep not even I could find it, I'll hire him myself as my replacement." His tone relays the truth in his bold statement.

At my request, Hunter undertook a background search of Isabelle the weekend she stayed at my apartment. His investigation failed to yield any real results. He supplied me with an expired copy of her learner's permit from when she was sixteen. It revealed that she resided in a coastal town near San

Francisco called Tiburon, but other than that, her file was as scarce as her bank accounts.

It may seem pretentious of me to investigate people in my life, but in my position, I have no choice. I've been burned in the past, so I'm cautious about who I allow into my life. Generally, my searches are reserved for staff or business associates, but Isabelle intrigued me enough to warrant her own special investigation. Although frustrated with Hunter's lack of information, it made the chase even more inspiring.

Hunter plops into the leather chair across from me. "This lady, on the other hand, reads like an open book." He tosses a manila folder filled to the brim with papers onto my desk. "Was there something you failed to mention when you asked me to investigate her?"

My teeth grinding together stuff his laughter into the back of his throat. While he scrubs his beard, a trait he always does when nervous, I open the folder. A grunt parts my lips when my eyes run over the extensively noted documents inside. Hunter is meticulous about the amount of information he unearths, but right now, I don't have time to read a one-hundred-plus-page report.

I sink lower into my chair. "I have a meeting with Regan in ten minutes. Can you give me a brief rundown?"

Hunter pulls an iPad out of the hemp bag he dumped on the floor upon entry. "Did Roger scan your office this morning?"

"Yes." I snap. "He didn't find anything... today."

After I was arrested, Hunter had my office, apartment, and private residence scanned for listening devices. Two bugs were found in my home, and one was in my office. Now, Roger examines my office twice a day instead of his usual once-over before I arrive.

"From what I unearthed, I'm assuming you know a good whack about her private life..." His arrogant smirk is wiped off his face when I growl. "All right, here are the basics. Theresa Veneto is thirty-two years old. She lives in Hopeton, she's unmarried, has one child, and her current position is an investigator in the Internal Affairs Department of the Federal Bureau of Investigation." His smile returns. "Oh, and last, but not at all least, she has a major lady boner for a businessman named Isaac Holt."

I shoot him a warning look. I'm not in the mood for his shit today. I'm at my tether. "How long has Theresa been with IA?"

"Since June thirteenth." Hunter doesn't sneak a glance at the information sitting in front of him. Hugo continuously jests that his brain is like a sponge. It absorbs every minor detail to retain it for future use.

"What was she doing before IA?"

Hunter arches his brow. "Investigating you."

"Was or is?"

"Was. Due to no credible evidence against you, she was removed from your case." His eyes snap to mine to give me a cheeky wink. "You can thank me for that later."

A subtle grin etches on my mouth. His skillset does warrant some credit, but I'll never tell him that.

"The details are a little shady, but Theresa was either demoted to IA or she asked to be transferred there." His tattoo-covered hand darts across the table to flick over a few pages of the extensive report he presented me with. "That's her current target."

Blood surges through my veins when my eyes drop to the surveillance photos displayed. The top picture is a photo of Isabelle and Theresa standing eye to eye in the entranceway of Isabelle's apartment.

"Why is IA investigating Isabelle?"

Hunter places his jean-covered ankle onto his knee before gliding his amused eyes to me. "For conspiring with you."

"They're investigating their agent for doing the job they paid her to do?"

Hunter's lips crimp as he shakes his head. "Now, the slap mark on your cheek makes sense."

His eyes float over my left cheek, which is still burning from the slap Isabelle inflicted on me over an hour ago. I'll be frank, my cock turned to stone when she slapped me. An angry Isabelle is just as ravishing as a jealous Isabelle.

Hunter drops his ankle from his knee before his elbow takes its place. "You probably don't want to hear this, but I'm gonna say it. Isabelle didn't rat you out."

A half-chuckle/half-grunt escapes my lips. "What is it with all the men surrounding me not seeing past Isabelle's ruse? First Hugo, then Cormack, now you. I thought I was the only fool who couldn't see past the wool she pulled over my eyes."

Hunter slants his head to the side, not the least bit confronted about the repercussion he may ignore by saying, "Because we'd happily rot in jail just for the opportunity of tapping a woman who looks like her, let alone having her more than once."

My back molars smack together when his eyes lower to the photo of Isabelle on my desk. Usually, my response would be much more severe, but I'm off my game, distracted by the momentous personal endeavors I'm currently undertaking. You'd think my arrest would be at the forefront of my mind. It isn't. I have more pressing issues to handle than the FBI's concerns about who I can or cannot dine with.

Hunter smirks, pleased with my response. "And from the way your jaw is spasming, and you look like you're about to kill me, I'll assume you'd accept the same fate for another night between the sheets with Isabelle."

I don't refute his allegation. There's nothing to dispute since it is factual.

"As I said earlier, Theresa's operating system is severely lacking in security. It didn't even take me ten seconds to get this."

He hands me the iPad device he earlier removed. It's open on an image of Isabelle sitting in a chair behind a white melamine table. The blond gentleman she kissed in her hallway nearly two months ago is seated across from her.

"Are you trying to rub salt into my wounds, or did you just set out to piss me off today?"

"Come on, Isaac. You know as well as anyone that not everything is black and white," Hunter waves his hand to the iPad. "Press play and watch the shadows turn to gray."

After shooting him a wry look, warning him I've reached my quota of smart-ass remarks, I press play on the iPad. My brows shoot up my face when "Are you in a relationship with Isaac Holt?" comes squawking through the speakers. My heart stops beating as I wait for Isabelle's response. Her pupils are wide, and her face is flushed. She looks like a deer caught in the headlights.

"I plead the fifth."

A smirk curves my lips. I'd break out a full smile if I didn't recognize the voice of the person interrogating Isabelle. Her nasally pitch is easily distinguishable. It belongs to Theresa Veneto.

My jaw muscle tenses when Theresa taunts Isabelle about being a paid mistress. It also makes sense as to why Isabelle reacted so fiercely earlier. I treated her just as poorly as the person attempting to railroad her.

When the video ends, exposing that Isabelle denied all interactions with me, my eyes shift to Hunter. "You couldn't have brought this to me an hour earlier?" *Then I wouldn't have insulted Isabelle so bluntly.*

"With everything going on with Nick and his fucked-up stalker, and those other matters you have me looking into, my resources are stretched thin. By thin, I mean I'm exhausted. Something had to give. Unfortunately, it was that." He jerks his head to his iPad.

My first response is to retort that I don't pay him to rest, but his tired eyes shelf my retaliation. He looks as exhausted as I feel. "Could Theresa's investigation have any legalities for Isabelle?"

Hunter runs his hand along his jaw as he slumps deeper into the chair. "I'm not a lawyer, but unless they can prove she was financially rewarded for supplying you with information, I don't see their investigation being anything more than hearsay."

His gaze shoots up to mine. "Did you ever discuss anything with her that could warrant their investigation?"

I shake my head. "We didn't discuss business matters." We barely discussed anything as we were too busy acting on our desires for one another.

"Then she should be okay. If you're not sure, maybe have Regan look into it for you."

I scratch my brow. "Regan is busy handling another matter for me."

Hunter nods. "Speaking of situations, Peters spotted Nick's stalker purchasing a bus ticket to New York earlier this morning. Did you want me to send someone with her? Or..." He stops talking mid-sentence, awaiting further instructions.

"Cormack has a security detail watching Nick from afar in Los Angeles. When he returns home, send one of your guys to keep an eye on him."

"All right." Hunter rises from the chair, snagging his bag from the ground on the way. "Let us know when he's back in town, and I'll send Peters over there." He strides toward the door before stopping abruptly and spinning back around. "You need to be careful with how you tread with this Theresa issue, Isaac. She could squash Isabelle if she wants to. I know you're pissed Isabelle wasn't forthright with you about what she did for a living, but does a small amount of deceit warrant her spending years in jail?"

Not giving me a chance to reply, he briskly exits my office.

14

ISABELLE

My eyes stray to the door of my apartment when a brisk tap booms through it. After gathering up the documents scattered around me, I hide them in the coffee table drawer. I'm not usually so suspicious, but I'm supposed to buzz in visitors before they gain access to my floor, so my distrust is higher today.

I realize the errors of my ways when I swing open my door. Hugo's big, brooding frame hogs nearly every inch of the doorway. He's once again dressed down in ripped Henley jeans and a dark blue, long-sleeve shirt. He wouldn't need to be granted access since he lives in my building.

"Hey, Isabelle," he greets me with his familiar drawl and a broad grin.

I open my door wide before gesturing for him to come inside. "Morning, Hugo."

He takes three steps into my apartment before swiveling

around to face me. His brows are drawn together, his lips pursed. "Where are you going?"

Before I can advise why I have a heap of moving boxes scattered around my living room, the intercom rings. Raising my index finger into the air, I request a minute before pacing to my intercom.

"Hello, Ms. Brahn, we have a Brandon James here to see you," advises a male voice over the intercom receiver.

"Thank you. Please send him up."

I place the intercom phone back onto its receiver before spinning back around to face Hugo. The suspicion I felt earlier flourishes when I notice he's rummaging through a box of knick-knacks I'm in the processing of packing. When he sees my watchful eye, he paces to the double door leading to my small but adequate balcony. "So, you're really moving out?"

I nod. With the end of the month approaching more quickly than I anticipated, I've commenced packing in preparation for my big move.

"Where are you going?"

After blowing a wayward hair out of my face, I shrug. I haven't worked that part out yet. Regina said I could move into the room I used when I moved to Ravenshoe, and Harlow offered me the couch in her tiny flat, but I haven't decided what I want to do just yet. With everything going on, I'm feeling a little homesick, so half of me wants to scurry back to my hometown with my tail firmly planted between my legs, whereas the other half is adamant we stay and defend both Isaac and my name.

"Do you miss your hometown, Hugo?"

From the limited information I expelled from his sister's police report, Hugo and his siblings were raised in Rochdale. Marjorie was born and buried there.

Hugo takes a moment to contemplate my question before shaking his head. "Home isn't where you're born, Izzy. It's where your family lives." His words are extremely soft for a guy of his size. "Family also doesn't mean they're related to you by blood."

My cheeks chuck a stink about the fast incline of my lips. Hugo is very built. His biceps are wider than my head, and his thighs are the width of my waist, but his buzz-cut hair and vast tattoo collection could have you mistaking him as a brainless brute. Only once you unearth the real Hugo do you realize his heart is the biggest muscle in his body.

I lose the chance to reply to his statement when a heavy knock sounds at the door. When I pull it open, I'm greeted by the brightly smiling face of Brandon. He's also dressed casually, but the price tags of his garments are more pricy than Hugo's. His Nieman Marcus Benn stretch-cotton pants and black cashmere and wool blend trench coat cost more than I earn in a month.

A much-needed smile stretches across my face when Brandon pulls out a bouquet from behind his back. One dozen long-stemmed yellow roses with whispers of baby's breath weaved throughout are arranged in a beautiful crystal vase.

"Brandon, you shouldn't have."

He smiles his trademark lopsided grin. The slight fault in his smile makes him even more appealing. Not many people are faultless, but Brandon's handsome boy-next-door looks and an even more stellar personality are cutting it closer. The slight wonkiness of his near-perfect smile makes him more realistic —an everyday person instead of an unattainable man. I've only met one unattainable man before. That man is the incredibly alluring Mr. Isaac Holt.

"I thought they'd brighten your day."

Smiling, I accept the vase before placing a kiss on his cheek. I grin like a Cheshire cat when he blushes from my friendly gesture. With a wave of my hand, I motion for him to join me inside. While peering my eyes around my apartment, endeavoring to find a suitable location to place my flowers, I stumble upon the infuriating glare of Hugo. He's shooting daggers at Brandon, his stance nowhere near as casual as his outfit. If he's striving to intimidate Brandon, he's failing miserably. Brandon hasn't even noticed his brooding presence lurking at the side of my living room. His eyes are fixated on me.

I give Hugo my 'behave' face before placing the vase on the entryway table, rotating it until I'm happy with its position. The crystal vase catches the morning sun streaming through the window, sending rainbow hues dancing across my living room.

When I twirl back around, I offer to take Brandon's jacket to hang it in the entry closet. A scratchy sensation hits my throat when Brandon's removal of his coat reveals a white, long-sleeve Armani polo shirt. It hugs his frame so snugly, it showcases him in a light I've not previously seen. He isn't as built as the other male agents in our unit, but I had no clue he was hiding *that* body under the business attire he regularly dons.

My chest expands when Brandon tilts in intimately close to

my side. He isn't standing close enough to make me feel uncomfortable, but to a stranger, it could look a little too chummy, which means it elicits the warning growl bellowing out of Hugo.

"Isn't he Isaac's bodyguard?" Even with Brandon's close proximity, my ears struggle to hear him.

My shoulder touches my ear when I shrug. "He isn't Isaac's bodyguard. He's more an... *associate* of his."

Smiling to ease the confused expression crossing his face, I head to Hugo to offer an introduction. Considering the circumstances, the giddy feeling in my gut is extremely ill-timed. I'm not liking the tension radiating out of Hugo. I'm just loving that even being unjustly fired by Isaac hasn't stop Hugo from defending him.

"Hugo, this is my *friend*, Brandon." I overemphasis the word 'friend,' hoping Hugo will get the hint that Brandon will never be anything more than that. "Brandon, this is my... *friend*, Hugo."

Unappreciative of my stumble, Hugo gawks at me. I mouth an apology. I was genuinely unsure about how I ought to introduce him. He's always been friendly, but most of our interactions occurred while he was an employee of Isaac's, so I wasn't sure if our interactions were because he liked me, or if he were doing the job he was paid to do.

"It's nice to meet you."

When Brandon extends his hand in greeting, Hugo accepts it, albeit hesitantly. "Pleasure."

After they shake hands, the whole gathering plunges into an awkward silence. As they gawk at each other, my eyes bounce between them, pondering as to why I've gone from having no visitors to two within minutes of each other.

When did I become Ms. Popular?

I realize I mumbled my last comment out loud when Brandon and Hugo's eyes snap to mine in sync. Over the silence, much less their dubious glares, I spread my hands across my cocked hip. "All right, spill, what are you two up to?"

Brandon is confused by my bold statement, but Hugo smiles so vividly, only the sturdiest pair of sunglasses could reflect the glare of his vibrant grin. "I've got nothing better to do with my time anymore, so I may as well hang out with you."

Regret stabs my chest. Although Hugo's comment is painful to hear, it holds merit so that only leaves one mystery remaining. Turning my gaze, I peer at Brandon with my brow cocked and my lips twisted.

He shifts from foot to foot as the natural hue adorning his cheeks reddens. "I need to talk to you." His gaze strays to Hugo, who is watching our exchange eagerly, not even pretending he isn't eavesdropping. "In private."

When Hugo gives him a look as if to say, *fuck you, I'm not going anywhere*, I clasp Brandon's perspiration-soaked hand in mine before guiding him into the hallway of my building. Hugo doesn't attempt to follow us. It's for the best. I might have shot him if he did.

After swallowing bleakly, Brandon's gaze floats up from his shoes. "I need a favor."

"Anything, Brandon."

He's been nothing but supportive of me the past six

months, so this is a prime opportunity for me to return the favor.

Relief skims over Brandon's face. "Thank you, Izzy." With how many times he wets his lips, I'm expecting something more profound to come out of his mouth than what he says next. "I need a date." When I stiffen, he coughs to clear nerves from his voice. "My mom's chairman of a charity that holds an annual gala. I tried to get out of it, but she won't accept any of the excuses I'm giving." He takes a step closer to me, his glossed-over eyes begging. "I don't want to go alone because Melody will be there."

Pain claws my chest. Melody was his first love. They were high school sweethearts who only ended their relationship when he joined the Bureau. Although Brandon assured her they'd make it work, Melody didn't want a long-distance relationship. Before I begged Brandon to communicate with her, so I could gain access to Hugo's sister's sealed file, they hadn't spoken in years.

"I'm so desperate for a date, I'm not below getting on my knees and begging. Please, Izzy. I'll do anything, anything at all if you'll just fake liking me for a night."

"I do like you, Brandon." The apprehension straining his face softens from my admission. "So, I'm sure it won't be hard pretending I'm your date for a night."

Brandon flashes me a killer grin. "Thank you, Izzy, thank you."

"You're welcome." Now he isn't the only one nervous. "But now, I need a favor."

My heart warms when he nods without pause.

"I've been looking a little deeper at Megan Shroud." I stop talking, anticipating backlash. When it doesn't come, I continue, "There are a lot of holes in her file I could fill in by driving out to her hometown to check things out." I swish my tongue around my mouth to soothe its dryness. "The thing is, I don't have a car, so can I please borrow yours?"

I slap his chest when he chuckles, "It hasn't recovered from the last time you drove it." He winks, loving my dropped lip. "But I'm more than happy to drive you there."

"Really?"

Grinning, he nods. "I still have nightmares from when you went to her hotel room alone. I refuse to make the same mistake twice. I have the weekend off, so why not go on an adventure?"

"Thank you, Brandon."

He squeezes my hand. "You're welcome. I'd do anything for you."

After arranging for him to pick me up the following morning, I pace back into my apartment. Happiness is beaming out of me until I spot Hugo standing near my vase of roses. When he absorbs my excited expression, silent accusations bound out of him so hard and fast, they nearly knock me onto my ass.

"He's a *friend*, Hugo." My voice gains an edge of annoyance to it. I'm sick of being accused of things I'm not guilty of. "Our relationship is no different than the one I have with you."

"*Friends*? Come on, Izzy, who brings roses for a *friendly* visit."

Needing distance before I say something I'll regret, I head

to my bedroom. I have a whole heap of stuff in there I need to pack before the end of the month.

"Can't deny it, hey?"

I whip around so quick, my hair slaps my face. "Yellow roses mean friendship. Every girl this side of the planet knows that!"

Hugo huffs. "Jeez, Izzy, don't be stup—"

I hit him with a stern finger point. "Don't you dare. If one more person calls me stupid, or any other name this week, I'm gonna... I'm..."

A low, simpering growl is the only way I can express my genuine anger, so that's what I do. Within the last week, I've been called stupid, naïve, a paid mistress, and a range of other nasty names, but the most stinging of all was when Isaac called me a prostitute. He may not have directly said the word, but he alluded to it. That hurt. It was the biggest hit below the belt this week. Not even getting suspended from my job hurt more than his comment.

With my fists clenched at my side, I step closer to Hugo. "It's been over a week since I confronted Isaac, and I've heard nothing but crickets since. I know you're loyal to him, Hugo, and I'll be forever grateful for that, but I have enough people dictating my life. There's no room for another. If you truly want to be my friend, do that, but you need to leave your judgment at the door."

Stealing his chance to reply, I storm into my bedroom. My front door slams shut not long after.

15

ISABELLE

"Stupid piece of shit."

The zipper on my suitcase just burst open for the second time today. I had forgotten about the busted fastener until I pulled it out of my closet to pack an emergency bag of essentials. Megan's hometown is nearly four hundred miles from Ravenshoe, so I'm not sure if Brandon and I will make the trip in one go or stay at a hotel. I could purchase a new suitcase, but after the massive withdrawal from my bank account last week to pay my backdated rent, my funds are best described as limited. So, busted zipper or not, my old bag must do.

When I drop down to my knees to wrestle with my suitcase, my memories drift to the last time I'd done the same thing. Even though it took us weeks to sort our shit out, I still class that morning as the beginning of my relationship with Isaac. The instant he stepped into my apartment, I no longer had the strength to fight a battle stronger than I could have ever imagined. My body craved him more than its next breath—it still does. If Harlow and Cormack weren't in the room with us that day, I would have shamelessly crawled to him on my knees and begged for him to claim me as his.

My heart leaps into my throat when a loud tap sounds at my front door. I know it isn't Brandon—he texted earlier saying he'll collect me at ten tomorrow morning. My heart is praying it's Isaac, but it will most likely be Hugo since security didn't call to say I have a visitor.

After zipping up from the floor, I pace to the door, cringing when I catch my reflection in the entryway mirror. In an attempt to improve my gloomy mood, I spent my morning binge eating. When it made me feel worse, I went on an afternoon run, doing anything I could to lessen the chocolate bars making their way onto my already curvy backside. I only just returned, so I'm still wearing black running shorts, a hot pink crop-top bra, and a thin mesh shirt. My shirt is so drenched with sweat, my crop-top is visible underneath, my once-high ponytail hangs loosely halfway down my back, and my face is devoid of makeup. I would get changed if my caller wasn't knocking like they're the police.

I realize how accurate my statement is when I swing open my door. Theresa and her still-unnamed male partner are standing on the other side. I thought the disdain crossing Theresa's face would be the only skin-crawling moment I'd handle today. It isn't. Her partner's vomit-provoking assessment of my body lasts for several uncomfortable heart-thrashing seconds, only stopping once he reaches my sweat-soaked socks.

From the way his tongue is hanging out of his mouth, anyone would swear I was standing before him naked.

When the male agent takes his eyes off my chest to follow Theresa into my apartment, I block their entrance. "I'm not talking to you without a lawyer present."

My abrupt closure of the door wavers when, "Only people with something to hide need a lawyer," sounds through the wood.

I said that exact statement to Isaac only a few months ago, and it would be hypocritical for me to pretend I didn't. I've been called many names the past week. I don't want another added to the list.

Against my better judgment, I swing my door back open. "I don't have anything to hide. *Nothing* I have done since I left the academy has been illegal."

"Then you'll have no problems talking to us."

Without seeking permission, Theresa enters my apartment. Her strides are efficient and confident as stuck-up as the expensive-smelling perfume she's wearing. The unnamed male agent shadows her the best he can without taking his eyes off my boobs. He must be several years older than Theresa as his hair has an abundance of gray strands throughout it, and his face is heavily wrinkled. If I had to guess his age, I'd say mid-to-late fifties. They're an odd partnership, but I'm confident Theresa always plays the bad cop during their interrogations. Excluding the occasional snicker, I've barely heard a peep come out of the male agent's mouth, proving that Theresa is the alpha in their duo.

After bouncing her eyes between the moving boxes scattered around my apartment, Theresa spins around to face me. She'd be a lot prettier if she mixed up the grim expression she frequently wears. She carries herself well, but her lips are always set in a thin line, and she's forever frowning—even when she's smirking.

"Trouble in paradise?"

I cross my arms in front of my chest before glaring at her. Her insensitive question doesn't warrant a reply, so I remain quiet, silently brooding instead of nibbling at the bait she's leaving out.

A triumphant grin tugs my lips high when Theresa's gaze turns away first. As she paces deeper into my living room, I study her more adeptly. She carries herself with stature. It's a stance I've witnessed many times before, generally when friends of my Uncle Tobias would visit. Just from her composure, I highly doubt she started her career in IA. It might not have even been at the Bureau. Her poise and the way she moves points more to her being a police officer or perhaps even a detective.

My heart squeezes when she picks up a photo of my Uncle Tobias and me from my mantel. It's a photo Tobias's *Dedushka* took the day I arrived in Tiburon. It was the same day my auction was held. My eyes are open in fright, and my expression is puzzled. I was only six years old, so I was incapable of comprehending what had happened that day, but most of my fright was because I had just undertaken my first flight. My fear of flying wasn't something I developed as an adult. I was born with it embedded deep into my veins.

"Is this the man who raised you?" For the first time ever, Theresa's tone sounds neutral.

After swallowing the rock lodged in my throat, I nod. "That's my Uncle Tobias."

My high pitch relays my fondness for my uncle. If he hadn't come into my life when he did, I would have most likely become the person Theresa thinks I am—a prostitute. Tobias hid most of Vladimir's criminal activities from me when I was younger, but once I joined the Bureau, every sordid aspect of his empire was unearthed in pain-staking detail.

Vladimir Popov and Col Petretti's names were regularly exploited during my training at the academy. Col is no doubt an evil man, but Vladimir is a true monster. Drugs, guns, kidnapping, prostitution, his family business dabbles in it all. He's so ruthless, he doesn't care if you're related to him. Unless you're making him a profit, you're worthless to him.

"Isabelle?" Theresa paces to stand in front of me, eyeing me curiously. I must have zoned out thinking back on my memories.

I shake my head to clear my thoughts. "I'm sorry, what did you say?"

She pompously smirks. "I asked, what's your knowledge of Col Petretti?"

"Other than what his FBI file informs me, I don't have any further knowledge of Mr. Petretti."

My reply isn't a total lie. Although I ran into Col on the weekend Isaac and I went away, and he threatened me, I have no further knowledge of him.

"Why are you asking?"

The back of my neck beads with sweat when Theresa hands me a photo from her leather handbag. It shows Col Petretti's righthand man lying in a hospital bed. His body is severely injured. One of his legs is hoisted in a sling, and his face is covered in bruises of different colors and shapes.

Not trusting Theresa to give me an honest answer, I stray my eyes to the male agent, who is wandering aimlessly through the boxes stacked at the side of my living room. "When was this photo taken?"

Theresa steps in front of me, blocking him from my view. "The weekend you and Isaac stayed at the McGregor residence."

Bile rises from my stomach to my throat. Isaac did threaten Col's right-hand man. He was pissed he displayed that he was carrying a weapon during Isaac's confrontation with Col. Isaac's file reveals he was a skilled fighter years ago, but I didn't realize he could still inflict so much damage to another person.

"How were his injuries obtained?"

Theresa's condescending shrug reveals I just walked straight into her trap. She's not only baiting me. She's laying out traps left, right, and center. "I was hoping you'd elaborate on that for me, considering you were there when it happened."

I shake my head, denying her false accusation. When she steps up to within an inch of my face, her rich-scented perfume makes my stomach swirl more.

"How many weeks did you sleep with a man you hardly knew?"

I stare her straight in the eyes before snarling, "I plead the fifth."

I'm not usually a catty bitch—*jealous, yes, bitchy, no*—but Theresa makes me want to bring out my claws and scratch them down her obnoxious face.

Theresa's eyes snap to the male agent who is watching our exchange with caution. "Let's go, this tap has run dry." For the first time ever, her smile appears genuine. "Ms. Brahn isn't a viable asset. She's just as *clueless* as the rest of us when it comes to Mr. Holt."

I don't give her the satisfaction of prying a reaction out of me. Instead, I fold my arms in front of my chest before returning her evil glare. Smirking like the smug bitch she is, she saunters to my front door, her hips swinging. The male agent shadows her, nodding farewell on the way by.

Just as she's about to exit, Theresa's shoddy gaze turns to me. "Enjoy your weekend, Isabelle, because it may be the last one where you're not sleeping in a four-by-four cell."

16

ISAAC

When gravel crunching under tires rumbles through my ears, I lift my gaze, spotting a dark black sedan pulling in next to my Bugatti Veyron. It kicks up dust when it comes to a stop outside the warehouse I own. My jaw quivers when Theresa climbs out of the driver's seat to saunter my way.

"Isaac Holt all alone on a Saturday morning, what are the odds?"

Her obnoxious smirk falters the instant my gray eyes glare at her. Stopping halfway between her car and mine, she crosses her arms in front of her chest, hoisting her fake breasts up high in her white blouse. Although she's dressed more casual than earlier this week, she's still on the job as her pistol is holstered on her hip.

"What do you want?"

My tone is short and clipped. I'm generally a tolerant

person. I take the punches life inflicts as well as anyone else, but my back gets up when someone hounds an innocent who should have never been dragged into the saga to begin with. Theresa despised Isabelle on sight, and she's only targeting her because of me.

As Theresa moves in closer, she studies my body, which is leaning against the hood of my car. I've just finished working the bag in the derelict warehouse. I'm wearing black Nike gym shorts and cross- trainer shoes. I removed my sweat-drenched shirt and have it hanging over my right shoulder.

Once her heavy-lidded gaze returns to my face, I snarl, "Never going to happen."

I drop my eyes back to my phone to see if I missed any calls from Hunter or Regan while I was working out. Upon seeing I don't have any missed calls, I jog around my vehicle to dump my gym bag into the trunk. After slipping a dark blue t-shirt over my torso, I stride toward the driver's side door.

"You think you're clever, but you'll slip up eventually." Theresa's tone is doused with arrogance.

"I don't think I'm clever, I know I am. You'll never find anything on me or anyone on my team as I always ensure my hands are thoroughly clean."

Ray-Ban sunglasses cover her eyes, but I can feel them drifting over my face, absorbing every detail that makes the girls go weak at the knees.

"I just realized I forgot to thank you." I stare into her mirrored glasses, which reflect my gray eyes. They're darker than usual due to enlarged pupils.

Theresa swallows before her tongue darts out to moisten

her lips. "For what?"

"For pointing out an oversight in my accounting." My smirk picks up right along with my attitude. "Your invaluable information earned me thousands of dollars."

Her head slopes to the side, apparently confused. "What information?"

"When you left my office, I realized I had heard of Ms. Brahn before."

Theresa sucks in a quick breath that puffs her chest out.

"Once I dug a little deeper, I discovered Ms. Brahn is one of my *many* tenants. During examinations of her account, my real estate agent found an oversight in the processing of her tenant application."

She pulls off her sunglasses, so her icy blue eyes can glare into mine. "What kind of oversight?"

"My real estate agent failed to lodge Ms. Brahn's application for expenses contributing to her move. Since she relocated to Ravenshoe for work, she had her rent reduced for the first twelve months. Because of your due diligence, my real estate agent has now lodged her application. The bureau contacted my agent earlier today, and they've assured us Ms. Brahn's backdated rent will be paid into my account by the end of the month." A smug grin curls my lips high. "So, Ms. Brahn's rental statement now reflects she was indeed paying the full and *fair* amount for her apartment."

Theresa's eyes narrow into thin slits as her stance stiffens. "Even if Isabelle gets cleared of all charges by my department, she'll never talk to you again after the information I've shared with her this week."

Other than my jaw involuntarily ticking, my outward appearance gives no indication her statement has affected me.

"You should have seen the tears in her big brown eyes when she watched the video of Ophelia begging you to stop senselessly beating her brother." She steps closer to me, her glare vicious. "Isabelle thought she knew the real Isaac Holt, but she's learning she doesn't know you at all."

My nostrils flare as blood courses through my body at a rapid pace.

"Have a pleasant day, Mr. Holt." Her voice drips with sarcasm.

After placing her glasses back on, she returns to her vehicle. Only once her government-plated sedan is nothing but a blur in the distance do I slam my fists into the hood of my car. The dark metal crumples from the brutal force of my knuckles, but I don't hold back. The night she referenced earlier forever haunts my dreams. It changed me to the man I am now. It's the reason I became the myth. The unattainable. The ruthless enigma...

Months and months of relentless chasing, denied requests, and returned flowers all came down to this. Ophelia had accepted my pleas, and our date had gone well. I impressed myself with how much of a gentleman I was. I opened her car door, pulled out her chair, and participated in an intellectual adult conversation. Then it all came down to dropping her home after the date. Was I supposed to kiss her? Should I invite her on another date right then or wait a required amount of time? It was a new experience for me.

Don't get me wrong, I was certainly not a fumbling virgin who didn't know what he was doing. I had bedded plenty of women before

Ophelia. I just never dated any of them. Even the best lays I had didn't compare to how I felt when Ophelia's translucent eyes glanced into mine. The chase was enthralling and addictive. My heart would constrict, my palms would sweat, and all I wanted to do was claim her as my own.

That night, when I pulled into her driveway, my mouth was unexpectedly engulfed by warm and soft lips. "Pick me up tomorrow at six," she instructed before jumping out of my car and walking toward the dorm she lived in without a backward glance.

One date turned into six, then six dates turned into three months. Time was flying by. Ophelia blew my mind. She kept me fascinated. She was unlike any other girl I'd been with before, but it all changed when I received a call during one of our weekly dates.

"Twenty Gs! Are you fucking serious?" My tone indicated my disbelief, confident I didn't hear Cormack right as there's no way twenty thousand dollars was being offered for one fight. I received the occasional higher offer from Col, but they rarely went over seven thousand.

"Yeah, man, twenty thousand, but your ass has to be here within an hour, or the deal falls through."

My eyes darted to Ophelia. I hadn't been entirely honest with her about what I did for a career. I mentioned it was sports-related, but when she failed to probe me any further, I neglected to mention it again. Although I was unsure about what her reaction would be, there was no way I was giving up that amount of money for one night's work.

"I'll be there in forty-five."

After disconnecting my call, I gathered Ophelia's jacket, hat, and scarf from the coatrack in the diner where we had just finished eating. Her beautiful giggle echoed around the grease-smelling space when I wrapped her scarf around her neck before plopping her beanie on her head. I plucked her from the chair by a tug on her wrist, then eagerly ushered her out of the diner.

"Where are we going?" she questioned curiously, still giggling.

"You know that car you've been saving up for?" I stopped to help button up her jacket. Snowflakes were already making the little point on the end of her nose turn bright red, I didn't want her getting sick.

"Yeah..." Her high pitch exposed her hesitance.

"We're going to buy it... tonight." I waggled my brows. "We just have to make a little detour first."

I grasped her hand within mine before jogging down the slippery, icy grounds, dragging a giggling Ophelia behind me. Once she was buckled in my car, I slid into the driver's seat and took off down the street. The massive compression of my foot on the accelerator made my car skid out of control on the icy roads.

Once I righted my wrong, I peered over to Ophelia. Her eyes were slitted, and she was glaring at me. After mumbling a quick apology, I continued on our route. She had been working at Buck's Diner the past six months, saving up to buy a car. All the money I earned fighting was locked in a high-interest account, and with the way the stock market was going, it would have been ludicrous for me to sell any shares I had, but with the money from the fight that night, I could buy Ophelia the car she had been working so hard to save for.

When I pulled into the old gym where the underground fights were located, Ophelia's fretful eyes turned to mine. "What are we doing here?"

"This is the quick detour I need to make first."

I jumped out of my car before darting around to the passenger side to help her out. Before I could get to her door, she opened it and stepped outside. Her hands splayed across her hips, and her nostrils expanded with every breath she took.

"Please, Isaac, tell me you don't participate in the events they hold here."

I balk, unaware she knew about the events held in that old gym. Before I could answer her, Cormack was at my side, slapping my shoulder in greeting. "Can you believe it? Twenty Gs."

After curling his arm around my shoulders, Cormack guided me toward the entrance of the run-down warehouse. Ophelia followed behind us but remained quiet. Needing time to prep my body for the fight, I headed straight into the locker rooms at the back of the arena to commence a dynamic warm-up routine. While I did that, Ophelia nervously paced back and forth. She mumbled incoherently and cursed several times in a row, her angry strides only halting when Cormack left the room.

"Please don't do this, Isaac."

I placed the jump rope onto the wooden bench before standing in front of her. Her pupils were wide, her face pale. She looked like she was going to be ill at any moment.

"I won't get hurt." Call me cocky, but the chances of me being beaten that night were non-existent as far as I was concerned.

"This isn't you, Isaac." Ophelia thrust her hand to the door that had roars bellowing through it. "This isn't the person I fell in love with."

My heart leaped. That was the first time she had told me she loved me. Hearing her say it made me feel invincible.

Grasping both of her cheeks in my hands, I kissed her firmly on her gaped-open mouth. "I love you too, baby," I spoke over her lips.

"If you love me, you won't do this." With my heart in my throat, I inched back. "If you fight tonight, you'll never see me again."

"What?" I was baffled. Some people see boxing as brutal, but at the end of the day, it's still a sport. It's included in the Olympics, for fuck's sake.

Ophelia folded her arms in front of her chest. "I love you, Isaac, but if you do this, I'll leave you."

My mind spiraled out of control. She was the first girl I'd ever loved, but she stood in front of me, giving me an ultimatum. She was forcing my hand. At the time, I was conflicted. I'd never been issued an ultimatum before, but I loved her enough, I would have done anything for her. So, with a small amount of hesitation, I put my shirt back on, grasped her hand in mine, then exited the locker room.

We weaved in and out of the hundreds of attendees preparing to watch the fight. The atmosphere was electrifying. A constant hum thickened my veins when we briskly strolled down a narrow hallway, but the pit in my stomach became heavier with every step I took. I was walking away from the one thing that gave me the financial security I so desperately craved.

Cormack's brows lowered when I walked by him, exiting the registration room. The confusion tainting his face slipped away when he spotted Ophelia's panicked expression. In silent support, he patted my shoulder on the way by.

When I took a left at the end of the corridor, I crashed into a solid chest. Every attempt I made to sidestep the person was fruitless. They kept moving back in my way, blocking my exit. With my blood black in annoyance, I lifted my slit eyes, coming face to face with Col

Petretti—the most ruthless man I'd encountered in my time in the underground fight circuit. He never threw in the towel, even when his fighter was close to death, and he didn't bat an eyelid when his fighters were stretchered off the mat. He was a monster, and I was desperate to get Ophelia far away from him.

My chances were lost when Col snarled, "If you leave now, you'll never see Ophelia again."

My eyes darted between his while striving to work out how the fuck he knew Ophelia's name. It was unearthed in the most horrid way.

"Papa." My head flung back to Ophelia, assuming I hadn't heard her right. If the gleam in her eyes was anything to go by, I had heard her right. She didn't just know Col Petretti; she was his daughter.

"You not only betrayed yourself, but you betrayed your family," Col spat in disgust, his angry eyes glaring at Ophelia.

I placed myself between him and Ophelia. I didn't care if he was her father or not, he was not allowed to threaten her in front of me. The instant I seized Ophelia's wrist to pull her behind me, the gentleman at Col's side pinched my left temple with his gun. Although pissed he brought a weapon into a fight that only needed fists, I learned early on that in my industry, I was never to show fear. Fear made you weak, and your competitors fed off it. So, instead, I strengthened my stance before glaring into the eyes of the soulless man in front of me. Our standoff only lasted seconds, although, at the time, it felt like hours.

"If you want to date my daughter, you must first prove your worth." Col drifted his eyes from Ophelia to me. "You'll fight my toughest competitor tonight. If you win, you'll become my fighter and have permission to date my daughter."

"And if I refuse?"

Col didn't grace me with a reply. He only smiled, a menacing, evil grin that showed the true monster he was.

"Be in the ring in five minutes," a gentleman at Col's side instructed.

When Col and his entourage left, I shifted on my feet to face Ophelia. Tears were welling in her eyes, and she was nervously fiddling with the button on her coat jacket. "You don't have to do this, Isaac."

I stepped closer to her. "Yes, I do."

"No, you don't. Just walk away, and don't look back." She scanned the arena, seeking the closest exit.

"Will you come with me?" She shook her head before yanking her hand out of my grasp. "Then, I'm going to fight."

Before she could rebut, the brute who pointed a gun at my head stood next to her. His semi-automatic was aimed at her rib. "Let's go." He motioned his head to the ring, indicating he wasn't leaving Ophelia's side until after the fight.

After curling my hand around Ophelia's clammy one, I made my way down the corridor that was filled with spectators. When we broke through the bleachers, the hum of the crowd lessened. Eyes of all ages and genders were gawking at me.

Once I reached the ring, a ragged gasp expelled from Ophelia's lips. She tugged out of my hold before darting to stand in front of me. "Please don't do this, Isaac. I'm begging you not to do this."

"I have to. If I don't, I'll never see you again." I stared into her glistening eyes, hating that I was disappointing her but not having any choice. She had a gun pointed at her. I had to protect her. "It'll be five minutes, tops, then we walk out that door and never come back."

My guarantee the fight would be over in minutes didn't award her any reassurance. If anything, it made her more panicked. I discovered why when she sobbed. "He's my brother."

---

*"*THROW IN THE TOWEL,*" I pleaded, staring into the eyes of a monster. "He's your fucking son."*

Ophelia's brother, CJ, had given a stellar performance. He was a competitive fighter, handling the match better than I had expected, but he was done. From the way his chin was dangling, I was confident he was sporting a fractured jaw. The cracking that expelled from his ribs when I punished him with a grueling left and right combination guaranteed he had numerous broken bones, and his right wrist was contorted in a weird angle. His body had endured as much hell as my mind had, but no matter how many times I pleaded with Col, he wouldn't throw in the towel.

There was no doubt in my mind CJ had impressive combat abilities, but my capabilities were stronger. When I peered into his bloodshot eyes, even they reflected his defeat, but Col refused to give in. The only way our fight was going to end was when CJ was stretchered out of the ring. If I were responsible for that, I'd lose Ophelia forever, but I had no choice. Col's goon was still at her side with his gun drawn. I had to pick between saving CJ or Ophelia. I was always going to choose Ophelia.

Every punch and kick I inflicted on CJ over the next ten minutes were met with Ophelia's panicked screams or gasps of disappointment. Halfway through the match, I realized no matter what I did, I'd lose her. If I walked away, ending the fight against Col's wishes,

Ophelia would be punished. If I seriously injured her brother, she'd never look at me the same again.

It was a lose-lose situation.

As CJ staggered to the middle of the ring, I locked eyes with Ophelia. Her beautiful face was contorted with sadness, and tears were streaming down her flushed cheeks. "I'm sorry. I promise I'll make it up to you."

Her tearful pleas faded into the background when I strayed my eyes back to CJ. He was cradling his broken wrist with his knuckle-busted hand. When his eyes lifted to mine, a sharp niggle hit my chest. He acknowledged my regret with a brief nod, aware I didn't want to do what I was about to do.

After strengthening my stance, I peered into his dark eyes. "I'm sorry," I murmured a mere second before completing a roundhouse kick to his right temple.

His eyes rolled to the back of his head as he plummeted to the ground in slow motion. The sickening thud of his unconscious body hitting the mat was so loud, it was heard over the screaming cheers of the spectators.

"Nooo!" Ophelia yelled in a blood-curdling scream.

The wild thrashing of my heart lessened when Col's righthand man holstered his gun before walking away from Ophelia. Since I had done as requested, he no longer had a reason to continue with his aggressive stance.

After diving through the ropes, Ophelia crawled on her hands and knees to the middle of the ring, her eyes never leaving her brother. Once she reached him, she cradled his bruised head in her hands, trying in vain to wake him up. I didn't kill him, but I did knock him out cold.

When Ophelia refused to relinquish CJ to the medical team assessing him, I wrapped my sweat-drenched arm around her petite waist and pulled her back. She kicked and screamed, fighting against my hold.

"Let them help him," I whispered into her ear as I dragged her to the other side of the ring.

Once she stopped thrashing against me, I lowered her back onto the ground. She turned to face me so fast, hot air blasted my face. Her beautiful eyes were tainted with hate, and she came out swinging. The first time she slapped me, I was so surprised, I didn't register it. The second time, its impact was felt more by my heart than my face.

I don't know how many slaps she inflicted before Cormack stood between us, so his body blocked her from imposing more punishment. "Let's go."

I shook my head. I wasn't leaving without Ophelia.

"She needs time, Isaac. Give her some time, then she'll understand you didn't have a choice."

When Cormack curled his arms around my shoulders to guide me out of the ring, I should have fought harder for Ophelia. I shouldn't have given up. I should have begged for forgiveness then and there, then she wouldn't have been in the car the night she was killed. But I was a coward who walked away. I left her crying over her brother splayed unconscious on a dirty boxing ring floor, meaning her devastated, tear-stained face was the last image I had of her.

My memories are interrupted when my phone vibrates. After unclenching my fists, I answer the call.

"Boss, we have someone in pursuit of Izzy."

17

ISABELLE

"I appreciate you doing this for me, Brandon."

I peer at him sitting in the driver's seat of his car. No words spill from his lips, but a fretful mask has slipped over his usually expressionless face. As his brows lower, his lips form into a harsh line. After coughing to clear his throat, he adjusts the tilt of the rearview mirror. Curious as to what has caused his sudden change in composure, I glance out the rear window of his blue BMW. Air snags in my throat when I spot a dark blue sedan tailing us.

Brandon's foot flattens the accelerator, increasing his speed to well above the signed limit. Burning rubber lingers in the air from his tires squealing from his acceleration. He weaves and darts between a handful of vehicles in front of us, but because it's mid-morning, the traffic isn't as dense as it would be during peak hour, although there are still a decent number of vehicles on the highway.

Even though the blue sedan remains a good three to four cars behind us, it continues following us down the side streets and back alleys Brandon turns down in an attempt to evade them.

"How long have they been following us?"

Brandon's gaze drifts to me, his Adam's apple bobbing up and down as he swallows harshly. "I thought I'd lost them, but they've been with us since we left your apartment."

My mouth becomes parched. We left my apartment well over two hours ago. "Do you think it's IA?"

He shakes his head. "No."

I wait for him to pull down another isolated street before asking, "How can you be so sure?" The drumming of my heart against my ribcage is heard in my voice.

Brandon glances at me from the corner of his eyes. "They don't have government-issued plates."

Conflict makes itself known with my gut. I thought the blue sedan was Theresa or one of the agents she assigned to surveillance me. A car with a similar make and model as the one tailing us was parked on my street when I returned from a run yesterday afternoon. Not long later, Theresa arrived at my apartment. Putting two and two together, I thought I was onto a winner. Her investigative tactics have been so heavy, I wouldn't put rummaging through my garbage past her. She'll do anything she can to get a shred of evidence against me, so surveillance seems like an action she'd utilize during her investigation.

Annoyed, I lift my gaze to Brandon. "Pull over. If it isn't IA following me, I want to know who it is."

Brandon's thigh muscles spasm before he does as requested. Ignoring the tremor rattling my hands, I yank my satchel off the floor while scanning our nearly-isolated surroundings. Other than a derelict building to my right, the rest of the street is nothing but paddocks of overgrown, vermin-infested grass.

I peer at Brandon's anxious face. "You never witnessed this."

Not giving him a chance to reply, I pull my government-issued gun out of my bag then throw open my door.

"Jesus, Isabelle..."

As I move for the long grass on the road edging, I see Brandon's hands dart under the driver's seat. While using the tall weeds for cover, I brace my revolver high on my chest, then peer down the sight. Approximately thirteen heart-thrashing seconds later, the sedan that was following us pulls down the deserted street, stopping a few spaces behind Brandon's car.

A cool breeze flicks up my hair when I sprint toward the stationary vehicle with my gun aimed at the driver's side front window. My heart beats wildly against my chest, and my thighs are quaking, but my shakiness isn't from fear, it's from the adrenaline surging through my veins.

Brandon approaches me from the left. He also has his gun directed at the unknown assailant and is demanding for him to switch off his ignition. Ignoring our repeated requests to surrender, the driver reverses back two places before he attempts to complete a three-point turn. As trained, I aim my gun at the back, right tire. My pistol recoiling is almost deafening in the quietness of the crisp winter day, but it has the effect I was aiming for. The back tire blows out, and the assailant's three-point maneuver crawls to a snail's pace. Once I shoot out the back-left tire, his getaway halts altogether.

After jerking up my chin, requesting for Brandon to have my back, I cautiously approach the stationary car. The patter of my feet on the asphalt is the only sound heard in the eerily quiet morning. Once I reach a close but safe distance from the car, I spread my feet to the width of my shoulders before adjusting my pistol, so the barrel faces the driver's side window.

"Slowly wind down your window and throw your keys onto the roadside." My voice is surprisingly firm for how fast my heart is hammering my ribs. "Or the next time I shoot, I won't aim for a tire."

Time stands still when the heavily tinted driver's side window slides down. A vibrant-colored, tattooed arm with keys dangling from its index finger pops out of the opening a short time later. With a swift flick of the wrist, the keys plummet onto the asphalt, mere feet from the driver's side door.

Brandon's eyes lift to mine in silent questioning. When I nod, he bridges the last few steps to the vehicle. I'm so nervous, I have to keep re-attaching the grip of my gun to ensure I don't drop it. I have no reason to be nervous, I've trained for this—not just at the academy, but at the gun range with my uncle as well, but something about this feels wrong.

I discover why when a thick familiar voice says, "Hey, Isabelle," from inside the vehicle I'm in the process of apprehending.

When I slant my head to the side, clearing my eyes from the mid-morning sun, Hugo's mischief-filled eyes peek out from behind the steering wheel. I exhale sharply before lowering my gun, so it's no longer aimed at his chest. Brandon's stance remains solid with his feet planted at the width of his shoulders, and the barrel of his gun is aimed at the pinched skin between Hugo's brows.

Sensing Brandon's hesitance, Hugo warns, "You better point that somewhere else before someone gets hurt." His voice is a threatening snarl someone as cheeky as him shouldn't be able to pull off. "And it won't be me who gets injured."

When a tick hits Brandon's freshly shaven jaw, I run my hand down his arm. His muscles bunch from my unexpected touch, but it relays to him that I want him to drop his weapon without a word needing to spill from my lips. The gleam that generally clusters in his eyes returns when he holsters his gun into the waistband of his trousers.

Happy I've diffused one dangerous situation without carnage, I walk straight into another. "Why are you following me?"

Hugo stops shooting daggers at Brandon to drift his eyes to me. Although they're narrowed, I can see the remorse settled behind them. "It's my job—"

"You never got fired, did you?"

The crisp dew-filled air burns my nostrils when Hugo shrugs. "Not technically. Isaac did take a swing at me, and he said a few things he didn't mean, but he never fired me."

My fists curl into tight balls as my chin trembles. "You son of a bitch."

Hugo's lips tug higher. "It's all that gray..."

"What about the intense stare-down between you and Isaac at the record company last week?" My high tone conveys my utter confusion. They seemed as if they hated each other that day.

"Isaac prefers me to watch you from a distance. Come on, Izzy, you know what he's like when it comes to any man getting close to you."

Watching over our exchange like a spectator at tennis, Brandon joins in. "Yeah, she does know what Isaac is like. That's why she needs to get as far away from him as possible."

Hugo's eyes snap to Brandon as quickly as mine. That wasn't what I was expecting him to say. "You can't fight fate, blondie."

Although grateful Hugo is backing up my relationship with Isaac, I'm still angry. He said that exact thing to me last week when he was *pretending* to be my friend. "So, for the past week, the whole, *I'm your friend, Izzy,* was that part of your job description or you fighting for fate?"

This proves why I hesitated during my introduction yesterday. I should have trusted my intuition. It's never steered me wrong before.

"I'm still your frien—"

"Don't even go there, Hugo. You're *not* even close to being my friend."

Hugo has a rough exterior, but the cheeky gleam in his eyes dampens from my harsh words. "Everything I said the past week was true." Hugo keeps his tone low, hoping Brandon won't overhear his confession. "Whether you believe it or not, I'm your friend. Everything I've been doing is to help you."

Out of the blue, a cell phone rings, startling me so much my heart almost leaps out of my chest.

As Hugo's hand slips into his jeans pocket, he grins. "I'd say that's for you."

Unappreciative of his disappearing hands, Brandon redraws his gun. With his vibrating cell phone halfway out of his pocket, Hugo cocks his head to the side. "Easy there, blondie. If you keep drawing your gun on me, I'll be forced to retaliate."

Snubbing the fact he has a gun pointed at him, Hugo hands me his phone. It's an ancient-looking cell that requires me to flip open the screen to answer it. My knees weaken when the seductive purr of Isaac sounds down the line a mere second after I squash it to my ear. "You drew your gun on one of my staff members?"

I swallow the lump in my throat before nodding. "Yes." I hate the nerves projected in my short reply, but in my defense, adrenaline is surging through my body so hard and fast, thinking rationally is above my caliber right now.

Isaac remains quiet, but I can hear his jaw ticking. I keep my gaze planted on the asphalt, not needing to look up to know Hugo and Brandon are watching me. Their heated gazes are all the indication I need to know they're spying on me.

After a short period of silence, Isaac speaks, "You had a tail—"

"I know, hence the drawing of my gun."

My attitude gets nipped in the bud when Isaac snaps, "It wasn't Hugo, Isabelle. It was a white Range Rover that's been following you the past week." Although his tone is stern, nothing can take away the concern in his rough and rugged voice. "Hugo ran a decoy to get them off your tail."

"What?" My hand not clutching my phone shoots up to cradle my neck. My pulse is racing so fast, I'm afraid I might burst an artery. I was so concerned about the dark blue sedan, I didn't check my surroundings for an additional threat. "I have a lady from the Internal Affairs Department investigating me."

"I know." Isaac's tone is less harsh. "But the plates on the Range Rover aren't government-issued. I have my security team looking into whom the car belongs to, but for the time being, Isabelle, Hugo will be your shadow."

My heart plummets into my stomach when I hear something he didn't mean to express. "Do you think it's Col?"

He sighs heavily. "I don't know, but I'm not taking any chances. I promised to protect you, so that's what I'll do."

Even though he can't see me, I nod. He isn't the cold-hearted, ruthless man everyone makes him out to be. He told me he'd keep me safe, and I trust he'll follow through with his pledge, even if he can't stand the sight of me.

"For once, please do as you're told, Isabelle, and don't let Hugo out of your sight," Isaac requests before disconnecting our call. Although his voice was clipped, his request still came out more like a plea than a demand.

In a blur of confusion—and a slight haze of lust—I attempt to hand Hugo's phone back to him. He shakes his head before he commences gathering his possessions from inside his car. My brain is so fried, I can't get any words to form in my mind, let alone spill from my lips. Brandon seems just as perplexed. His handsome face is stained with uncertainty, and his eyes are flicking between Hugo and me.

The only one who doesn't look like a stunned mullet is

Hugo. Without seeking permission, he exits his vehicle then cockily strides to Brandon's. My mouth gaps when he slides into the driver's seat. He pushes it back as far as it can go, ensuring his large build can fit comfortably.

Once he has made himself at home, I drift my eyes to Brandon. "I'm sorry, Brandon." I have no clue what I'm apologizing about. It just seemed like the right thing to do, so I ran with it. "I understand if you want to turn around and go back to Ravenshoe."

My suggestion is met with awkward silence. I never knew thirty seconds could feel like a lifetime until now.

"I know this is hard for you to understand, but Isaac is trying to protect me—"

"From what?" Brandon interjects, his voice loud. "Himself?"

Even though I'm mad at his snapped tone, I shelf my retaliation. He has a right to be angry. I just put him in a horrible predicament.

"Six weeks ago, I was threatened by Col Petretti."

Brandon's brows draw together as his eyes dance between mine.

"Isaac said a tail has been following me the past week."

Nothing but panic is heard in his tone when he asks, "Does Isaac think it's Col?"

I halfheartedly shrug. "He doesn't know, but he doesn't want to take any chances either. That's why he wants Hugo to join us."

Although his eyes show his apprehension, an uneasy smile forms on his face, silencing some of my uncertainty. He runs his sweat-slicked hands down his pants. Despite it being a crisp winter morning, the air surrounding us is stifling.

Once his hands are free of sweat, Brandon jerks his head to Hugo, who is pretending not to watch our exchange from Brandon's car. "Do you trust him?"

I nod. Even though he was deceitful to me this week, my intuition is telling me I can trust him.

"All right. I have no reason not to trust your instincts." A ghost of a smile cracks my lips at the actuality in Brandon's tone. "We're already halfway there, so we may as well continue on our journey." After offering me the crook of his elbow, he locks his eyes with mine. "Are you ready to find out where every guy's worst nightmare grew up?"

Cringing, I nod while silently praying weird stalker fetishes are the only hazardous things we stumble upon today.

18

ISAAC

"**B**oss."

"Where is she?"

"Talking to blondie outside of the car," Hugo responds.

My jaw clenches as my top lip sets into a straight line. "Do you know where they're going?"

"Not yet, but I'll soon find out. I just confiscated blondie's car for my own personal use. You'll have to send Roger to pick up the Audi." His chuckles fuel my annoyance instead of dousing it. "You know you could ask Izzy where she's going. I'm sure she'd tell you."

Snubbing his relationship advice, I sternly request, "Watch her, Hugo."

"She won't leave my sight." His tone relays the truth in his statement, and it eases the uncertainty weighing down my chest. "Hey, Boss..."

I press my phone back against my ear. "Yes."

"What I said to you the other night is true. If you don't hurry up and pull your head out of your ass, someone will swoop in under your fucking nose and steal her."

"Over my dead body."

I disconnect our call, but not before his loud chuckle screeches down the line. It takes all my strength not to throw my phone onto the blue-carpeted floor beneath my feet. Just knowing Isabelle is associating with a man whose eyes light up like a Christmas tree every time she's near has blood racing through my body, but I need her to leave town as it will give my security team time to work out who's been tailing her the past week.

I'm reasonably confident it isn't Col. He rarely takes business matters outside of the family, but who else is a threat to Isabelle? The only respite I have is that I trust Hugo when he says he won't let her out of his sight. He's my most loyal employee, and the only person I trust to look after Isabelle when I can't. Under my lawyer's advice, I've kept my distance from Isabelle the past week. Our relationship must remain a secret until Theresa's investigation is found unwarranted. By not associating with her, the risk of me unwillingly implicating her in their investigation is significantly reduced. I won't lie. It's been a hard endeavor.

After housing my unregistered phone in my suit's top pocket, I pace into Isabelle's apartment. My cock twitches when I catch the tiniest whiff of her scent infused in the air. Hunter acknowledges my presence with a bob of his head before squashing his index finger to his mouth, requesting for me to remain quiet. His unusual quiet piques my interest. His scan of Isabelle's apartment must have unearthed something.

He places the all-in-one frequency scanner on the dining table before dragging a wooden chair to a hanging pot in the corner of the room. With pursed lips, he digs his hand into the pot, scattering the marble floor with potted dirt. My jaw muscle spasms when he yanks a small black device out from beneath the rubble. Soundlessly, he nudges his head to a glass of water on Isabelle's table. When I hand it to him, he drops the bug into the glass.

"Give it two minutes, then take it out and stomp on it."

"It'll be my pleasure," I respond more to myself than Hunter. "Was there only the one device?"

After climbing down from the chair, he strolls into Isabelle's compact yet modern kitchen. The marble countertops are covered with the equipment he utilizes while searching for bugs or listening devices. "There was also a hidden camera."

My breathing stops as my eyes dart to his. "Where was it located?"

I swear the moon circles the planet three times before he finally answers, "In the living room."

My breathing returns to a normal rhythm, grateful it wasn't housed in Isabelle's bedroom. Hunter scrubs his beard before plugging the USB port from a camera with a lens not much bigger than the tip of a ballpoint pen into a larger storage device. Once he inserts that USB into his laptop, he clicks a black camera icon on the monitor. Suddenly, his pupils widen, and he freezes.

"Fuck." He twists around, so his back now faces the laptop screen.

When my confused gaze drops to the computer screen, fury scorches through my veins so fast it burns. Inches of Isabelle's beautiful naked skin is plastered across the monitor. The first few images aren't too concerning because I'm covering most of her body, but as our vigorous morning activities progress, they grow more disturbing. Every inch of her delicate skin I devoured the morning I was arrested is on display.

I can still recall the smell of honey on her lips from the sweetened coffee she was drinking when she straddled my lap to nibble on my ear. Never able to restrain myself when it comes to her, I ended an important call to take her for the second time that morning on the red shag rug in her living room. The photos Hunter just downloaded gives a play-by-play recount of the activities we undertook that morning.

After yanking the USB out of Hunter's laptop, I store it in the breast pocket of my jacket. "Who has access to these images?"

Hunter shrugs. "This kind of device requires them to be downloaded from the apparatus. I'm hoping since the pictures weren't wiped, it means they weren't downloaded yet."

"Who do you think it is, Col or IA?"

He winces. "It's hard to say. Whoever it is, they're smart. They placed the camera high enough it gave them a bird's-eye view of the apartment." His eyes glance down to the original device housing the microscopic USB. "But this equipment is basic. You can pick it up at any spy shop." He grabs a second drive from his toolbox on his right. "This one, on the other hand, is more complicated. This is a government-issued device."

I snatch the plastic bag out of his hand. It looks like a small storage device you'd use in a digital camera. "Do they have to download this device as well?"

"No." Hunter shakes his head. "But if it were stored in Izzy's cell, every call or message she made would have been transcribed and sent to the owner's computer mainframe."

My heart beats at an unnatural rhythm. "What about private conversations while the phone is in the area?"

Hunter nods. "Any conversations, music, radio, etc. would have been transcribed."

Fuck! So, Isabelle was telling the truth. She wasn't the one who told the bureau about my call that morning.

I stop reprimanding myself when Hunter discloses, "The good news is that device has a serial number attached to it."

"Have you traced it?"

He smiles a slick grin. "It's running through my system now. Since I had to enter a few backdoors, it'll take a few hours to finalize."

"Be sure to inform me the instant you discover anything." My gaze shifts back to his laptop. "Can you adjust the perimeter of my google alert to include Isabelle? If those photos surface on the net—"

"I'll set it up. If they surface, they'll be immediately removed. I'll also corrupt their system with a few nasty viruses in return." His voice rattles with nerves when he suggests, "If you give me the USB from the camera, I can run it through a program to see when it was last accessed."

My nostrils flare as a growl rumbles in my chest.

"It's the only way we'll know if anyone else has viewed those images." He seeks my gaze. "I won't need to open the files to run the search, but I can't execute the program if I don't have the USB."

"Can you run it on any computer?"

He nods.

"Good. Then meet me at my office tonight. You can run it through my system there."

He glares at me. "If you don't trust me, Isaac, what the fuck am I doing working for you?"

"This isn't about trust, Hunter. It's about Isabelle and protecting her from having her naked body plastered around the country because someone has a vendetta against me that they're unleashing on her. You said my security servers are the best in the country, so it's the only system I trust to ensure these images remain private."

Hunter scrubs his hand across his hairy chin. "It's the best system... because I designed it. I'll drop by your office tonight."

The knot in my stomach relinquishes its firm hold. It doesn't last long. "There's something else..."

Hunter is interrupted by my ringing phone. After lifting my index finger, I pull it out of my pocket. The wild beating of my heart dampens when I discover the vibration is coming from my standard cell phone, not my emergency one.

My eyes float up from my phone to Hunter. "It's my brother, can this wait a minute?"

Hunter nods. "Yeah, I'll make it look like we've never been here before heading out."

An appreciative smirk etches onto my mouth. "Thanks. I'll meet you at my office tonight." As I stride to the entryway of Isabelle's apartment, I push my phone to my ear. "Nicholas, calm down, Nick... What? I'll be right there."

19

ISABELLE

Hugo's eyes dart to me, his scrunched-up face revealing his confusion. My lips curve into an uneasy grin before my gaze flicks to Brandon. He's sitting in the back seat of his car, his brows pulling together more the longer he peers outside. If I had to describe Megan's family home with one word, it would be 'ramshackle.'

Even in the rapidly setting sun, the white two story house doesn't look like it's seen a coat of paint in centuries, let alone years. Numerous tiles are missing from the stained brown roof, and three out of the four windows facing the road have had their holes repaired with duct tape. Yellow-tipped, overgrown grass stands as tall as the first story of the worn, rundown house, and weeds have confiscated any garden beds. In the far right-hand corner of the property, there's a red barn that's at least double the size of the house, and a big, old rusted truck is parked at the front of it.

"Are you sure this is the address you're looking for?" Hugo questions after pulling into the long dirt driveway.

After double-checking the number hand-painted on a microwave at the front of the property with the records I've gathered on Megan the past week, I nod. Hugo's features harden before he continues driving down the dirt driveway. The only sound heard in the interior of the car is my heart madly beating against my chest. I'm not concerned about my safety. It just seems as if we're walking straight into the set of a horror movie.

Hugo is only driving five miles per hour, but the tires are kicking up the dry dirt from the ground, leaving a cloud of dust trailing behind us. Ignoring the particles of dust scratching my eyes, I absorb the properties surrounding us. Other than another white barn on the horizon, there are no houses within eyesight.

"Whose house is this?" Hugo's tone is flat and apprehensive.

My gaze drifts to Brandon. His eyes meet and lock with mine before he shrugs. After returning my focus to Hugo, I answer, "Megan Shroud."

Air puffs out of his nostrils as his lips etch into a thin line. Apparently, he's heard of Megan before. When he parks in front of a set of rickety steps, I swing open the passenger door. I don't even get one foot out of the car when Hugo's arm splays across my chest to pin me into my seat. "Let us check it out first." He waves his spare hand between Brandon and himself.

"I'm a federal agent, Hugo. I'm *not* a child."

"Yeah, and that's Freddy-fucking-Kruger's house." His voice is riddled with both nerves and cheekiness. "If Isaac finds out I let you go in there without me first scoping the premises, I won't be on his Christmas card list anymore. He gives very generous bonus checks in his Christmas cards."

Even in the tense circumstances, I can't help the smile that tugs my lips high. His playfulness suffocated the despair ridding the air of oxygen, but there's no way in hell I'm staying out here by myself. Even from the outside, this place gives me the creeps.

After gathering my pistol from my satchel, I shadow Hugo and Brandon onto the leaf-covered veranda. The old wood creaking under my feet gives away my silent follow.

"Stay behind me."

Hugo's tone conveys he's not requesting, he's telling. Nodding, I position myself behind his left shoulder. I hate that he's babying me, but now is not the time to argue protocol. Other than wind whistling between the cracks in the floorboards, no sounds come out of the house. The frayed curtains on the grime-covered windows are open, and the paint-peeled door is hanging by the one hinge still attached to the doorframe.

I stop drinking in the rundown home when Hugo pulls out a gun from the back of his jeans. I didn't know he carried a weapon. He takes on an active stance before straying his eyes to Brandon. With a nod, he instructs Brandon to knock. When Brandon does as requested, a loud creak screeches through the air. His tap was so firm, the door swung open. A foul stench penetrates my nostrils. It's the smell of trash, rotten food, and something else that makes my stomach churn.

"I'm an FBI field agent, is anyone home?"

Hugo's eyes snap to Brandon, making me realize I failed to mention that Brandon is also an agent. *Oops!* I was under the assumption he was aware of that fact.

When the tenant fails to respond to Brandon's question, he turns to face me. "Did you hear that?"

I eye him curiously. I didn't hear anything.

"I think I heard someone yelling for help."

Hugo clicks onto Brandon's ruse quicker than me. "Yeah, I heard it, too. We should probably check on them."

Since we *hear* pleas for help, we make our way into the house. The aroma of rotting food scraps amplifies the further we walk in. The house is as desolate on the inside as it is outside. A square, box television sits on an old milk crate in one corner. It has a recliner sitting in front of it. The remaining chairs from the setting are squashed under the stairwell. They're covered in the plastic they were originally delivered in. From the material and design, I'd say they were purchased quite a few years ago.

Scary shadows dance around the room since a hill hides the sun. When I flick on a dirty light switch at my side, the tube light on the ceiling flickers a handful of times before illuminating the room with an unnatural yellow light.

Hugo silently signals for Brandon to clear the lower level of the property before gesturing for me to follow him to the stairs. As Brandon paces toward the kitchen with corkwood floors covered with trash and rotten food scraps, we head to the stairwell. Every step we take is met with a loud creak of the frail wood, but its faint squeals have nothing on the one I do when Hugo's boot falls through one of the steps.

I slap my hand over my mouth, my eyes darting up to the landing to make sure my squeal didn't gain any unwanted attention.

Confident we're alone, I return my eyes to Hugo. "Are you okay?"

Nodding, he pulls his foot out of the hole, sending splinters of wood onto the plastic-covered sofa below. We continue with our mission, my heart thrashing more with every step we take. The smell of unwashed laundry and another scent I can't work out becomes more apparent when we finalize the last few steps.

"You clear the left, I'll clear the right."

Ignoring Hugo's furious glare, I pace to the first door on my right. I'm not a baby, so I refuse to be treated like one. My heart freezes when sloshing filters through my ears a few seconds later. Peering down, I noticed the frayed red and black hall runner is saturated with water.

Well, I'm hoping it's water.

With my heart in my throat, my gaze floats across to the door adjacent to me. A clear liquid is seeping out from beneath it. Through trembling hands, I twist the white porcelain knob before pushing open the warped wood. I keep my gun up high as I absorb the basic yet spotlessly clean bathroom. The cold-water tap on the peach vanity sink is turned on full blast, toppling water over the edge like a rapid-flowing waterfall.

"Hello?"

When no one returns my greeting, I pace deeper into the room. While turning off the tap, I scan the space. The bathroom is outdated, but compared to downstairs, every surface is sparkling clean.

Once I've checked behind the shower curtain, and in the bathtub, I head back to the hallway in preparation to check the next room at the end of the corridor. My heart leaps into my chest when Hugo unexpectedly steps in front of me. I snap my mouth shut, suffocating the urge to scream.

After sucking in a shaky breath, I flutter my eyes back open.

"Sorry," Hugo mutters, genuinely remorseful that he scared me. "There's nothing down there but a bedroom with a double bed. The closets and drawers are full of clothes, but the bed hasn't been slept in recently."

"Okay." I shift my gaze to the last door in the corridor. "That just leaves one room."

Brandon climbs the stairs two at a time, narrowly missing the hole Hugo's boot left, his head shaking when he spots my silent question. "Excluding a dozen rats, there's nothing down there but rubbish." His face scrunches up when he mentions the vermin.

In sync, we turn our heads to the one room that has yet to be searched. A bead of sweat rolls down my back as I follow Brandon and Hugo to the end of the hall. Hugo wraps his hand around the doorknob before cranking his head back to Brandon and me.

"One... two... three."

On three, Hugo flings open the door for Brandon and me to rush in with our guns drawn. My eyes go crazy, rapidly absorbing every confronting detail while also making sure the room is secure. When my search comes up empty for potential threats, I lower my gun before shifting my attention to Brandon.

He's pivoting in a circle, taking in the entire room. "Holy shit."

His response is more reserved than Hugo's. He bites out a string of curse words as he takes in wall after wall of photos, magazine cut-outs, CD covers, and posters of Isaac's brother, Nick. Some images appear to be taken by paparazzi, but at least half of them aren't professional pictures. There are hundreds of long-range shots of Nick in various poses, but the ones that make my stomach churn are the up close and personal ones.

A handful are of Nick sleeping, but most are of him in various stages of sexual activities with a young lady with strawberry blonde hair. I thought the bathroom in Megan's hotel room was bad. This room is ten times worse.

My stomach tenses when I reach a desk in the corner of the room. "Is this Jenni, Nick's fiancée?" I lift one of the many photos with her eyes gouged out and blood trailing down her legs.

After drawing in a long, shaky breath, Hugo nods.

"Does Isaac have someone watching them?"

"He has Peters watching Nick from a distance, but I don't know about Jenni. His security team determined the threat pertained more to Nick than his fiancée."

A dull ache gnaws in my chest, my intuition warning me that something isn't right. "You need to get protection for Jenni." I shift on my feet to face Brandon. "What's the closest division associated with this district?"

Hugo exhales raggedly. "Don't call the authorities until Isaac's security team gets a look at this first. If you bring in the feds, this will get shut down quicker than Hunter turning down an offer to dance."

I hate what he's saying, but it's true. With Isaac being investigated by the Bureau, they won't let him anywhere near the scene, much less share confidential information with him. But can I do this? Can I go against everything I've been taught for a man I've only known for months?

With my stomach too twisted up in knots to think straight, I seek Brandon's opinion. He takes a few moments to deliberate on my soundless question before mumbling, "It's up to you, Izzy. I'll go along with whatever you decide."

A tense stretch of silence crosses between us. The only audible noise is my big pants of breath. I'm terrified of what Isaac's reaction will be, but nothing he's done the entire time I've been a part of the team investigating him has been classified as illegal, so I can trust him. I'm just worried this will force him to do something unlawful. He loves his brother, and he'd do anything to protect him—*anything at all*—but if I keep this from him, and something happens to Nick or his family, I'll lose Isaac forever. That's something I'll never handle.

With that in mind, I remove a layer of sweat beaded on my neck before digging out the cell phone Hugo gave me earlier. When I thrust it to him, the tension straining his face slackens. The cuff of Brandon's shirt tickles my wrist when he moves to stand next to me, but I can't take my eyes off Hugo. He dials a number he knows by heart before lifting the burner phone to his ear. He's making a call I know will break the heart of the man I love. Nothing is more important than this.

Just as faint ringing stops sounding through my ears, Hugo's eyes rocket to mine. "She's fine. She's right in front of me."

My heart swells, pleased Isaac still cares enough about me to be concerned about my welfare. My happiness dampens when Hugo says, "You need to send the security team to Parkerville. Tonight. This isn't about Izzy. It's Nick."

20

ISABELLE

"Feel free to tell me to buzz off, but what's a beautiful girl like you doing in a shithole like this?"

When I turn toward the voice, I'm met with the grinning face of a ruggedly handsome man. His jawline is covered with a thick, full beard. His dirty blond hair is pulled back into a messy man bun. His red and black checked plaid shirt rolled up at the sleeves showcases his vast collection of tattoos, and a pair of well-fitted jeans and black boots finalizes his outfit.

"That was the worst pick-up line I've ever heard."

He smiles so broadly, wrinkles crinkle his murky blue eyes. "I highly doubt that, sweetheart."

When he waves his hand at the stool Brandon just vacated, I say, "Feel free, but just a warning, I'm not the greatest company tonight."

His chuckle vibrates my toes. "That's okay, I'm never good company, so I'm sure I can handle your moodiness for a night."

His witty comment awards him my first genuine smile of the night. It doesn't linger for long. Just one sip of my wine the bartender just replenished has my happiness stepping back to when I was born. My taste buds were spoiled the past month with expensive bottles of wine I've never heard of, so they're protesting about the harsh bitterness that comes with a three-dollar glass of house wine.

After ordering a drink, my new companion drags his eyes down my body. I don't feel threatened by his enthusiastic review. He doesn't give out threatening vibes.

"Let me guess what brings you to this fine establishment this evening." He adds a fake amount of poshness to his deep timbre. "Relationship problems?"

"All that from a glance of my body?"

He scrubs at his beard to hide his smile. "Nah. It's the fact every guy in this place is gawking at you, but not one has been brave enough to talk to you."

He pulls a packet of cigarettes out of his jeans pocket, yanks out a cigarette, then twists the packet my way. When I shake my head, he dumps the packet onto the counter between us before placing the unlit cigarette between his plump lips.

"The leave-me-the-fuck-alone vibes are bouncing off you, sweetheart. It's scaring all the guys away, so if you're out here prowling for a man to heat your sheets, you might want to shut down those vibes."

A rowdy giggle escapes my lips before I can stop it. Hugo, Brandon, and I chose this pub as we'd be less likely to get hassled by locals, wondering why strangers have suddenly arrived in their derelict town. We don't want any unwanted attention while waiting for Isaac's security team to arrive. I'm only alone because Brandon left a few minutes ago as he wanted to reach out to some contacts he has in the FBI in the hope of unearthing Megan's current location, and Hugo needed to use the bathroom. He was apprehensive about leaving me alone, but since I refused to follow him into the men's restroom, he had no choice.

Besides, I don't feel in any danger. When I was younger, I went with my Uncle Tobias to old run-down pubs all the time. It's amazing the wonderful people you come across in the sleaziest looking places. Usually, they're the ones with the biggest hearts as they've been through the toughest struggles. I probably also feel safe as I have my pistol in my bag.

After checking his phone in the top pocket of his flannel shirt, my mystery companion props his elbows onto the countertop before inclining close to my side. "Unless you want a drove of men running toward you, you probably shouldn't giggle."

When I eye him curiously, his float over the poorly-lit space. When I follow the direction of his gaze, I do notice several pairs of male eyes watching me.

"Thanks for the warning. I'll keep my mouth shut." I return my eyes to his. "I'm not on the prowl tonight." *Or any night.*

"That's my cue to leave." He stands and swiftly walks away, getting halfway to the door before turning back around. I watch him with a hint of amusement, tugging my lips when he strides back to slip back onto his stool. "Ah, stuff it. I only have another five minutes before I'm due back at work, so I may as well spend it talking to a beautiful lady."

I grin at his cheeky demeanor as he once again pulls his cell phone out of his top pocket to peer down at the screen. Noticing he still hasn't lit the cigarette dangling from his mouth, I question, "Do you need a light?"

I stop grabbing for the box of matches on the sticky bar top when he replies, "No, thanks." He pulls the cigarette out of his mouth. "I gave up smoking weeks ago." He stabs out the unlit cigarette into an ashtray. "Old habits die hard."

After downing the cloudy brown liquid in the shot glass the bartender just set down in front of him, he signals for another before tilting my way. "So, what caused all this worry to your pretty face?"

"No offense, but you don't look like a therapist."

He flashes me a cheeky wink. "Don't judge a book by its cover, sweetheart. Under this God-gifted sexiness is a real heart of gold."

Another broad smile stretches across my face. I have to give it to the stranger. He oozes cockiness, and he has a real bad-boy sentiment, except he's one hundred percent man. But even more appealing than his rugged good looks is his cheeky personality.

When he shifts his head to the side, waiting for me to answer, I shrug. I don't want to be rude, I just don't know how to answer him without bringing Isaac into the equation. When my attention returns to my glass of wine, in the corner of my eye, I witness him once again checking the screen of his phone.

He must be waiting for an important call. Otherwise, why would he constantly check his phone?

"Are you waiting for a call?"

He grins again. It's a little shyer this time around. "Nah. It's another bad habit of mine."

"There could be worse habits you could have."

"True." This smile is genuine. "Such as?"

I roll my eyes, not falling for his tricks. He laughs before nudging his head to my nearly empty glass of wine. "This round is on me, Izzy."

My eyes snap to his as panic surges through me. *How does he know my name? I never told him my name.*

After pushing off the barstool, I scamper backward. The stranger's shoulders stiffen as he scrubs his hand down his face. "I'm not here to hurt you, Izzy." He stares straight at me, stupidly believing his honest eyes will quell the panic radiating out of me. "My name is Hunter. I'm Isaac's head of security."

I huff in disbelief. Other than when Hugo was faking being my friend, I never saw him out of a suit. Nothing against this man, but he doesn't seem the type to wear a suit. Lumberjack, yes. Head of security for the most fascinating man I've ever met —unlikely!

Sensing my silent grilling, his brow arches high into his hairline. "Hey, don't judge a book by its cover, remember?"

As he assures me he's worthy of my time, I examine the space, seeking any exits that won't require me to walk past the man claiming to be the head of Isaac's security. My heart beats wildly. Because soot and dust cover the windows, I can't make out anything but shadows milling in the moonlit night. For all I know, I could be walking straight into a trap by leaving, but I don't have much choice.

Anxiety plays havoc with my vocal cords when I say, "I'm carrying a weapon. If you attempt to stop me from leaving, I'll shoot you."

The bearded man referring to himself as Hunter smiles while standing. Although I'm warning him to stay away, he takes a step closer to me. Meaning I have no choice. I must protect myself.

In less than a heartbeat, I snag my satchel off the counter, shove my palm against the bridge of his nose, then bolt for the exit door as quickly as my quivering legs will take me. His groans sound through my ears as I break through the barn-style wooden door. The coolness of the night gives calming relief to my overheated flushed cheeks, but nothing will ease the panic curling around my throat.

As my eyes dart up and down the deserted street, endeavoring to find a secure location to hide, I'm grabbed from behind. Their hold is so powerful, my feet lift from the ground at the same time my satchel skids across the concrete path. When my frightened screams are muffled by a hand, I kick out my legs wildly, ensuring the heels on my boots connect with my attacker's shins. I dig my French-tipped nails into his exposed arms before biting at his hand, my furious battle only simmering when the rugged voice of Hugo whispers into my ear. "It's me, Izzy. It's okay. Don't scream."

My lungs hunt for air when he removes his hand from my mouth, but their campaign is cut short when my eyes lock in on the bearded stranger briskly pacing toward us. Blood is dribbling from his right nostril, and his eyes are narrowed into tiny slits.

Sensing my panic, Hugo spins around while discreetly removing his gun from the back of his jeans. The worry straining his face eases when he spots the bearded stranger. He returns his gun to the waist of his jeans before greeting him with a pat on his back. "Hey, Hunter, what happened to your nose?"

Hunter's heavily shadowed eyes shift to me. Even though he's angry, his dark eyes still have a sparkle of amusement in them. "I had the pleasure of meeting Izzy without a formal introduction."

Cringing, I mumble, "Sorry."

Hugo muffles his chuckle with a cough when Hunter glares at him.

Certain he has the situation under control, Hunter snatches my satchel off the concrete sidewalk and rummages through it.

"Hey!"

Hunter's eyes snap to mine, his vehement gaze cutting through me like a knife. I'm tempted to hit him for a second time when he yanks my sleek black iPhone out of my bag before smashing it onto the ground. It shatters on impact, but that's not good enough for Hunter. He has to get his boot in on the action as well. He stomps on it three times, rendering it as useless as he'll be once I rearrange his nose for the second time.

Hugo seizes my elbow, halting my angry strides. It's for the best. If he hadn't stopped me, I would have never witnessed Hunter removing a small flat device from my phone. It looks very much like a bug. After assessing it under a street light, he drops the offending product into a half-empty glass of beer discarded on a table outside the pub.

"How did you know she had a listening device in her phone?"

Hunter shifts on his feet to face Hugo. "The scanner in my pocket was picking up a signal."

So that's why he was obsessed with checking his phone.

"It looks similar to the one I removed from Izzy's phone yesterday morning."

My eyes snap to Hugo. "You what?"

He coughs to clear his throat. "You had a bug in your cell. We don't know how long it's been there, but we believe it may have been how the FBI discovered Isaac's private residence."

"We?" Nothing can iron out the hope in my tone.

Air whizzes out Hugo's nose. "Yes, *we*. Isaac was the one who suggested I scan your apartment for bugs. Unfortunately, blondie didn't distract you long enough for me to do a thorough search."

My heart rate quickens. Does that mean Isaac believes I didn't divulge any of his private life to the FBI? I wonder why his opinion on the matter altered so quickly?

My deliberations stop when Hunter digs his fingers into the glass of beer to remove the bug. He places it into a plastic bag he pulled out of his jeans pocket. Once he has the device secured in the top pocket of his plaid shirt, he moves to stand in front of me. "Who's been in your apartment since yesterday morning?"

Before my brain can sort through any facts, Hugo answers

on my behalf. "Only one person." His tone is low and danger-ous. "Blondie."

He strides down the street, his steps quick and precise. After snatching my satchel out of Hunter's grasp, I take off after him. "Hugo, wait!"

Because his strides are so long, I have to sprint to catch up with him. I call his name several times, but he ignores every request I make for him to calm down. My eyes dart back to Hunter to seek his assistance. He's following us but doesn't offer up any support.

I gasp when Hugo draws his gun from the back of his jeans before kicking open Brandon's hotel room door. As he enters the room, he aims his gun to Brandon, who is sitting on a hideous green floral bedspread, talking on his cell phone.

Brandon swallows bleakly when he notices the fury clouded in Hugo's eyes. "I-I-I'll call you back," he stammers into the phone before disconnecting his call.

When I place myself between Hugo and Brandon, Hugo adjusts his gun so it no longer faces me, although it could still inflict harm to Brandon. "I trust Brandon; he wouldn't do this." I stare into his barren eyes, my voice quaking. "He's my friend. He's been helping me."

I don't turn my head, but I see Brandon rising from the bed in Hugo's dilated eyes. "What's going on?"

"Why don't you tell us, *blondie*?" Hugo spits out Brandon's nickname like it's trash.

After giving him my best 'warning' look, I spin around to face Brandon. His eyes flick between Hugo and me for several heart-thrashing seconds before he shifts them to Hunter, who is leaning in the doorjamb of his hotel room.

His focus returns to me when I divulge, "They found a listening device in my cell phone."

He nods a mere second before reality dawns on his face. "I didn't plant the bug. It wasn't me. Izzy, you know me. I've been helping you—"

"You're the only one who's been with Izzy since I removed the last bug yesterday morning."

Hugo's angry sneer reverberates through me so well, it clears some of the bewilderment in my head. "No, he wasn't." I crank my neck back to face Hugo, my legs shaking. "Theresa Veneto and a male agent came to my apartment yesterday afternoon. She showed me photos of Col Petretti's right-hand man in a hospital bed. She said he was beaten the weekend Isaac and I went to club 57. She was trying to coerce me into unwillingly incriminating Isaac."

Hunter's deep snicker sounds through the room. "That's bullshit. For one, if Isaac had tracked him down that night, he wouldn't have left breathing. And two, Col would never file a police report on the assault, let alone have an FBI agent consider it. He'd have swept it under the rug like he always does."

Hunter squeezes Hugo's shoulder, wordlessly suggesting he stand down. After working his jaw side to side, Hugo does precisely that.

I eye Hunter in suspicion when he moves to stand in front of a quiet and white-faced Brandon. With the veins in his neck pumping, he asks, "Who are you?"

"Brandon James."

When Brandon offers him his hand to shake, Hunter snubs his offer.

"What's your real name?" He crosses his arms in front of his chest. "Because I did a search on a Brandon James after your *date* with Izzy a couple of months ago, nothing came up."

"Just like your search on Izzy failed to yield any real results?"

I'm not the only one shocked by Brandon's brash statement. Hunter and Hugo are also taken aback.

"I buried Izzy's private life as much as I did mine." Brandon's eyes stray to mine. They're clouded with intrigue and anxiety. "I knew they'd be looking."

He doesn't need to say any more. His truthful eyes communicate the entire story. He knows my secret. He knows who my dad is.

"Isaac already knows—"

"I'm not talking about Isaac," Brandon interrupts, stepping closer. "I'm talking about the bureau." After smiling to ease the turmoil swirling in my stomach, he strolls to the other side of the room to secure some papers from a black briefcase. "You're not the only one who's been doing some research the past few days."

When he hands me a printed document, my eyes drop to scan it. The more I read, the closer my brows become. "The bureau paid for me to fly business class?"

Brandon shakes his head. "Not the Bureau, Izzy. Alex signed off on it."

"That son of a bitch," I growl, baring teeth. "Why would he do that?"

When Brandon shrugs, I clench my fists into a tight ball, fighting with all my might not to curse the quiet night air. I shouldn't be surprised by Brandon's admission. Alex was adamant from my very first day that I was only brought in as a piece of eye candy for Isaac. I just had no clue how vigorous his attempts were to force me to go undercover until now.

21

———————

ISABELLE

My bleary eyes float over the black shadows dancing on a water-stained ceiling. I've just awoken from another sexually graphic yet unsatisfying dream. My imagination has always been wondrous, but knowing first-hand how impressive Isaac's sexual prowess is has my dreams being the most vivid they've ever been. My body must be punishing me for betraying the man who sparks my every sense with the simplest touch of his fingertip because every time I'm on the cusp of a climax, I wake up.

Although they're only dreams, I'm beyond frustrated. Before I met Isaac, I could go months without sexual stimulation. Now, I can't even last a few measly days. My dreams are so convincing, I swear I can smell Isaac's seductive scent filtering through my nostrils right now. It's so strong, it's overtaking the horrid smell of wet carpet plaguing the badly outdated motel room I'm sleeping in.

After Brandon's revelations about Alex, I went to lie down in an attempt to unjumble some of the confusion clustered in my head. Hugo would only leave me alone on the agreement that the interconnecting door between our rooms was to remain open, and I place my loaded gun on the bedside table. I didn't expect to fall asleep, but with my sleep lagging the past month, exhaustion must have overtaken me.

I pant, hoping to calm down the erratic beat of my heart. The pulse in my neck intensifies as warm dampness pools between my legs. My body is craving Isaac's touch so much, it's convinced it can sense his closeness.

Stupid, traitorous body.

When I turn my eyes to the bedside table to see what ungodly time it is, my heart leaps out of my chest. There's a dark shadow standing near the window of my room. After shooting my hand up to stifle my terrified scream, I scamper up the mattress, my movements so fast, the sheets bunch under my bare legs. While flattening my back on the headboard, my hand creeps to the rickety bedside table, trying in vain to locate my handgun I'd placed there earlier.

My pulse skyrockets when my search comes up empty.

"Looking for this?"

My eyes snap shut as an inappropriate swear word seeps from my mouth. "Jesus, Isaac, you scared the shit out of me."

Every nerve in my body prickles to attention, but now, it's more associated with excitement than fear.

After taking a moment to discharge the panic scorching my body, I flick on the bedside table lamp. Isaac is standing next to the motel window. His impressive body is encased in midnight black running pants, a black sweater, dark sneakers, and a baseball cap is pulled down low, concealing his enthralling eyes.

When he heads my way, my heart beats out a funky tune. Even dressed down, his stature demands my attention. While peering at me from beneath his cap, he places my unclipped gun and removed magazine onto the bedside table.

"Hugo made me put it there."

"I know," he interrupts as his lips curve into a mouthwatering smirk. "He's trying to protect you, Isabelle. You need to let him do the job he's paid to do."

"He drew his gun on my friend, Isaac. That's beyond his job description."

"And your *friend* drew his gun on him," Isaac snaps back. "Doesn't that now make them even?"

Before I can verbalize a response, my heart leaps into my chest for the second time in under a minute. Hugo barrels into the room with his gun drawn in front of his chest, his pistol only lowering when his eyes collide with Isaac's halfway across the room.

"I guess it's lucky it was me sneaking around Isabelle's room and not Col."

Hugo's throat works hard to swallow. "Sorry, boss. I'll get Hunter." When my eyes narrow into thin slits, he adds on, "and blondie."

Because of the low angle of Isaac's cap, I can't see his entrancing eyes, but I do feel the heat of his gaze running over my barely-covered body. Wanting to get comfortable, I was resting in my long-sleeve shirt and a pair of panties. My inner vixen cheers when his gaze loiters on my exposed thighs longer than what could be categorized as an acceptable glance.

No longer able to reel in my overwhelming desire to touch him, I crawl across the bed on my hands and knees. Air puffs from Isaac's lips when I raise onto my knees in front of him. I peer into his shadowed eyes that are murkier today than last week. "I'm sorry for everything that happened, but I swear to you, I never divulged anything about your personal life to the bureau. Even if you never want to see me again, I need to know you believe me."

Several heart-clenching seconds of silence pass between us. Even with unease being the forefront of our gathering, intimacy is also paramount. It zaps in the air, heating my skin and the area between my legs.

"I know you lied to me, Isabelle."

Moisture burns my eyes as a sob tears at my throat.

"Let me finish," he requests when he notices my sullen expression. "I know you lied when you said you led the FBI to my private residence." Because of our closeness, my breaths flutter his mouth. "I just don't understand why you did it."

I fist his jacket, tethering him closer to me while also soundlessly signaling that I'm not letting him go without a fight this time around. "That night, you fired Hugo even though he didn't do anything wrong. With everything that was happening, you needed him by your side. That's why I lied."

Isaac remains quiet, his breathing the only audible noise over the rapid beat of my heart. I stare at him, wishing he'd take his cap off so I could see his eyes. I've missed them so much the past week.

Sensing my private bidding, he removes his cap to rake his fingers through his luxurious hair that's a little overdue for a trim. My fingers itch, dying to join the party. Before they can, he puts his hat back on. When I nibble on my lower lip, battling not to yank his hat back off, Isaac saves it from my menacing teeth.

My breaths become delayed when his thumb drags over my parched mouth, lingering on the cupid's bow on my top lip longer than the rest. The air is stifling with an equal amount of lust and testosterone. When my tongue darts out to moisten my dry lips, I accidentally lick Isaac's thumb. Anticipation clusters in my pussy when he sucks in a sharp breath from my frisky tease. Acting on the prompts of my body, I sway nearer to him, craving his closeness. I've missed his touch so much the last two weeks, I'm willing to put everything on the line to feel it again.

A rock settles in my stomach when he grumbles, "No, Isabelle." His intense glare emerging from underneath his cap makes my pussy throb. My horniness doubles when he mutters, "You still lied to me. Not just Friday night, but for the past month, so if I were to touch you right now, I'd spend more time punishing you than pleasing you."

My pulse thrums in anticipation as warmth slicks between my legs. "I'll take any punishment you want to give if it means it will end with you touching me."

I press my thighs together when the most deliciously wicked smile etches onto his sinful mouth, revealing he heard my mumbled comment. I can barely control my breaths when his eyes snap shut so he can inhale a huge whiff of air through his nostrils. "Fuck, you smell good." His growl wets my panties. "I've missed that scent."

My smile is so broad, my cheekbones hurt from their quick incline. When he tilts toward my heaving chest, desire scorches through me. I'm unable to move as the lips I can't stop fantasizing about inch toward mine. Just as his perfectly carved mouth brushes my hungry lips, Hugo re-enters my room with Brandon and Hunter on his tail. Sensing that we have company, Isaac yanks back, leaving nothing but the smell of his expensive cologne in his wake. I try to conceal my frustration, but the smallest groan still escapes from my lips. I'm beyond frustrated.

"Are we interrupting?" Hugo asks, fully aware he is.

When my eyes snap to him, he grins a full-toothed smile before he continues sauntering into the room. They're halfway to my springless mattress when all three men stop dead in their tracks. Hugo's brows stitch together, Brandon swallows bleakly, and Hunter's beard-covered mouth carves into an illustrious smirk. My eyes bounce between them, striving to work out why they look so petrified.

I discover the cause of their fret when I follow the direction of their gazes. Isaac is staring at them. His infuriating glare is so downright dangerous, it makes my pussy throb.

"We'll meet you in there." Hugo hooks his thumb to the room they just emerged from before scurrying away even quicker than they arrived.

The hairs on my neck prickle when Isaac presses his lips to my ear. "When you're *adequately* dressed, meet us next door."

I smile, suddenly aware of the men's wish to flee. Isaac is

even more ruthless when he's bombarded with jealousy. My shirt covers my backside, but only just.

When Isaac arches a brow waiting for me to respond, I nod. He appraises my face in devoted, pussy-wetting detail before doing one last brush of my lips with his thumb. "We'll discuss this more once we're alone."

After pressing his lips to the edge of my mouth, he strides into the room next to mine, not once glancing back my way.

22

ISAAC

Three sets of eyes track my every move as I walk across the room. This isn't uncommon. When I was younger, the attention used to bother me. I couldn't fathom why I always gained watchful stares. Now, it's customary. Wherever I go, I acquire the devotion of others. Some are unwanted, but most are a necessary requirement in my industry. The more attention I receive, the more my business ventures succeed.

After removing my cap and jacket, I place them on the dilapidated two-seater table at the side of the room. This motel hasn't been remodeled in the past three decades, but it was the only motel in Parkerville, so Hugo had no choice but to stay here with Isabelle.

It took me so long to arrive as I had to fly in the wrong direction to elude the surveillance team that's been shadowing me since my arrest. As far as the bureau is aware, Isaac Holt is currently in deep negotiations in a boardroom in the heart of

New York City. No one paid any attention to the busboy leaving the restaurant after his evening shift, not even when he jumped into a car that cost more than ten times his annual salary.

"Where are you on tracking the source of the listening device in Isabelle's phone?"

Hunter's eyes pop up from the report he's perusing. "The serial number corresponds with the one Hugo got out of her phone yesterday, but it's also untraceable."

"I know someone who could look into it," Brandon, who is sitting on a double bed at the side of the room, pipes up. "I just need the serial numbers."

My gaze drifts from Hunter to Brandon. Victory heats my blood when Brandon returns my intense stare-down for a miserable three seconds before he succumbs to the pressure. Once his gaze drops to his polished shoes, I drift my eyes to Hugo. "Why is he here?"

Hugo's lips twitch, but before he can speak, a voice that makes my cock turn to stone just from hearing it says, "Because I trust him."

Isabelle enters the room wearing more clothing than she was mere minutes ago. Although my eyes just assessed every inch of her delectable curves, I can't help but scan her seductive body again. With a mouth that would bring mortals to their knees, eyes that see through to my soul, and a body made to be pleasured, she's too enticing to only warrant one glance.

There's no doubt I'm a sucker for punishment. I scrutinized the surveillance video of Isabelle and Brandon kissing in the hallway repeatedly the past week. Although Isabelle didn't jerk away from Brandon's embrace, her body didn't melt either. She didn't react with half the intensity she does when I kiss her. Call me conceited, but I only need to glance at her, and she responds with more intensity than she did while Brandon kissed her. I only need to rake my eyes over her body, and evidence of her arousal filters through my nose. Isabelle's seductive scent is the most intoxicating thing I've ever smelled. My cock flexes just thinking about how delicious she smells when she comes.

"Brandon has done nothing but help us, Isaac." When she stops in front of me, her intoxicating smell permeates the air surrounding us. I clench my fists at my side, battling not to mark and claim her in front of the three men whose eyes haven't left her since she joined us. "You can trust him."

When she stares up at me with her big chocolate eyes, my anger wanes. Her eyes are my eternal weakness. Not only can they see my soul, they consume it as well.

I take several long moments to appraise her beautiful face before shifting my focus to Hunter. "Give him the serial numbers." I nudge my head to Brandon.

I don't need to see Isabelle to know she's happy with my reply. I can feel her smile defrosting the ice that formed around my heart the past two weeks—ice only she can thaw.

"Thank you."

When she balances on her tippy toes to place a kiss on my cheek, my cock stiffens. I'd give anything to be in an empty room with her right now—anything at all. Then, once she begged for forgiveness, I'd spend hours becoming reacquainted with her body. It's only been two weeks since she was underneath me, but it feels like months.

My eyes shoot across the room when Hugo asks, "Do you two need a minute to finish, or can we get this show on the road?"

His smile sags when I retort, "You may only need a minute, Hugo, but most men require a lot longer than that to pleasure their women."

Hunter and Hugo's boisterous chuckles bounce around the room. Even Brandon snickers. The only person who stays quiet is Isabelle. Her pert nipples bud against her thin shirt as her beautiful scent infuses the air. My lips thin into a hard line. I'm barely restraining myself from touching her as it is, and she's making my struggle ten times worse. I wouldn't hold back if the chuckles booming from the other side of the room didn't clue her on to the fact we have company. She's just as proficient about failing to notice anyone else in the room when she's in my presence as I am with her.

She claps her hands two times, waking herself from her trance. "Okay, let's get down to business."

She pads to the other side of the room to gather a bursting-at-the-seams manila folder from underneath her dowdy satchel. When she twirls back around, the smile curving her lips slackens so a rueful frown can take its place. After returning to my side, she gestures for me to sit on the sofa across from the double beds Hugo, Hunter, and Brandon are sprawled on.

When I do, she removes several printouts from the folder, fanning them out on the chipped coffee table wedged between us. "These were taken at Megan's hotel room in Ravenshoe."

After scanning the photos, I lift my eyes to hers. "My security team supplied me with similar photos."

The day before I was arrested, Nick had a run-in with a lady at my nightclub. I immediately had a security detail placed on him. I also updated Cormack on the situation the days following my arrest so Nick would have adequate protection while on the road with his band. The photos Isabelle supplied are nearly identical to the ones Hunter took.

After sitting next to me, Isabelle splits the photos into two separate piles. Although her outward appearance doesn't reveal that she's affected by my closeness, her body gives away her deceit. The hairs on her arms bristle as her breathing shallows. Once she has them sorted, she angles her body to face mine. "These are from today."

She hands me a stack of images printed on plain white paper. When my eyes roam over them, my jaw quivers. This evidence proves Megan's obsession with Nick is more than the random groupie/rock star fascination my security team has been running with the past month.

My gaze floats up when Isabelle places her hand over my fist to give it a reassuring squeeze. The concern relayed through her eyes has me on edge. "When the bureau first stumbled upon Megan, we were under the assumption she was one of your... *flings.*" When she said 'we,' her eyes flicked to Brandon. "It was only when I followed Megan the day before your arrest did I discover her interests centered around Nick."

She followed Megan? My furious eyes snap to Hugo. "Where were you? You were supposed to be her shadow!"

"I asked him to collect those documents you required from

Regan," Hunter informs me on behalf of Hugo. "We thought Isabelle would be safe as she was scheduled to remain at her workplace for several more hours."

Ignoring the thick stench of awkwardness plaguing our gathering, Isabelle shuffles through the photos on the coffee table. When she finds the picture she's after, her eyes return to mine. "Megan had a baby crib set up in her hotel room, indicating that she may have been pregnant. When I saw this ultrasound photo, it all but confirmed it."

She hands me a picture of a crib and an ultrasound photo. "Megan was pregnant, but it wasn't Nick's baby. He had an in-utero paternity test done a few months ago—"

"No. Megan wasn't pregnant because she's *never* had the chance to be pregnant."

Isabelle passes me a stack of documents Brandon just gave her. He gathered them from a portable printer at our right. The papers are the itemized bill Nick's lawyers sent me after representing him in his paternity case. She flips through a handful of pages. Her teeth catch her bottom lip when she finds the place she's searching for.

My knuckles popping echo around the room when she points to a vitally imported section in the middle of the medical report. "Are you kidding me?"

Isabelle shakes her head. "No, Megan has never had sexual contact with anyone, let alone Nick."

I throw the documents onto the coffee table so I can rake my fingers through my hair. My hands twitch in sync with my jaw, my anger so potent, I'm on the verge of cracking. "If she never had sex, why did she have a crib set up in her room?"

"Because she's extremely unwell." Isabelle's voice shudders as she scoots closer to me. "She's been in and out of mental hospitals since she was a little girl. During her latest stint, the doctors diagnosed her as having pseudocyesis. Even though she isn't pregnant, she truly believes she is."

My limbs suddenly feel heavy as anger overtakes every inch of me. "If she's so unwell, why isn't she admitted to the hospital now?"

Isabelle coughs to clear her throat. "She was, but she escaped after she struck an orderly with a steel chair."

I jump up from my seat so abruptly, Isabelle startles. "So, she isn't just a psychopath, she's dangerous!" I glare at Hunter, beyond pissed that he failed to pick up any of this during his many reports on Megan the past month.

"We assessed the situation before acting on the information we had on hand at the time, Isaac. That's why Nick has Peters shadowing him," Hunter remarks, speaking for the first time since I arrived.

I know what he's doing. He assigned the talking to Isabelle as he knows I won't lash out at her as I would him. He's being a coward, and he'll be reprimanded for it the instant I fix the monumental fuck-up he created.

My eyes fall to Isabelle when she says, "Brandon, Hugo, and I believe Jenni and her unborn baby are more at threat than Nick." Her eyes shift to Hunter. They're full of silent apologies. "Nothing against Hunter and his team, they could only go off the information they had before them, but after we called you, we completed an in-depth search of Megan's room. The threat to Jenni and her unborn baby is credible."

Hugo moves to stand next to me. "When I couldn't reach you earlier tonight, I called in a favor. One of my guys is watching Jenni's house. He's been reporting back to me every thirty minutes. The house has remained dark throughout the night. I assure you he's good, Isaac. He won't let anything happen to them."

I scratch my brow while drifting my eyes between the four sets watching me with concern. I wasn't reachable today as I've been at the hospital, and then on a plane. I just had no clue both my distractions today were for the same thing.

"Jenni gave birth this morning."

A deep sigh spills from Isabelle's lips as the strain marring her beautiful face relaxes. "Oh, thank God," she mutters under her breath. "Is everything okay? Is the baby safe and healthy?"

"They're both fine. He was five weeks early, but he's doing well." I halfheartedly shrug. "Jenni seemed a little rattled, but she's in good spirits."

Isabelle scoots to the edge of her chair, her concern undeniable. "Did she give birth naturally?"

When I nod, her eyes snap shut so fiercely, two tears drip down her pale cheeks. Even irritated over the situation with Megan, my heart stops beating. I fucking hate when she cries, but not any more than I hate how tired she looks. Dark rims are circling her eyes, her face is gaunt like she hasn't eaten a proper meal in days, and her hair is well overdue for a washing.

While she brushes away the tears on her cheeks with a sweep of her finger, I stray my eyes to Hugo. "Can this wait until the morning?"

"Yeah." Hugo nods, understanding me more than I give him

credit for. "We searched Megan's residence as thoroughly as we could, but the lighting was poor, so we decided it would be best to return in the morning. We're planning to go back at sunrise." He gestures his head between himself, Isabelle, and Brandon. When his gaze settles on Brandon, he asks, "Since Jenni has had the baby, has the threat been stabilized?"

The tautness on his face eases when Brandon nods.

"My guy will stay on Nick's house until you tell me otherwise. Brandon has a lock on Megan's bank accounts, and he added her to a travel database, so if she makes a move, we'll be the first to know." Hugo drifts his eyes to Isabelle for the quickest second before returning them to me. "It's been a big day."

I nod, acknowledging his wordless distress for Isabelle. Anger is still coursing through my veins, but Nick, Jenni, and their baby boy, Jasper, are safe, so my focus can shift to taking care of Isabelle. It's been a draining two weeks on all of us, but Isabelle has had shit flung at her from all directions. Although I can't clear away all the mess just yet, I can soothe her as only I can.

I lock my eyes with Hunter. "Call Peters to give him an update on the situation, and make sure he stays on the hospital grounds. Also, supply those serial numbers to Brandon to run through his database. I want to know where the equipment that was in Isabelle's apartment came from." I shift on my feet to face Hugo. "Have your man stay on Nick's house, but when I return, I'll want to meet him. I need to ensure he's a good fit for Nick and Jenni before making him an official part of their security detail."

He nods, his smile one I haven't seen before.

"And you..." I drift my eyes to Brandon. He goes from gawking at the shaggy-stained carpet to looking at me. "Thank you for helping... *us.*"

I still have apprehensions about Brandon, but if Isabelle trusts him, I can decompartmentalize my jealousy for her benefit. It's the least I can do after what I put her through the past two weeks. The biggest grin stretches across Brandon's face before his twinkling eyes stray to Isabelle. Her mouth is gaped wide, and her pupils are the size of saucers. Anyone would swear I've never issued a compliment before from the shocked expressions on Hunter, Hugo, and Isabelle's faces.

I have, just not verbally.

23

ISABELLE

efore my brain can register the fact that Isaac complimented Brandon, Isaac scoops down to gather me in his arms. His intoxicating scent engulfs my nostrils, activating every one of my hot buttons. He carries me across the room, his speed faster than a bullet. I want to ask where we're going, but not a word escapes my parched lips. I have an inkling as to what is going on in that big head of his. Our undeniable urge to have one another will have a lot of people mistaking our relationship as only being based on lust, but that isn't the case. We have a connection that's hard to explain unless it's dispersed physically. That's why we indulge in our fantasies as often as possible.

I'll never be able to rein in my desires when Isaac is in my vicinity. Even in this complicated situation, I yearn to nurture him. If the massive erection jabbing into my backside is anything to go by, Isaac is craving the same thing.

Once he breaks into the poorly-dated room I was resting in only an hour ago, he kicks the door shut, then paces toward the bathroom. His warm breath tickles my nose when he says, "Shower and then bed."

I nuzzle into his neck, drinking in his delicious scent. "Okay."

His pec muscles flex when my lips brush the pulse in his jaw, but before I can relish in his body's response to my smallest touch, we enter the minuscule bathroom attached to my room. A toilet in one corner has the vanity balancing over the top of it, and an old, pink-tiled shower is in the opposite corner. Its curtain is riddled with soap scum and mold, and there's a giant rip down the middle of it.

"I think we should keep our shoes on."

Giggling, I nod. "Without a doubt."

After placing me onto my feet, Isaac tugs his shirt over his head before lowering his sweat pants down his splayed thighs. I strive with all my might to keep my eyes planted on his sculptured face, but the pull to glide them over his body is too great to stop me. I float them over his smooth, hairless pecs, down the six bumps in his midsection, before darting them between the scrumptious V muscle I love tracing with my tongue.

Just when I think the visual can't get any better, Isaac ups the ante by yanking his boxer shorts down. I become wet when his cock springs free from his trunks. It's thick, pulsating, and has a perfect drop of pre-cum beaded at the top. While licking my parched lips, I wrap my hand around his densely veined shaft. Isaac stops kicking his clothes to the other side of the room, his hiss coming out with a moan. As he stares into my eyes, the walls close in on me. They're so intensely beautiful, I could topple into ecstasy without stimulation.

No words are spoken between us. We don't need them to express ourselves. Everything is reflected in his beautiful eyes. His forgiveness for my betrayal. His sorrow for his harsh words. It's all said without a word needing to escape his lips. This is us. This is how we show our affection to each other. We communicate our feelings through touch, not words. Besides, nothing he could say would change how I feel about him, so why waste time rehashing old issues?

When Isaac steps closer to me, I'm rendered motionless, mesmerized by the perfect specimen of a man displayed in front of me. His eyes stay locked on mine, only breaking for the quickest second when he lifts my shirt over my head to discard it on the floor. His cock twitches when he unclasps the button of my jeans before sliding down the zipper. Tingles spasm my spine when he crouches down to guide the stiff material down my quivering thighs before steering them over the ballet flats I'm wearing.

My knees curve inward when he places a kiss above my right ankle. A gentle bite closely follows it. Then another kiss, before another bite. He presses a trail of kisses and nips from my right ankle to my thigh, making my left leg jealous. After every bite, his tongue soothes the sting his teeth made, his eyes never leaving mine.

Pleasure rockets through me when his teeth graze my throbbing panty-covered clit on his way to pay the same dedication to my left leg. He gives it just as much devotion as he did my right leg, except this time, he goes from my hip to my ankle.

By the time his thorough dedication is complete, my panties are drenched, and my nipples are capable of cutting diamonds. I'm not the only one getting carried away. When Isaac stands to his full height, his cock digs into my stomach. He's the thickest I've ever seen him, and I can't wait to taste him.

"I need hours, Isabelle." His voice is hoarse with lust. It makes me even wetter. "But you need to rest."

While my inner vixen screams vulgarities at the top of her lungs, I pout. Isaac smirks, loving my unashamed response. I'd make him pay for his ill-timed smile if his next set of words didn't steal the air from my lungs.

"I'm still going to fuck you, Isabelle." His cocky confirmation sends a thrill of excitement to my core where it clusters and tightens. "It'll just be hard and fast against that wall." His commanding eyes flick to the only wall in the bathroom that doesn't have some sort of contraption attached to it. "Then you'll sleep, and I'll have the remainder of the weekend to devour you."

The scent of my arousal lingers in the air, revealing how close I am to the edge. One touch, one brush, one pound of his cock, and I'll be toppling into orgasmic bliss. I should be ashamed of how aroused I am, but I'm not. After two weeks of turmoil, I'm going to soak up every little drop of attention he's giving me, starting with his cock.

As I fall to my knees, I grasp his densely-veined shaft. Air whistles between his teeth when my tongue darts out to lap up the bead of pre-cum pooling on his swollen knob.

"Fuck, Isabelle." He rocks his hips forward, ramming inches

of his delicious cock into my mouth. I take as much of him as I can, my lips burning from their wide stretch.

The grunted moans spilling from his lips make the burn worthwhile. He's loving this as much as I am, appreciating that I'm just as incapable of harnessing my desires as he is. While sucking him down deep, I relish his musky scent. He smells so manly, so scrumptious, so toe-curling delectable. When I fail to get half of his impressive cock into my mouth, my hand works on the sections missing out. I drag it up and down his shaft in sync to my lips, taking him a little deeper with each suck I do.

My strokes become needy when his dirty mouth spurs on my pursuit to unravel him. I want him incapable of rational thoughts, to make him speechless like he forever makes me.

"God, Isabelle. Even in my dreams, it didn't feel this good. Those lips, that mouth, your velvety tongue... I'll never get enough." His cock hardens with every word he speaks as does his grip on my hair. "I'm going to come in your mouth before coming in your tight pussy. Are you ready for that, Isabelle? Are you going to swallow my cum like you were born to do it?"

Our combined purrs of ecstasy bounce around the small bathroom. I stroke him harder, faster. I draw him into my mouth so deeply, I gag. It adds to the heat teeming between us. He loves nothing more than dominating me, and gagging on his big dick does precisely that. He feeds his cock in and out of my mouth, groaning when he hits the back of my throat.

When my tongue swirls around his knob, eagerly lapping up every delicious drop of liquid formed there, he begins to pant. The veins on his glorious cock throb, revealing he's seconds from coming before the first spurts of seed violently erupt from his cock's head. My name tumbles from his mouth in a grunt as his clutch on my hair tightens. I milk him greedily, pumping him furiously with my hand as my throat works hard to swallow down every delicious drop of his cum.

Once his violent shudders dissipate, I release his cock from my lips with a pop, place a kiss on his God-crafted V muscle, then stand to my feet. I sway in an invisible breeze, my legs quivering so fiercely, I can barely stand. It would be easier if Isaac's knee-buckling eyes weren't staring straight at me. Add that to the delicious smirk etched on his handsome face, and you've got more than a panty-wetting situation.

Several heart-clenching seconds pass in silence as we participate in a lust-filled stare-down. My breaths are so ragged, my bra-covered chest thrusts up and down with every inhalation I take. When Isaac cups my cheek in his spare hand, I nuzzle into his embrace. After tracing the dip in my top lip, he arrows his mouth toward mine. Stars form in front of my eyes when the mouth that keeps me up for hours every night seals over mine. His kiss bursts with intensity, love, and devotion. Every lash of his tongue and nip of his teeth increases the dampness between my legs. It takes my breath away, making me feel weightless.

When my legs wrap around his waist, I capture his rough moan in my mouth. Without relinquishing my lips from his, Isaac carries me to the discolored, paint-peeled wall he gestured to earlier. With a flick of his fingers, my bra is unclasped and dumped onto the once white-tiled floor. With one hand cupping my ass, holding me in place, the other one slithers up my body, only stopping when he reaches my breast.

He kneads and caresses it, stiffening my nipples to the point it's almost painful.

After a final nip to my bottom lip, Isaac inches back from my tingling mouth. His pupils are so large, I can see my reflection in them, and his plump lips are swollen from our kiss. "Lean back, baby. Let me see you."

Flashbacks of the first time we had sex in the private jet rush to the forefront of my mind. He loves seeing me. If he could fondle me and watch me at the same time, I'm certain he would. When my back braces against the wall, my breasts are propelled into his face. He traps one of my erect nipples into his mouth before swiveling his tongue around the peaked bud. As his talented mouth speeds up my sprint to orgasm, I snap my eyes shut.

"Oh god... that feels so good."

After paying dutiful attention to each of my breasts, he presses a trail of kisses up my chest, past my neck, and along my chin. My core tightens from his tantalizing tease, bringing me so close to ecstasy, my mind is nothing but a hazy blur of lust.

"More. Please. I can't wait any longer."

"Not yet." He tugs on my earlobe with his teeth before sucking it into his mouth. "I want to be inside you when you come. I want to feel your drenching wet pussy convulsing around me as you greedily beg for my cum, but more than anything, I want to hear my name torn from your pretty little throat like it did earlier tonight in your dreams."

My eyes pop open before drifting to his. I stare at him in shock, unaware he heard my dream. When he takes in my bewilderment, the most delicious, roguish grin stretches across his sinful mouth. "I heard every perfect little moan. You were so close, I was tempted to strum your clit to get you over the line, but I was greedy. I wanted to feel you come, not just see it."

The ruggedness of his voice nearly topples me into ecstasy. "If you still want to feel it, you better hurry because I'm dangerously close to the edge."

In the blink of an eye, my panties are shredded off my body, and the crown of Isaac's cock is braced at the entrance of my pussy. His intense, unique-colored eyes rake my torso before assessing my face, swelling my heart with the possessiveness beaming out of them.

He leans his forehead against mine, saying my name in a raspy groan when he slowly inches inside of me. A shiver surges through my body once he's fully seated. After adjusting my hips to a better angle, his fingers digging into the fleshy meat on my sides, he withdraws to the tip. A groan shudders from my lips when he slams back in one fluid motion. My pussy convulses around him, sucking at him as my mouth did his cock earlier.

"So silky and tight. Your pussy was built to be fucked by me, Isabelle."

His dirty words and each precise stroke of his thick cock has the fiery warmth in my stomach amplifying. Even in the crisp, near-winter morning, my body is so overheated, and a fine layer of sweat is slicking my skin. My rush to climax is so frantic, my body tightens in fear, scared of spiraling out of control. It's genuinely terrifying how much my body relinquishes its power to Isaac.

Sensing my hesitation, Isaac says, "Let it go, baby," while not once diminishing his relentless, mouth-watering pounds. He knows the hold he has on me. With his power and dominance, he knows my body solely belongs to him.

As shivers wreak havoc with my body, I lift and lock my eyes with his. When our gazes collide, I fall into the most violent, earth-shattering orgasm I've ever had. Shockwaves tremble through my body, and my vision blurs when a climax shreds through me so hard and fast, I can't withhold the screams of ecstasy tearing from my throat.

"Fuck, Isabelle," Isaac groans before sealing his mouth over mine.

He kisses me like he's never kissed me before, like a man starved for my taste. Like he'll never get enough. Our tongues frantically collide, desperately exploring each other's mouths. It's a hot and heavy embrace that's full of intensity and mutual understanding. I return his kiss with as much passion, expressing to him that I'll never give him up. I'll fight for him —*for us*—until my very last breath.

As Isaac pulls his torturous lips away from mine, he slows the pace of his frantic pumps. He coerces my eyes to his without a word spilling from his lips. When he gets them, a familiar tightening sensation builds again in my womb, my next orgasm spurred on by the dominant gleam in his beautiful eyes.

"I'm yours. I've always been yours. I'll always be yours."

His sexy-as-sin growl vibrates through my body, heightening my senses to never-before-reached levels. As his pupils dilate in the most knee-clanging way, a seductive smile stretches across his face. It isn't a smirk, it's a genuine smile that wipes away every bad thing that's happened between us the past two weeks.

When a second climax rockets through my body like fireworks exploding in the sky, it is the fight of my life to keep my eyes open, but I do it just because there's nothing more captivating in the world than the strikingly gorgeous face of Isaac Holt in the midst of ecstasy.

24

ISAAC

"I don't care what you have to do, Regan, I want it squashed."

Regan sighs down the line. "Okay, I'll do my best."

"Good. I won't be back in town until Monday afternoon, and no cell service from midday, so if you need me, you'll need to contact Hunter or Hugo."

"I won't need to see you before then. Unlike you, some of us have an occasional weekend off," Regan replies brashly. "I'll meet you at your office Tuesday morning with my findings."

After finalizing my call, I place my burner cell into the breast pocket of my suit jacket. I'm grateful Catherine insisted she pack me an overnight bag before I left the hospital yesterday afternoon. Otherwise, I would have been left wearing that hideous getup I was prancing around in last night. There's nothing wrong with gym clothes when you're at the gym. If you're not, you have no reason to wear them.

As I pace closer to the open window of Isabelle's dirty motel room, my gaze catches sight of the sun rising over the flat, barren horizon. The town of Parkerville would be best described as a dump. It's one main street has more closed shops than open, the land is unusable, and the facilities in the township are less than stellar. I can't wait to pack up Isabelle and leave this wretched town for good. But first, I need to return with Hugo and Hunter to Megan's family residence. I don't know what it is, perhaps intuition, but I can't shake the feeling there's something more to Megan's story than what's been unearthed so far.

My lips curl when the husky mumble of, "What time is it?" comes tumbling out of a mouth that took me to the brink three times last night.

I did have every intention of fucking Isabelle hard and fast so she could get some rest, but she altered the course of my moral compass when she dropped to her knees to devour my cock like she's never been fed. All my good intentions were left for dead when her velvety tongue licked up the beady drop on my crown.

When I spin around, my eyes widen when they're rewarded with the visual of Isabelle stretching her arms well above her head. Her dynamic stretch has the shirt I discarded on the bathroom floor last night riding up high, exposing inches upon inches of the luscious skin on her smooth thighs. Her hair is a tangled mess, her face is void of makeup, and she looks exhausted, but she's still the most ravishing woman I've ever laid my eyes on.

Her eyes wander over my body before flicking to the alarm

clock that displays it's a little after seven o'clock. "Life isn't fair," she harrumphs before flopping onto the lumpy mattress that kept me awake half the night. "How come you get to wake up looking like that..." she throws an arm my way, "... and I wake up looking like this?" She gestures her spare hand down her luscious body.

Smirking, I stride toward her. Since the room is so small, it only takes a few lengthened steps to reach her. She's lying flat on her back with her arm covering her exquisite eyes. The hairs on her arm bristle when I glide my index finger along it. Her mouth curves into a grin before she peers at me from behind her arm.

"Three times in one night still not enough to satisfy your appetite?"

A broad smirk stretches across my face, but I don't formulate a response to her question. She's acutely aware of my answer as her eyes are locked on the crotch in my trousers, which is struggling to contain my erection. As her teeth munch on her bottom lip, she glances into my eyes.

"Don't look at me like that, Isabelle." My tone is low and dangerous, revealing how close to the edge I am.

After relinquishing her lip from her gentle nibbles, her tongue darts out to replenish her dry lips. She knows her lips are my eternal weakness, so she's using them to her advantage. Her breathing shallows when I tilt my head closer to her. Her beautiful scent infuses the air, making what I'm about to say ten times harder. "If Hugo weren't outside that door waiting for us, I'd make you pay for that tease."

When I lick the shell of her ear, a jolt shivers through her body. She sighs when her eyes snap to the open interconnecting door between our room and Hugo's. I face my second fight this morning when her lower lip drops into a pout. I want to suck it. Taste it. *Bite it.*

Before I can, Isabelle jumps out of bed and scurries toward the tiny bathroom. "Give me five minutes, then I'll be ready to go."

Halfway there, she stops, then pivots around to face me. The biggest smile stretches across her adorable face as she rushes back to me. After slapping my cheeks, she stares lovingly into my eyes. "Good morning."

Any response planning to seep from my lips is halted when she presses her mouth to mine. A warning growl rumbles up my throat when she fails to open her lips at the request of my lashing tongue.

"No," she murmurs over my mouth. "Or we'll never leave."

With that, she spins on her heels and skips to the bathroom.

"Isabelle..." My grumble is rough and sharp, freezing her halfway between me and the bathroom door.

With quaking thighs, she turns around to face me. My lips crimp at her submissiveness. She's a strong and independent woman, but the instant we step into the bedroom, she surrenders all her power to me. Nothing in the world has made me feel more influential than that. Not takeovers, not business ventures, and not how much capital I have in my bank accounts. Nothing compares to the feeling I get knowing she trusts me enough to relinquish control of her body to me.

I stride toward her, my shoulders sitting higher than they

were this morning, my walk cocky. I grip the back of her slender thighs, coercing her legs to wrap around my waist. When they do, her sweet-smelling pussy heats my cock. I rock my hips upward, dragging my erection through the material clinging to the lines of her wet pussy. When her mouth falls open, I slip my tongue between her pouty lips. I nip, lick, and explore her succulent mouth like it's the first time I've sampled it.

We kiss for several minutes, the heat in our exchange enough to keep the country warm through a prolonged winter. Once I'm happy I've inspected every scrumptious portion of her mouth, I inch back until my forehead rests against hers, and her beautiful chocolate eyes are peering down at me.

"That's a proper good morning," I greet her with a wolfish smirk. "And it's how I plan to greet you every day from here on out."

My smirk enlarges to a full grin when I place her back onto her feet. Her wobbly strides as she makes her way into the bathroom have me wishing I hadn't made the promise I did years ago. Alas, I am a man of my word. I told my brother I'd forever have his back. I plan to keep my promise.

ISABELLE's nervous fidgeting becomes more apparent the closer we get to Megan's family residence. Hugo is driving my car with Isabelle and I sitting in the back seat. Hunter and Brandon are following behind us in Hunter's van that's stacked with the best computer equipment and surveillance devices money can buy.

When Hugo pulls my car into a long dirt driveway, Isabelle's panicked eyes rocket to me. "When we show you the information we gathered yesterday, I need you to remember Jenni and Jasper are safe and unharmed." Her voice is surprisingly smooth considering how hard her hands are shaking.

My eyes shift to Hugo, who's eyeing me with caution through the rearview mirror. "Did you discover anything that would warrant the authorities being called in?"

Hugo nods. "Yes, but Isabelle and Brandon agreed they wouldn't call it in until your security team was first given access to it."

I run my hand along my jaw, tracking the tremor there. "This won't keep your hands sparkling clean, Isabelle."

"I know, but I love you," she replies without pause. "Wouldn't you get your hands a little dirty for someone you love?"

Her words impact me more today than they did the first time I heard them. Because this time, they weren't said during intimacy. She said it because she truly means it.

When the car comes to a stop at the front of a derelict farmhouse, Isabelle scoots across the leather seat to clasp my hand within hers. "I trust that the man I've fallen in love with will handle this in an appropriate and *legal* manner." Her eyes dance between mine. The moisture in them sets my nerves on edge. "You're not the man your FBI file says you are, Isaac, so I'll trust that you'll uphold my beliefs on that."

I take a moment to ponder her statement. Like any good myth, the reality barely corresponds with the fabricated fiction, so I'm confident my police record is full of half-truths and misrepresentations of who I am, but, even so, I'm a protector. It's who I am. Nick is my responsibility. He's my blood. He gave me the gift of life, so it's my job to protect him from any potential threats just as I'll protect Isabelle from Col and Theresa. To me, there is no difference.

"I protect what's mine, Isabelle." My tone is as surly as my mood is becoming.

Isabelle's shoulders hunch forward as a sigh spills from her lips. "I know that, Isaac, but there are *legal* ways to handle this. The bureau or even the local sheriff's office could assist with this."

"Like how they handled my arrest?" A vicious snarl forms on my face as my anger transcends. "They *illegally* detained me for hours while they barbarically destroyed my house under the legality of a warranted search the Judge signed off on under false pretenses. Are they really the people I should seek out during a crisis?"

When Isabelle shifts her focus to the passenger window, I force her eyes back to mine via her chin. "Answer me, Isabelle! Are they truly the people I should trust?"

"Those people are me, Isaac! I'm *those* people." As her eyes bounce between mine, they're dangerously close to spilling the moisture flooding them. "Are you saying you don't trust me?"

Needing to escape before I say something I'll regret, I swing open the door and curl out. "Please stay in the car. You'll be safer here." My tone is firm, but my suggestion still comes out as a plea.

My jaw muscle tenses when Isabelle snubs my suggestion

by pushing open the back passenger door to step onto the dirt driveway, mumbling something about not being a child.

"One thing at a time, Isaac," I murmur to myself while joining Hugo at the front stairs of a rundown house.

The pain weighing down my chest intensifies when Isabelle twists her body, so her back is facing us before her hands dart up to scrub across her cheeks with a sense of urgency.

"Boss..."

I shoot Hugo a wry look, stopping him mid-sentence. "I'll fix *that* after I handle this."

During the 'that' part of my statement, I nudge my head to Isabelle. I hate the way I'm acting, but I need to focus on one task at a time. I'm juggling so many things at the moment, mistakes are bound to happen if I don't start being more cautious.

Hugo's thinning lips reveal his annoyance, but he nods all the same. He's aware of the mammoth tasks I'm undertaking as he's part of most of them. As I shadow him up the farmhouse steps, I absorb each unique feature. It reminds me of my dad's house before he renovated it. He's very much like Nick—stubborn to the point of being annoying. No matter how many times I offer to buy him a more suitable house, or to pay for his renovations, he always refuses my proposals. "You don't spend anything you haven't earned yourself," he commonly quotes.

"Give Brandon and me ten minutes to clear the premises before you and Hunter enter," Hugo requests when Hunter's van pulls in next to my town car.

I nod. "You have five minutes." The longer I'm here dealing

with this, the longer it'll be before I can repair the mistakes I made with Isabelle.

The house is cleared by Hugo and Brandon in under three minutes. A lack of floor space aided with their staunch search. The inside of the house needs even more repair than the outside. It's rundown and old, smelling like a garbage truck that's on the brink of retirement.

Hugo gestures his head to a rickety stairwell on the left. We climb them shoulder to shoulder, which isn't the smartest thing we've done this week. It barely looks capable of holding my weight, much less Hugo's.

"My boot," Hugo murmurs when my curious gaze takes in a hole halfway up. "Last door on the right."

The hallway reeks of stale water and mold, but compared to downstairs, the space is spotlessly clean. Fear tears me in two when I enter the room at the end of the hallway. Understanding Megan's obsession with Nick via pictures has nothing on seeing it firsthand. Every inch of her room, including the ceiling, is covered with photos of him. They range in dates from when his band was hardly known in its heydays at Mavericks, to pictures of him on a stage during a morning breakfast show a couple of weeks ago.

"How could you fathom the threat was to Jenni and Jasper? This room makes it pretty fucking obvious who the threat pertains to—"

"Not everything is black and white, Isaac. You need to look for the gray." Isabelle floats across the room, whisking up her beautiful scent that lessens the fury burning me at the stake. I wish I could take away the moisture brimming in her eyes just as quickly. "Remember, they are safe and protected. She can't hurt them anymore."

Pain rises in my heart knowing I caused her tears when all she has done is support me. As I run my hand down her cheek, breathing a sigh of relief when I discover it's dry, I nod. A smile tugs on her lips before she heads for a set of double doors in the far corner of the room. She wants this over as quickly as me, aware I need more than ten seconds to fix the mistakes I made.

When I join her at the side of the room, she grips a white door handle that's only just visible between the posters of Nick's band, Rise Up. The scent of bleach and disinfectant filters through my nostrils when she pushes the door open. Unlike Megan's bedroom, the white walls of this room are untouched and immaculately clean.

As I step into the sanitary-smelling space, my eyes dart in all directions. There isn't much to see. Other than a melamine table with a stainless-steel chair underneath it, the room is barren.

My jaw tenses when my eyes roam over the open textbooks on the desk. There's a range of articles and documents high-lighted on how to complete an illegal cesarean. The images are so graphic, even with having a cast-iron stomach, I still feel squeamish.

"Don't touch anything."

Isabelle's command freezes my hand halfway to a white sheet draped over the desk. When she raises it with a pen on my behalf, a knot twists in my stomach. Medical equipment that includes forceps, umbilical clamps, scissors, and a razor-sharp scalpel are stored inside a stainless-steel kidney-shaped bowl.

My nostrils flare when I drift my eyes to Hunter. He's the most deserving of my wrath considering it was his job to unearth everything he could about Megan after she attacked Nick at my nightclub.

Hunter holds his hands out in front of his body, mindful I'm two seconds from snapping. "Nothing like this was in her hotel room, or in *any* of the searches I completed."

I clench my fists so fast, the air ripples.

"Megan doesn't use a computer. Her cell phone is a burner, and she mainly relies on cash." Isabelle places herself in the firing line by standing between Hunter and me. "Her books were borrowed from the library or purchased at flea markets." She stares at me, begging for me to hear the truth in her words. "This isn't Hunter's fault, Isaac. Megan is unstable. She needs more help than any of us could have fathomed."

The genuine remorse in her beautiful, rich eyes subdues my anger. I do believe her. I also trust her. While replenishing my lungs with oxygen, I study the space, contemplating my next move. Any decisions made while angry will most likely result in an irrational reaction, so I need to quell my fury to ensure I think sensibly.

After a few moments of pondering, I turn to face Brandon. "Give Hunter an hour to document everything in this room, then call in local authorities." Isabelle looks at me with loving eyes as Brandon nods. "Hunter, I need you to hack every local CTV camera in Ravenshoe and two towns each side of it. If

Megan gets within a foot of my town, I want to be the first to know."

"Already done. After Hugo updated me on the situation last night, I knew you'd suggest it. I also updated Ryan. I kept the details vague, but he's passing Megan's photo onto his reputable officers," Hunter informs me.

"Good." My gaze shifts to Hugo. "Have your man sitting at Nick's house switch with Peters. I need Peters on the first flight to New York."

Hugo nods while pulling his dated cell out of his pocket.

"Get this wrapped up quickly and effectively. We don't have any time to waste."

While briskly strolling out of the room, I remove my untraceable cell from my pocket. I move to a room at the opposite end of the hall. Although I trust Isabelle, I can't put her at risk of prosecution, so this call must take place in private.

After dialing a number I know by heart, I squash my phone to my ear. Henry answers on the very first ring. "Isaac, you haven't rung me on this number in years. What do you need?"

"I need to call in that favor."

Henry's chuckle sounds down the line. "If my son can't find a loophole for your fighter, I won't be any more help."

"It's not for my fighter. There's a family situation I need your help with."

AFTER TALKING to Henry and my lawyer for thirty minutes, I re-enter Megan's bedroom. Brandon is taking a call in the corner of the room, and Hunter is digitally categorizing the space.

"Where's Isabelle?"

Hunter jumps off a step ladder in the middle of the room. It has a circular camera mounted on a tripod. It will record the area in 3D format.

"She and Hugo went to check on the outbuildings."

Nodding, I pace to a cracked window that looks out at the overgrown fields below. Because of Hugo's large size, it doesn't take me long to spot him standing next to a black truck at the front of a wooden shed. The vehicle must be locked as he's ramming a flat steel bar down the driver's side window to jimmy the lock.

I stray my eyes away when Brandon stops to stand next to me. "Boss.... umm... Isa..."

A grin spreads across my face. I shouldn't relish in his nervous response, but I do. He has a gun and badge on his hip, yet he still fears me. My ego has never been stroked so well.

"You can call me Isaac. I'm not your boss."

Brandon nods as a smile curls his lips. "I called in a favor with a girl I know. The owner of this property is Carlyle Shroud. He's fifty-eight years old, and has been receiving disability checks since a workplace injury nearly two decades ago." He drops his eyes to the notepad. "His disability checks have been deposited each month, but none of his bank accounts have been utilized in months, which is surprising. Carlyle is what you might call the local drunk. More than eighty percent of his support payments are spent at the liquor store in town."

The heaviness that's been weighing down my chest the past two weeks amplifies. "Does he have any vehicles registered in his name?"

Brandon flicks through his notepad. "Yes, one. A black Dodge truck, license plate number 44W—"

"2285?" I interrupt, reading the plate on the black truck Hugo has just entered.

When Brandon nods again, dread overwhelms me. Why would Carlyle's only source of transportation be parked in the front of his barn when he lives in the middle of nowhere, miles from the nearest town?

He must still be here.

In urgency, I yank on the cracked window. It doesn't budge. It's locked, held in place by rusty nails hammered into the frame. My heart thrashes against my chest as my suit-covered elbow smashes through the thin glass. Shards of glass jab into my skin, but my brain doesn't register the pain. It's too panicked to register anything.

Hearing the shattering of glass, Hugo emerges from the black truck and glances up at me. "Where's Isabelle?" My voice rumbles in the crisp morning.

He cranks his head to the left before pointing to the far corner of the property. Isabelle is walking toward a white barn on the very edge of the horizon. Compared to the filthy paint-peeling barn Hugo is standing next to, the one she's approaching is spotlessly clean, glimmering in the morning sunlight—just like Megan's secret room.

Panic scorches through my veins. "Get Isabelle!"

Hugo freezes for all of two seconds before he takes off in her direction, the urgency in my tone undeniable.

When the seriousness of the situation dawns on Brandon, he shadows my rush down the rickety stairs. My body doesn't appreciate the cooling effects of the crisp morning on its over-heated skin when I sprint out of the house. Nothing but reaching Isabelle is on my mind.

Due to the overgrown fields, only the roof of the barn is visible as I sprint to Isabelle. Terror thickens my veins as horrid thought after horrid thought filters through my brain. My lungs burn from a lack of oxygen, but I continue. I'll never breathe unaided again if Isabelle gets hurt on my watch.

"My name is Brandon James. I'm an FBI field agent. My number is 443567. I need an ambulance, and a police unit brought to 15634 Snow Mountain Road, Parkerville," Brandon pants heavily into his phone.

My concern for Isabelle outweighs the fact he's calling in the authorities. He can call anyone he wants as long as it means Isabelle is safe.

When I reach the clearing on which the barn is located, I spot a cracked open door at the side. I race for it, my legs pumping as fast as my heart. When I break through the partially opened barn door, my stomach launches into my throat. A horrific smell is lingering in the air. It smells like death and hell all rolled into one.

"Holy fuck," Brandon mumbles when he too discovers the horrifying image in front of us.

I shoot my eyes sideways when a sob sounds through my

ears. Huddled in the barn is Hugo. He's sitting on the hay-covered ground with Isabelle cradled in his lap. Her face is buried into his chest, and his hand is covering her eyes.

With my heart in my throat, I rush for her. She jumps out of her skin when I remove her from Hugo's lap. "It's okay, Isabelle." My eyes rake her body to ensure she's uninjured. The wild beat of my heart weakens when I discover she's unharmed. "I've got you."

When she burrows her nose into my neck with the assistance of Hugo, I remove my jacket to place it over her shuddering shoulders. Once she's secure in my lap, my eyes shift to the man hanging from the beam. The unnatural color of his skin reveals why the smell is so potent. He's been deceased so long, his skin is no longer covering his body.

"We need to move quickly. The authorities have been called in." Although I'd love nothing more to comfort Isabelle for a few more minutes, here is not the place to do it. I also don't want it done in an interrogation room at the Parkerville Sheriff's Office. "Go help Hunter pack up his equipment, then we'll head to my cabin..."

I stop talking when Isabelle suddenly leaps out of my arms. She makes a beeline for the barn door, barging past Brandon a mere second before her heaving petite body breaks through the eerily quiet morning.

25

ISAAC

"Take her to the cabin as originally planned. We have every angle covered. Megan won't get close to Nick or his family without us first knowing about it. You need to concentrate on Isabelle."

Hunter's eyes drift to Isabelle, who is sitting in the back passenger seat of my town car. She's far away in thought. Her beautiful tear-stained eyes are peering up at the brilliant blue sky. After she was sick, I carried her to the car in my arms. Her body felt warm, but shivers still racked through her during our short trip.

Hunter gathers a satellite phone and a charger from his van to hand them to me. "I'll call you if anything comes up."

"I'll drive you out to the cabin, then I'll head back to Raven-shoe to update my guy." Hugo shifts his focus to Brandon, who is standing at his right. "Brandon will stay here until the authorities arrive. He has assured me he won't mention that we were here."

Brandon nods. "I'll tell them I was conducting further investigations on Megan as part of your case." Nervousness is heard in his tone. I don't know if he's scared or worried. Considering he's peering at Isabelle, I'd say it is the latter. "I'll take care of everything here as long as you promise to look after her. I still recall the first time I saw a dead body. I'll never forget it, and my discovery wasn't as gruesome as that."

I tilt my head to Isabelle. She's no longer looking up at the sky. Her beautiful eyes are locked on me. When she notices she's captured my attention, her lips curve into an uneasy smile.

"I'll take care of her." Eager to get things wrapped up, I devote my focus back to Hunter. "Call Ryan to give him the latest. It's out of his jurisdiction, and most likely a suicide, but I don't want him in the dark. He has resources the rest of us don't, and he owes me, so if the need arises, I'll call in a favor."

"All right." Hunter jerks up his chin before straying his eyes to the horizon. "But we should get moving before we lose the opportunity."

I nod. Sirens are growing louder with every second that passes. Hugo and Hunter shake hands before sliding into their transportation of choice, leaving me standing across from a man who falsely believes he cares for Isabelle as much as I do. He's wrong because nothing could compare to the feelings I have for her. They're irrepressible and unexplainable.

"I'll ensure you're compensated for your assistance with this matter."

Brandon's lips crimp. "Thanks, but payment isn't necessary. I don't do this for money."

I halfheartedly nod. "Then, I guess I'll owe you."

"That's got to be more valuable than any monetary amount, surely." Even though his comment could be construed as witty, his tone doesn't allude to that. "It was a pleasure meeting you, Isaac."

When I accept the hand he's holding out, I'm shocked by how firm his handshake is. He seems a little too timid to pull off such a firm shake. "Likewise."

After a final glance at Megan's house, I slide into the back seat of my town car. My mind is jumbled with the diverse range of situations I've been hammering with it the past two months. So much is happening in my private life right now. If I don't stop and assess each task, mistakes are bound to happen. By sticking with my original plan of taking Isabelle to my cabin in the foothills of the mountain, it'll give me a chance to evaluate everything while also taking care of her. It will also bide some time for Hunter and his team to trace who placed the equipment in Isabelle's apartment before she returns there.

As Hugo glides my car down the dusty driveway, I seize Isabelle's wrist and carefully pull her over to sit side-straddled on my lap. She plasters her body as close to mine as possible before burrowing her nose into my neck.

The pulse beeping through her body is heard in her words when she murmurs, "The academy tries to prepare you for stuff like this, but nothing can prepare you for the smell. It was..." A shiver runs through her body before her tears wet the collar of my shirt. "I can still smell it on my skin."

Hugo's eyes meet mine in the rearview mirror. After a swift lift of my chin, he raises the privacy partition without a word spilling from my lips. Once the barrier is in place, I undo the top three buttons of my business shirt before tugging it out of my trousers.

Isabelle's tear-filled eyes stare into mine. "I... can't."

"I'm only going to hold you, baby," I promise, staring into her glistening eyes. "I'll remove the smell from your skin with my own. Then, once we arrive at the cabin, I'll wash it all away."

After sucking in a shaky breath, she nods. Because of the confines of the backseat, she has to assist in yanking her tight jeans down her shaking thighs. Once they're dumped onto the floor, I raise her long-sleeve shirt over her head. Her hair flicks out a mere second before it falls down her back in dark, shiny waves.

Once she's in nothing but her bra and panties, I draw her back into my chest. She splays her body into mine, every soft curve melting against me. When she trembles as if she is cold, I snag my jacket from the floor to cover her shoulders and back. She's shaking more from shock than the temperature. Hugo turned the heat up the instant he raised the barrier, but I'm happy to pretend she's cold if it keeps her tears at bay.

In silence, I glide my hand up and down her back, offering her wordless comfort. The scene she just witnessed was horrific, and the smell was unlike anything I've ever sampled before, so I can comprehend her shocked reaction. Yes, she's a federal agent, but she's still a human being. I'd be more concerned if she weren't reacting the way she is. Only a woman without a heart would witness something so horrific and not react.

* * *

BY THE TIME we arrive at my cabin, Isabelle has stopped shuddering, and she managed a few hours of restless sleep in my arms. My eyes float to the privacy partition when Hugo lowers it down an inch. "Give me a few minutes to scope the premises."

I nod, acknowledging his request. "Make it quick."

The deep rumble of my voice causes Isabelle to stir, but when Hugo closes his door with more force than needed, her head rises off my chest. She scans our location for a few seconds before the faintest smile creeps onto her lips.

Noticing angry black marks careening down her cheeks, I lick my thumb before rubbing it under her eyes, clearing away the smears of mascara formed there. Once all the evidence of her tears has been removed, my thumb lowers to the cupid's bow in her lip. My touch is as soft as a feather, but a shiver still darts through Isabelle's body. A smirk etches on my mouth, loving that even in the most distressing circumstances, she can't help but react to my touch.

When three brief taps hit the driver's side back window, Hugo's way of indicating the cabin is clear of any threats, I place Isabelle onto the seat next to me. After adjusting my jacket to ensure she's covered, I fling open the car door. Pine trees and varnished wood infiltrate my senses the instant I step outside. Out of respect for Isabelle, Hugo has made himself scarce, but just in case, Isabelle holds down the hem of my jacket to maintain her modesty.

As we pace toward the log cabin, her freshly-woken eyes eagerly absorb all its quirky features. This is where I come when I need to get away. I came here the weekend I was arrested. I had to put distance between Isabelle and me, or I would have ended up at her apartment, seeking answers to the hundreds of questions filtering through my mind after she left Friday night.

There's no cell phone reception or internet connection in this part of the forest. Power is supplied by a generator in a shed attached to the back of the property, and an open wood fireplace heats the living room. Catherine organized for the cabin's caretakers to crank the generator, ignite the fire, and replenish the fridge when I called her on the drive to Parkerville last night, so we have everything we need for a two-day stay.

Freshly picked wildflowers infuse the air when we walk into the living room of the cabin. The caretakers are a retired couple who live next door. Catherine must have told them I was bringing Isabelle as this is the first time they've left flowers.

After placing my keys onto the side table, I shift on my feet to face Isabelle. "Do you want something to eat before you shower?" She hasn't eaten anything but the sugar-coated donuts Hugo arrived at our room with this morning. It's now a little after noon, so she may be hungry.

She shakes her head. "No, I'd rather shower first." Her voice is low, but it isn't as shaky as it was earlier.

"Okay. Give me a minute to see Hugo off, then I'll come shower you."

Her pupils widen before she nods. She heard my comment as I had intended. I'm going to take care of her as I've craved from the moment she crashed into me at the airport.

"The main bedroom is just through that door."

When I point to the wooden door on her left, she cranks her neck back to peer at it. "Okay, I'll wait for you in there." She paces toward the door, spinning back around just before she enters. "Can you thank Hugo for helping me today?" Her brows pull together tightly as her teeth get friendly with her lower lip. "My screams will be ringing in his ears for weeks to come."

"It's his job to protect you, Isabelle, so you don't need to commend him for doing the job he's paid to do."

"I know, but I still want him to know I'm grateful." She stares at me with begging, tear-filled eyes. "Please tell him."

She waits for me to nod before entering the main bedroom. Once she closes the door, I walk back out onto the veranda. After scanning the densely treed property, I find Hugo near the driveway talking on the satellite phone Hunter gave me earlier.

"We'll go over more specifics when I return... all right... I'll speak to you tonight. Bye, Hawke." After disconnecting his call and handing me his phone, Hugo gestures his head to the cabin. "How is she?"

"She's all right, a little rattled, but proving to be stronger than I thought."

Hugo grins, the twist of his lips amusing. "Yeah, I've seen a different side to her the past week. She's a powerhouse when she wants to be. At least I was left uninjured after our run-in. Hunter learned the hard way that she isn't to be messed with."

My brow arches. This is the first I'm hearing about any confrontation between Isabelle and Hunter.

Hugo chuckles. "Hey, I'm no snitch. If you want to know all the deets, you'll have to pry it out of Hunter or Izzy."

I shove my hands in the pockets of my suit before glaring at him. Hugo is the first man I've come across who doesn't quake in his boots from my furious glare. *Stupid bastard.*

As my brain tries to devise acceptable praise for Hugo, I remain quiet. It isn't that I don't like issuing praise, but my staff's acclamations usually come in a monetary form. Hugo will be rewarded for aiding Isabelle today with a hefty bonus check, but I told Isabelle I'd thank him on her behalf, so I'll follow through on my agreement.

"Isabelle wanted me to thank—"

"Don't thank me, Isaac." Hugo swipes his hand in front of himself. "I should have never let her out of my sight."

I don't refute his statement since everything he said is true.

Happy to avoid an awkward conversation, Hugo heads back to my town car. "Do you want me to collect you tomorrow afternoon?"

A switch inside me flicks on as excitement heats my blood. "No, I'll take the DB out for a spin."

Hugo waggles his brows before securing the charger for the satellite phone off the passenger seat. "Just in case you need it."

After handing the equipment to me, he thrusts out his hand in offering. With a wry grin, I shift the satellite phone to my left hand before accepting his gesture. He uses my imbalance to his advantage. He pulls me in for a man-hug, his hand slapping my back as if he's more a friend than an employee. "Call if you need me."

"Thanks. I will."

I walk back into the cabin without a backward glance, hating the mirth his tone was dripped in.

26

ISABELLE

I've always trusted my intuition. From now on, I'm going to listen to it. Something was drawing me to the barn, but every step I took had my legs quivering more. It wasn't just the horrifying visual that caused my distress, it was the unimaginable smell.

I never want to smell anything like that ever again.

When I joined the Bureau, I envisioned that I'd help people like my Uncle Tobias helped me, but I haven't done anything helpful since I started my position six months ago. If anything, I've hindered more people than I've aided. And even more concerning than that is the fact I've hurt the people I care about the most. Maybe I'm not cut out to be an agent. Perhaps I'm not strong enough to handle this type of career.

My somber thoughts are interrupted by a door creaking open. My eyes float up from the brown shag rug to where the noise came from. When my eyes lock in on Isaac leaning on the doorjamb, watching me cautiously, my heart skips a beat. His white dress shirt is rolled up at the sleeves, and its collar is stained with the mascara that ran down my face when he carried me to the car.

After his eyes finish their lengthy appraisal of my body, he pushes off his feet and heads my way. Every step he takes makes my pulse intensify. My heart grew so large it barely fits in my chest from the attentiveness he displayed during our drive to the cabin. I've never felt safer and protected than I do now.

Without a syllable seeping from his lips, he scoops me into his arms, then carries me to the other side of the master suite. His manly scent invades my every waking sense. It's the only smell capable of removing the putrid odor embedded on my skin.

My breath hitches halfway between my lungs and my throat when the white-washed door is pushed open. The first thing my gaze locks in on is a canopy of trees swaying in the breeze above the glass ceiling. Potted plants and hanging pots cover nearly every free surface, and a double-headed shower sits on the right-hand side wall. The backsplash has been done with smooth pebble rocks, adding a touch of allure to the rustic design of the space. Bamboo walls cover three sides of the room, leaving one remaining wall, which is made entirely out of glass, providing endless views of the dense forest the cabin backs up to.

When I notice a copper clawfoot tub sitting in front of a glass wall, my eyes shoot to Isaac in silent questioning. A devilish smirk tugs his lips high before he nods. After placing me onto the speckled white stone countertop, he turns the bathtub faucets on full blast. Jasmine and lilies filter in the air when he places fragrant bath products into the massive flow of water.

Once the tub is full, he toes off his shoes, kicks them to the side, then turns around to face me. Tears once again well in my eyes, but this time they're from the tender possessiveness in his unique eyes.

"Isabelle... don't. Please don't cry."

Isaac crosses the room with a sense of urgency, reaching me in less than a breath. His thumbs brush away the tears before they fall on my face as his eyes nurture me as only they can. The steam from the water flowing into the bathtub and the heat radiating off him soon have my cheeks flushing.

The longer I stare into his mesmerizing eyes, the more my mind is freed of the horrific incident I witnessed. In no time at all, it's just the man who wakes my every sense with nothing but the brush of his fingertip and me.

The air shifts when he glides the back of his hand down my cheeks. He knows what has caused their change in coloring. He knows what he does to me. When his index finger traces my lips, his touch is so tender, it can barely be classified as a touch. It's like a cloud floating by my face—soft and gentle.

When my teeth graze the pad of his finger, the ache gnawing my chest lowers to my soaked pussy. He tastes delicious. Manly, yet oh-so-perfect. A needy, animalistic groan rips from Isaac's throat when I suck his finger into my mouth. He stares down at me with lusty eyes before taking a step back, freeing his finger from my mouth.

"I need to take care of you."

"You are." My voice is a husky whisper, full of unmissable yearnings. "In the best way you know how."

For the first time, a wash of hesitation crosses Isaac's face.

"I want this," I whisper breathlessly as my eyes dance between his. "I want you."

As I undo the buttons on his suit jacket, I keep my eyes planted on him. He maintains my eye contact until the very last button is unclasped. When I shimmy his coat off my shoulders, air hisses between his teeth. His gaze is hungry and wanton, and one hundred percent focused on me.

After flicking off my ballet flats, I pop down from the counter. I pace toward him with my hips swinging and my eyes wide, not the least bit confronted that I'm standing before him in mismatched panties and a push-up bra. I didn't expect to see him this weekend, so I didn't pack for the occasion. If the unbridled look of lust in his eyes and the massive bulge in the crotch of his pants is anything to go by, I don't think he's noticed my silk bra doesn't match my cotton panties.

I sway when I stand in front of him. The sheer sight of his handsome face takes my breath away. "Take it all away. Mark me with your mouth. Your body. Your scent—"

Before the final word escapes my mouth, Isaac pounces. A knee-knocking blur of teeth, lips, and tongue soon have me purring like a kitten. His kiss reflects his hunger. It tells me he's starved of my taste, and that he'll never get enough.

The coolness of the countertop gives relief to my over-heated skin when he plants my backside where he placed it when we entered the bathroom. Not relinquishing my mouth from his, his hand slithers up my damp, slick skin, only stopping to cup my aching breast. He rolls my nipple between his index finger and thumb, his talented hand turning my breaths ragged in under a minute.

When he slides a second hand beneath the waistband of my panties, the muscles in my stomach bunch. His thumb circles my clit, forcing my back to arch.

"Isaac..." I moan in a breathless pant.

His mouth steals every wispy moan and grunt erupting from my throat. He laps them up as effectively as he toys with my clit, bringing me to the edge so quickly, giddiness clusters in my head. My sprint to release gains momentum like a tsunami. It's a blinding, soul-stealing pace.

Isaac tugs on my bottom lip one last time before his dedication moves to my neck. My core tightens when he marks my skin with his teeth and lips. I love being claimed by him. Being devoured. Taken.

As his relentless circular pattern on my clit continues, my hips instinctively gyrate. I'm close to toppling over the brink, but my body is yearning for more. It wants more of him—his touch, his smell.

Just him.

Intuiting my needs, Isaac pushes two fingers into my soaked pussy. When he flicks the bud of nerves inside me, my head crashes into the vanity mirror. My body doesn't register the pain. All it can feel is pleasure. It's shivering in delight.

Storm clouds form in the sky just as fast as my looming release gathers intensity. It hisses and cracks as effectively as me when Isaac clamps his teeth on my erect nipple. His bite sends me freefalling over the edge.

As his name is torn from my throat, my hands dart out in search of something I can tether to, to lessen the spasms rocketing through my body. After one hand clasps the copper faucet and the other secures a firm hold on Isaac's shoulder, my pussy clenches around his fingers as I ride the intensity of my awe-inspiring orgasm.

"Eyes, Isabelle. Give me your eyes."

When I do, he watches me unravel beneath him, loving that my body submitted to him without him removing an article of clothing.

Several fierce, tremoring minutes later, I loosen my grip on his shoulder to tackle with the pearl buttons of his shirt. My movements are frantic and rushed. I'm incapable of thinking rationally when he's nearby. Pleasure shoots through my core when his trousers and black boxers closely follow the removal of his shirt. As my eyes scan his chiseled body, my mouth dries. It's too perfect to describe. Athletic, yet with a heart-cranking scattering of muscles in all the right places. I swear there's not an ounce of fat on him, except in much-needed regions. His cock is so magnificent, it almost hurts to look at it—thick, long, and mouthwateringly delicious.

After curling his arm around my back, he carries me to the double-headed shower. While he twists on the shower knobs, I nibble on the day-old stubble on his jaw. Once the water is heated to a comfortable temperature, Isaac positions us until we're under the spout of liquid flowing from the copper showerhead.

Warm water drenches my hair before sliding down my face to cling to the curve in my top lip. Isaac laps up every drop that fails to escape the bow of my mouth before adjusting my position. He tilts my back to a forty-five-degree angle, encouraging my feet to dig into his spectacular backside. He grips my neck with one hand before securing a firm hold on my right hip with the other. Even being slippery standing in the shower with no walls to support my weight, I'm not the least bit concerned that he'll drop me. His secure hold makes it seem as if I'm as light as a feather.

The muscles in his abdomen constrict when he lines up his cock with the entrance of my pussy. His eyes collide with mine for the quickest second before he hilts me in one swift, fluid motion. An aching zing fires through to my core from being stretched so wide, but it isn't a painful ache. It's so pleasurable, passion dashes through my body.

His hold aids him in gliding me up and down his rigid cock. He fucks me at a pace that has me eagerly chasing the next wave. The water tumbling down my chest, past my breasts, and over my throbbing clit adds to our combustible lovemaking. It makes me hot all over while giving relief to the brutal pounds my pussy is being hit with.

"Pinch your nipples, Isabelle." Isaac's deep timbre vibrates right through to my drenched pussy. "Show me how horny you are, baby. I want to watch you touch yourself."

Oh, god.

Confident he'd never drop me, I remove my arms from around his shoulders and cup my breasts. I squeeze them together before tweaking my nipples like he always does. It should feel stupid fondling myself while being fucked beyond recognition, but it doesn't. The wild grunts Isaac releases as I toy with my breasts have my core contracting so fast, my next climax is mere seconds away.

"Eyes, Isabelle," he demands, intuiting me as only he can. "I want to watch you unravel, to see your pupils dilate and your eyes spark before pretty little moans tear from your throat."

His pumps become more frantic, more precise. Every stroke hits that spot deep inside me making my core clench tighter and my pussy get wetter.

"Oh... ah... oh my god."

When Isaac shifts his head to the side, his nostrils flare, and his grip on my neck tightens. Its firmness sends bolts of pleasure down my spine. Immensely interested in discovering what he's glaring at, I stray my eyes in the direction he's looking. My pussy milks his cock when a visual too risqué for words enters my vision. Because storm clouds are hovering above our heads, and the bathroom light is switched off, our reflection is bouncing back from the darkened glass wall. It isn't as bright as a mirror, but it's clear enough I can see every muscle in Isaac's flawless body contracting as he pounds into me without restraint. The image reflecting back is so primal, so raw, so... *Oh!*

"Eyes, Isabelle!" His rough command adds to the violent shakes hammering me as another orgasm scorches through my veins. "You're so gorgeous when you come. So sexy. So fucking beautiful."

Isaac waits for my shudders to lessen before stepping us out of the spray. When he withdraws his still-throbbing cock, I feel instantly hollow. The empty feeling doesn't linger for long. The image of Isaac stroking himself sends fiery warmth spreading across every inch of my body.

He drags his hand to the base before returning it to the crown, his pumps quick, almost brutal. When his hooded eyes collide with mine, my name comes tearing out of his throat in sync with hot cum shooting out of his swollen knob. It splashes over my stomach and halfway up my chest, coating me as effectively as my arousal drenched his cock.

He continues his seamless pumps until every drop of cum is expelled, then he lifts his hand to rub it into my skin. My heart swells when he smears his still-warm semen over my chest, my stomach, around my neck, and down my arms. He's keeping his word on washing away the horrid scent embedded on my skin by replacing it with his own intoxicating smell. And, at the same time, he's once again claiming me as his.

27

———————

ISABELLE

"Isabelle," says a deep voice to my left. "Wake up!"

Jolting, my torso shoots off the bed as my bewildered eyes bounce around an unknown room. It takes me several terrifying seconds to realize I'm in the suite of Isaac's cabin. My shirt is damp from sweat, and my heart is wildly beating.

I suffocate a scream when Isaac's hand unexpectedly brushes my shoulder. "You're okay. You're safe," he croons, his voice low and nurturing.

Bedsheets shuffling sounds through my ears when he molds the front of his body to my heavily panting back. He cocoons his body around mine, making me feel safe and protected. No words filter from his mouth. He just patiently waits for me to regather the composure I lost in the midst of a nightmare. Yesterday morning's unfathomable event just replayed in explicit detail in my dreams. It felt so real, I thought

I was back in the barn watching Carlyle's skin drip from his body.

When a brutal shudder tremors through me, Isaac tugs me in closer. My chest puffs out to accommodate my enlarging heart when he presses his lips to my hairline before gliding his hand up and down my arm. His body heat eases the shivers rattling my bones, but it's his protective hold that's greater than any inferno. Now everything he said yesterday makes sense. He's a protector. It's how he keeps those he loves safe while also displaying how much he loves them.

Two-day-old stubble scratches my cheek when I crank my neck back to peer at him. "I love you, Isaac." My voice is still harsh from recently waking up, but it's also filled with emotions.

Isaac's chest swells when he sucks in a big breath. After releasing it, he lowers his eyes to mine. The admiration in them has fresh tears pricking in mine. These tears are more noble than the ones I shed while sleeping.

After kicking off the bedsheets covering my legs, I shift my position until my bottom rests on the balls of my feet, and my face is directly in front of his. He assesses my body with precise detail before the most deliciously wicked smirk curls his plump lips. Not waiting for permission, I seal my mouth over his. His lips are warm and taste like cinnamon and coffee. He must have eaten before rejoining me back in bed.

Our kiss is slow and tender, a sensual mix of gentle nips, plunging tongues, and soft moans. In the process of our heart-stuttering embrace, I somehow go from kneeling on the bed to straddling Isaac's lap. I grind down against him three times, loving that his cock lengthens with every grind I do.

Just as I'm about to rub against him for the fourth time, he slips off the bed, taking me with him. "I want to taste you, Isabelle." His needy words vibrate on my lips. "But first, I have to feed you."

His efficient strides have us reaching the wooden kitchen more quickly than a heartbeat. I huff when he places me on the granite countertop. His kiss awoke my libido, and it was hoping he was on the menu.

Hearing my shameful protest, Isaac pivots around to face me. I'm only wearing one of his short-sleeve t-shirts and modest panties, but he looks at me as if I'm the most precious jewel in the world. "Food first. Then you'll be dessert."

Several core-clenching seconds pass in silence. Isaac is the first to break our intense stare-down. He drops his eyes to watch my tongue leisurely slide across my top lip. Happy I have him right where I want him, I return my tongue to its rightful spot, then lock my eyes with Isaac.

Excitement shoots through me when he mutters, "You'll pay for that."

Stealing my chance to reply, he removes eggs, bacon, and a loaf of bread from the fridge. He doesn't ask what I'd like to eat. That isn't how he operates. He's so confident he can read me, he doesn't feel the need to seek assurance. I'm starving, so I'll happily eat anything he presents without protest. I did the same thing yesterday when he took care of me.

Isaac was attentive and gentle while also being firm when needed. He stressed that nothing I could have done would have made a difference because the gentleman hanging in the barn was most likely deceased before I became an agent. He gave me space to gather my thoughts in peace before offering a shoulder to cry on when the vivid images became too much to bear. He's been perfect in every single way, and my love for him has grown even more substantial the past twenty-four hours.

With loved-up eyes, I hop off the kitchen counter. "Did you need any help?"

Isaac stares at me, dumbfounded. He discovered the hard way that I'm not a skilled cook. One morning, I set the toaster on fire. It wasn't my fault. I wanted my toast a little browner, but when Isaac distracted me with his skillful tongue, I forgot I had pressed the toast button down for the second time.

I twist my lips. "I can make coffee?"

Isaac smiles before pointing to an overhead cabinet above my head. "Coffee and sugar are in there."

For the next twenty minutes, Isaac prepares scrambled eggs, maple syrup bacon, and French toast. The smell filtering through the cabin is nearly as intoxicating as him. I aid him the best I can. I gather the eggshells from the counter and place them in the waste bin before setting the small two-seater table in the living area with cutlery, placemats, and glasses. It's early in the morning, but the setting looks like a romantic date since it's next to an open fireplace.

When Isaac gathers two plates overflowing with scrumptious breakfast treats, I grab the pot of coffee and carton of orange juice. The only audible noise heard for the next several minutes are the moans erupting from my mouth as I sample each delicious item on my plate. Isaac remains quiet, but I can feel him watching me which, in turn, makes my moans more dramatic than necessary. I can't help but tease him.

Satisfied, and full to the brim, I push my plate away before leaning back in my chair. As I rub my almost bulging stomach, I scan the room. It's a decent size, nearly the size of the living room in my apartment, but exposed vaulted ceilings give it a homey feel. The roof is curved just like the half circle window in Isaac's bedroom, and it is varnished in the same color. A framed oil painting of a country setting hangs above the open fireplace, and a selection of framed photos are below it.

My inner monologue trails off when my eyes zoom in on a picture in the center of the mantelpiece. It's of me—sleeping.

I shoot my eyes to Isaac. "When did you take that?"

His lips lift against his mug. "The night you slept at my apartment. That was after you gave me your panties."

When my mouth falls open, he cockily winks. After standing from his seat, he gathers the picture I'm referring to. It's a close-up photo of my face. My eyes are shut, my mouth is ajar, and smears of mascara are under my eyes.

I gag. "Why would you frame that? I look wretched."

Isaac's grin slackens as he murmurs, "It's the only photo I have of you."

A dull ache hits my chest. Because we were forced to keep our relationship a secret, we never got to be an average couple. We didn't go on fancy dates or meet each other's friends and family. We kept our life hidden away, not just from the world, but ourselves as well. Our relationship was never given a chance to get out of the gates since it was shrouded in secrecy from the beginning.

"I'm going to resign from my position at the FBI."

Isaac places my photo back onto the mantel before twisting around to face me. "I don't—"

"I'm not just doing it for you, Isaac." I join him near the fireplace. "I'm also doing it for me. I can't live without you, but I can't have both you and my career, so I'm choosing you above anything else."

He cups my cheek, his thumb rubbing the invisible tears he thinks he sees in my eyes. "If Theresa's investigation is rattling you, don't worry about it. My lawyer is working on having her investigation squashed. She has no credible evidence against you. Once it's cleared, we can be together."

"It isn't IA or Theresa I'm worried about. It's me. I literally can't breathe without you in my life. The past two weeks, everything was numb. Not just my heart, but my entire body." Tears loom in my eyes. "Furthermore, the bureau could transfer me to anywhere in the country on a whim. I don't want that."

He clasps my hand in his, then lifts it to his mouth. Anticipation sparks through me when he kisses my palm. He doesn't need to speak any words to reflect that he cares for me. His actions show it. His dominance. The way he protects me. Every little thing he does demonstrates that he cares for me more than words ever could. Some people may call me naïve, especially since it's so early in our relationship, but I'd give up everything I have to ensure Isaac remains a part of my life.

"I don't care about anything that's happened in your past, Isaac. The vendetta with Col, your fighting career, I don't care about any of it. It's in the past, and it can stay in the past. I want to concentrate on our future. Right here and now. Nothing else matters."

His brows fetter. "So you want to sweep it under the rug, pretend it never happened?"

I shake my head. "No. You'll always remember what happened. Just like you'll always love Ophelia." His shoulders square at my comment, but he remains quiet. "I can live with that, Isaac. As long as I have you in my life, I can handle anything."

He takes a few moments to consider my statement before seeking my gaze. "And what happens if this doesn't work?" He gestures his hand between us. "What happens to you then?"

A painful knot twists in my stomach, but I'm confident enough in what we have to shut it down just as quickly as his worries. "That will *never* happen. I'm yours, Isaac, and you're mine."

Pride flashes in his eyes pleased I responded how he'd hoped. That's not the only thing they're displaying, though. Cockiness is also beaming out of him. I wonder if I can shut it down just as swiftly?

"But if it did..." His grin slackens as he glares at me. "... I'll just find another sugar daddy to take care of me."

My knees buckle when a sexy growl emits from his mouth. He yanks me closer to him by gripping my ass cheeks, plastering my body to his. When his mouth seals over mine, I inwardly cheer at the success of my tease. His kiss is dominating, greedy, and toe-curling good. It promises his next set of words is nothing but a guarantee.

"I'll ruin you, so you'll never want another man."

I stare into his heavy-lidded gaze. "You already have."

Plates shatter when Isaac clears the dining room table with his arm. Once the plates, cups, and cutlery are scattered onto the floor, he plants my backside onto the tabletop before inching his hand toward my shirt. A cool breeze buds my nipples when he shreds the rigid material straight off my chest. It falls to the ground like tissue paper, no match for his brutal force. The dominance radiating out of him steals the air from my lungs. I've never seen him so unhinged before.

He shoves my shoulder until my back is splayed on the table, and my legs are dangling over the edge. I eye him curiously when he glides my panties down my thighs. He's always been more a panties-shredder than a remover.

"I'm adding these to my private collection." Dampness pools between my legs when he raises them to his nose to take in a huge whiff. "You always smell so fucking good."

Oh, god. I think I just had a mini-orgasm.

After slipping the damp material into his pocket, he yanks his trousers to his knees. My eyes widen when his cock springs free from his trunks. It is so big, so thick, so drool-worthy.

"I'm dying to taste you, Isabelle, but you need to be taught a lesson, so it must wait."

A long, salivating groan rolls up my throat when he lunges forward, stuffing his densely-veined cock into my ravenous pussy. Because I wasn't prepared for his onslaught, it takes many frantic pumps for lust to overtake the pain associated with taking a man as large as him without foreplay, but when it does, our exchange is pure brilliance. His manly scent infuses the air as his big cock pounds me toward hysteria.

"Do you like teasing me, Isabelle?" A bead of sweat rolls down his cheek before splashing onto my stomach. The heat bristling between us is not caused by the fire roaring on our left —it is from him, the man who invades my every thought even when I'm asleep. "Answer me, Isabelle."

The rough arrogance of his voice sends tingles darting down my spine. My climax is teetering, dangerously close to freefalling, but it won't happen without Isaac, especially if I refuse to answer his question. So, with that in mind, I chew on my bottom lip before nodding. I love forcing his dominant side to be unleashed. Knowing I have the power to unhinge a man with authority like Isaac is euphoric. Nothing rattles him except his jealousy.

"Wrong answer," Isaac mutters before increasing the tempo of his hips, screwing me until I'm screaming like a madwoman.

28

———————

ISAAC

*I*sabelle learned a valuable lesson today. I do not like being teased, especially when it entails her being touched by another man. I may have sustained her orgasm until she begged for forgiveness. She's a stubborn little thing. Her pleas took longer to spill from her mouth than they did when I made her plead for clemency in my apartment. But, in some ways, I'm just as stubborn, so her begs for forgiveness soon filtered through my ears.

Isabelle rolls her shoulders before leaning deeper into my embrace. "Mmm."

"Does it feel good?" I add an extra squirt of shampoo to her hair before rubbing it into her scalp in a circular motion.

"Uh-huh. Sooo good."

We're lounging in the bath we planned to bathe in yesterday. I'm hoping it will relax my bunched muscles while also taking care of Isabelle. My muscles aren't tense from the vigorous activities we undertook on my dining room table, but because they're aware of the cruel world we must emerge back into this evening. It would be nice to stay out of the rat-race for a few more days, but unfortunately, that's not attainable for a man with my responsibilities.

The only time I turn off my thoughts is when Isabelle is beneath me, but since she can't be attached to my cock twenty-four-seven, we have no choice, we must face reality. Hopefully, someone there will be able to help Isabelle with the terrible nightmares she's having.

After our antics on the dining room table, I carried Isabelle back to our bed. Since she was nearly unconscious, I was confident she'd drift into a peaceful, undisturbed sleep, so you can imagine my shock when she woke up screaming, not even an hour later. When she realized it was just a dream, she tried to put on a brave front, but the fear in her beautiful eyes gave away her deceit.

That's when I carried her into the bathroom to have a bath. I've never been the nurturing type, but Isabelle brings out sides of me I didn't know existed. Caring for her is as natural as breathing to me.

Once the suds have been removed from her hair, I stand from the tub, taking Isabelle with me. Goosebumps prickle her skin when I stride across the room to gather a towel. Winter is approaching, impinging the cabin with a nippy chill—even more so since I didn't re-stoke the fire, knowing we'd be leaving shortly.

"Thank you," Isabelle whispers once I've dried her from the luxurious strands of her hair to the tips of her toes.

I dump the towel on the rail. "Get dressed, then pack your belongings. We should probably head out before the next storm rolls in."

When I peer up at the glass roof, Isabelle follows my gaze. Numerous dark clouds formed the hour we were in the tub. "Good idea." She presses a kiss to my mouth before scurrying into the main bedroom.

I pull on my black slacks and white business shirt left discarded on the floor before gathering my satellite phone off the bedside table. "I have a couple of calls to make before we head off, so I'll wait for you outside."

Isabelle stops yanking her jeans up her legs to turn her worried eyes to mine. "You don't have to hide away to make phone calls, Isaac. You can trust me."

"This isn't about trust, Isabelle. There are just some things I can't disclose to you yet." When she sighs, I bridge the gap between us, my steps fast and efficient. "When I can tell you what's going on, I will, but until then, you need to trust me." I lift my hand to cradle her cheek. "You trust me, don't you?"

She nods. "Yes, because without trust, we'll have nothing."

"Exactly. That's why you need to trust that I wouldn't keep anything from you unless it were important. I wish I could share everything with you now, but I can't... not yet. But when I can, I will. I promise. Okay?"

A smile curls on her lips. "Okay. I can work with that." After straying her eyes over her clothing discarded chaotically throughout our room, she returns them to me. "I should be ready to leave in around twenty minutes. Will that give you enough time to make your calls?"

When I nod, she stares lovingly into my eyes. "Okay, I'll meet you outside in twenty."

"Stop looking at me like that, Isabelle, or we'll never leave this cabin."

"Please."

When my brow arches, a pink hue flushes her cheeks.

"I said that out loud, didn't I?"

My cheeks groan when they rise high. "Do you need me to scratch your itch before I make my calls?" When I step closer to her, I rake my eyes down her seductive body, ensuring she didn't miss the innuendo in my tone.

Her eyes shift to the window at the same time a crack of lightning brightens the late afternoon sky. "Does your car have a hard-top roof?" Her bottom lip drops when I shake my head. "Then I'll meet you outside in twenty minutes."

She's as scared of storms as she is of flying. She must have a vendetta against the sky.

After assuring her I'll keep her safe, I head outside to make my calls. Parker answers his phone on the very first ring.

"Boss."

I drift my eyes back to the cabin to ensure Isabelle isn't within earshot. This is one conversation I never want her to overhear.

Confident the coast is clear, I ask, "Any updates?"

"Two point four million dollars is scheduled to be transferred Thursday morning at nine. The withdrawal will be distributed from your Cayman account."

"Will the funds be traceable?"

Parker barks out a laugh. "No. This isn't my first rodeo."

"Good. Let me know the particulars once it's been processed."

"Will do." His tone is as flat as his personality.

"Parker..."

I hear his phone hit his ear, before, "Yes, boss."

"I want to be there when it's done. I want to make sure it's handled right."

My request is met with a length of silence. I'm so convinced he has hung up on me, I lower my phone from my ear to check our call is still connected. It is. He's just quiet.

I discover why when he growls, "Boss—"

He only says one word, but his tone speaks volumes. "No, Parker. It wasn't a request. I'll be there." I disconnect our call, refusing to answer to a member of my staff. I am the boss. I pay his salary. That means he does as I tell him, not the other way around.

The hairs on my arm bristle when I gallop down the three stairs at the front of the cabin. While heading to the attached garage, I dial a memorized number into my satellite phone.

"Everything all right?" Hugo questions not even three rings later.

"Yes. We'll be leaving the cabin shortly. I want Roger to scan her apartment again before we arrive."

I hear him scrub his chin. "Shouldn't you be instructing Hunter that, since he's your head of security?"

"*Was.* That title is negotiable at the moment. Have Isabelle's apartment scanned and update the security personnel in her building. Tell them no one, not even if they have police credentials, is allowed access to her floor without first running it through me."

"All right." Hugo's reply is reserved like he's dying to say something, but unsure if he will. "What time are you arriving?"

My gaze lifts to the sky. "If the rain holds off, we should be there around four o'clock. I'll drop Isabelle off in the underground garage of her building. Until Regan gets the IA's case dropped, we can't be seen together."

"All right. I'll wait for her in the hallway of her apartment at four."

I cough, warning my throat it better not rattle with nerves before saying, "Isabelle is unaware of the surveillance camera that was in her apartment. I want it to remain that way. She's dealing with enough issues at the moment, we don't need to add more."

"I understand," Hugo replies coolly. "Won't say a peep."

"Because I don't want her left alone, I'll have you stay with her during the day, and I'll stay with her at night. She's still rattled about what she witnessed yesterday."

"Okay, that's understandable; it was pretty horrific." Hugo nervously coughs before asking, "Is Izzy aware of the circumstances that led to your arrest yet?"

My jaw tenses. "No, and I trust since I made you privy to that information, it'll remain that way until I decide otherwise."

"I'd never say anything, Isaac. I just know she'd prefer to hear it from you than another source."

"I plan on telling her when the timing is right. *Now* is not the right time." My tone indicates this isn't up for further discussion. "I'll see you in a few hours."

I'm lowering the satellite phone from my ear when I hear Hugo say, "Before you go."

"Yes," I snap, my agitation over his line of questioning clear.

"Hunter hasn't stopped since he arrived at Parkerville. Cut him some slack."

My back molars grind together when he hangs up on me. I understand what he's saying. Hunter is a loyal employee, and he's a hard worker, but he missed critical information about Nick's stalker, stuff that could have been fatal for Nick and his unborn son. If a mistake affects those I love, I refuse to let it go unpunished. Col's righthand man learned that the hard way.

29

ISABELLE

I flop back with a huff. It only took me two minutes to pack, but since I told Isaac I'd give him twenty to finalize his calls, I have to spend the next eighteen minutes sprawled on a rumpled bed that smells like Isaac and sex mixed together. It's a scent that could be bottled up and sold for millions, but it's making me more restless than calm. I don't even have a phone to occupy my time since Hunter smashed it. A few rounds of Candy Crush would have killed more boredom than brain cells right now.

As my head lolls to the side, I spot Isaac passing the bedroom window. He has a large phone attached to his ear, and his lips are moving. As much as my heart ached that he didn't want to make personal calls in front of me, I understand his hesitation. I deceived him for months, so it'll take even longer than that to regain his trust.

With that in mind, I roll onto my opposite hip, so I can

count the petals of the wildflowers in a vase on the bedside table.

That takes all of ten minutes—a very dull and boring ten minutes. With my boredom paramount, I snatch my satchel off the bedside table and dawdle toward the front door of the cabin. Ten minutes is close to twenty, right?

When cold winds blast through me, I drop my satchel to the ground to fasten the buttons on my Burberry trench coat. No, I didn't pay thousands of dollars for the jacket. Just like my Juicy Couture sweatpants, my coat was another San Francisco thrift shop diamond in the rough. It's amazing what people give to charities when it's no longer in season.

"Dammit!" I murmur when my satchel snags on a nail in the wooden deck, causing a hole approximately the size of a quarter in the bottom right-hand corner.

Wanting to ensure there isn't anything small enough to fall through the hole, I search my satchel. Considering how much it usually houses, it's reasonably empty. There are chocolate wrappers, my Kindle that hasn't been charged in months, my purse, and my FBI-issued pistol.

I stuff the chocolate wrappers into the front pocket of my jeans to ensure they don't slip out before securing the zipper on my satchel. When I take the last three stairs of the porch, in the quietness of the forest, I hear Isaac's deep voice penetrating from around the corner. After hooking my satchel onto my shoulder, I quicken my pace, eager to be near him again. His tone is flat, revealing his mood has somewhat dampened the past twenty minutes.

Panicked it could be something to do with his brother, I

walk even quicker. He notices my approach in an instant, encouraging it with a summoning wiggle of his fingers. When I reach him, I wrap my arms around his midsection before nuzzling my head into his chest. His seductive scent overtakes the dampness in the air compliments to the rapidly-forming clouds. He tugs me in closer before returning his attention to his caller.

"Henry, I have to go. I'll call you again tomorrow morning," he says into a phone that looks as heavy as a brick. "Yes... okay. Bye."

"You and Henry have grown friendly since our weekend away." When he stiffens, I lift my head off his chest to peer into his eyes. "That was Henry, wasn't it?"

Dread rains down on me when he shakes his head. "No, it wasn't."

I just heard him say Henry as clear as day, didn't I?

Oh no.

"Was that Henry's father?" *The suspected mob boss of New York City.*

Isaac hears the accusation in my tone I didn't mean to express. "Don't ask questions you don't want the answer to, Isabelle. I don't want to lie to you—"

"Then don't. Tell the truth."

Over my interrogation, he pulls away from me so swiftly, air blasts my face. When he strides to a vehicle housed under a white cover in a wooden garage attached to the cabin, I quickly follow after him.

"Who were you talking to?"

The low-hanging sun catches the dust filtering in the air,

making it look like fireworks exploding in the darkening sky when he yanks off the car cover. "It was Henry Gottle *Senior*."

The distress that's been plaguing my stomach the two weeks returns stronger than ever. "Why were you talking to him?"

Anger flashes across Isaac's face. "Stop interrogating me, Isabelle. You're not on the job."

"I'm not asking for my job. I'm trying to protect you—"

"You don't need to protect me! It's not your job to protect me!"

"Yes, it is!" My angry voice reverberates through the dense forest. "It's my job to defend you as honorably as you'll defend me." I step closer to him until our heaving chests battle for space. "You said you protect the people you love. It's no different for me. I love you, Isaac, so I'll protect you with everything I have until I take my last breath—"

Before I can comprehend what is happening, a set of delicious lips seal over mine. He attacks my mouth so savagely, my feet lift from the ground. They curl around his waist when he pins me to his car by his crotch. He kisses me senseless, holding nothing back until I'm struggling to remember my name, much less what we were arguing about.

After inching back, he rests his forehead against mine. The uniqueness of his eyes hits me full force from his closeness. They're so beautiful, yet trouble. "Trust me, Isabelle." His low tone indicates his statement is more a plea than a demand. "I'll tell you everything when I can, not when I'm forced."

When I nod, the vibe immediately changes from my submissive response. I'm not meaning to be a brainless bimbo.

I'm just not up for more fighting. Furthermore, he asked me to trust him. I can't do that and interrogate him at the same time. I also can't think straight when he kisses me as he did.

"You do realize, one day, I'll be strong enough to fight my attraction to you."

"No, you won't." His brow curls high as he shakes his head all cocky like. "Just like me hearing you say those three little words. It will forever take my breath away. It will never get old."

I think my heart just burst.

After cupping his jaw, I kiss him gently, relaying how much his words impacted me. My heart swells even more when he allows me to guide the pace of our kiss. That's a huge step for a man as dominant as him

By the time I pull back, I'm breathless and giddy, emotionally high from the raw passion displayed in our kiss. "I love you."

Smiling, Isaac gathers my hands in his jawline, kisses each palm, then places them over his heart.

Now I'm certain my heart has burst.

We stand across from each other in silence, no words needed to express our strange kinship. I never believed in soul mates, but as I stand across from Isaac now, I've never believed in something more. He completes me, he's my other half, and as I said earlier, I'll do anything to keep him safe.

A loud clap of thunder interrupts our love-filled staredown. It came from the clouds above our heads that have made the sky so dark—it seems a lot later than it is. When my eyes float over the classic- looking convertible Isaac pinned me to earlier, I shake like a leaf. It reminds me of a car James Bond would drive, and it's sexy with its top off, but I'm petrified of storms.

I dart my eyes back to Isaac. "Can we put the top on before we leave?"

He smirks a delicious smile before shaking his head. "You can't drive a classic with the top on."

His eyes hold the same glimmer Hugo's did when he told me all about his *baby*.

"Is this your *baby*?"

He nods again, his smile picking up. "A 1963 Aston Martin DB5." His voice is higher than usual since his fondness for his car is filtering through his tone.

When he runs his hand along the curved front fender, jealousy makes itself known with my gut. I have no reason to be jealous when he murmurs, "She rides me *nearly* as good as you do." He snickers at my reaction, loving the quick clench of my thighs. "Come on. Let me take you for a ride." He opens the passenger door before dropping his eyes to mine. "Then perhaps you can take me for one."

WIND WHIPS up my hair when Isaac maneuvers his car through the winding roads at the foothills of the mountain. For the past forty minutes, his concentration remained focused on the road, but I've caught the occasional glance he directed my way. He's loving me sitting shotgun in his baby as much as I'm loving the chance to witness all sides of his personality. He's in his element, and the sexiest I've ever seen him.

Leaning over, I give his trouser-covered thigh a gentle squeeze. When his muscles bunch from my meager touch, I smile, pleased to have sparked a reaction out of him.

The reactions keep coming when I tiptoe my fingers three inches higher. Isaac peers at me beneath lowered lashes, the material of his trousers bunching around his stiff cock. "As much as I'd love nothing more than to feel your lips sliding down my shaft, I need hours, Isabelle. We don't have hours. We only have minutes."

"I could make it quick?"

He smirks, loving my confidence. "Things will never be quick between us." He flashes me his eyes. They're full of honest truths. "Furthermore, what kind of man would I be if I let you please me without returning the favor?"

"Pleasing you pleases me, Isaac."

He growls. It's as hot as hell, but it ends our conversation.

When we arrive at the street my building is located on, my hair is blown out, and my cheeks are flushed from the fresh wind, but nothing can dampen the grin stretched across my face. Sitting in a classic car with a handsome specimen behind the wheel made me feel like Hollywood royalty. Like Frank Sinatra and Ava Gardner undertaking a leisurely Monday afternoon drive.

After lowering his speed, Isaac narrows a baseball cap onto his head before hiding his highly recognizable eyes with aviator sunglasses. "Hugo will be waiting for you in your apartment. I'll be back tonight."

He pulls into the manager's parking space at the front of the elevator banks. Even though I can't see his eyes through his mirrored glasses, I can feel their heat studying my face.

"Okay. I'll see you tonight." I press a kiss to his lips, lingering a little longer when his aftershave stirs up excitement. "I love you."

After kissing my palm, he places it on his chest, swelling my heart to a point of no return.

With reluctance, I climb out of his car and pace to the elevator banks. The flash of a sexy-as-sin smirk is the last thing I see when the elevator doors snap shut with me inside. When I catch my gaze in the mirrored wall, I do a little gig. My pupils are wide, making my brown eyes appear darker than normal, my cheeks are flushed, giving me an illuminating glow, and my lips are swollen from all the kisses we've shared the past two days. Signs of a person in love is all over my face, and for the first time ever, I agree with my body's judgment of the situation. I am in love. Wholly. Deeply. Will never be the same again.

I peer out the elevator when the doors pop open. It hasn't arrived at my floor. It's just conducting a brief stop at the lobby. My heart beats out a funky tune when I spot Brandon a mere second before the doors close. He's talking to a security officer near the reception desk. Things look heated.

"Brandon!"

I dash out of the elevator, scooting past an elderly lady hoping to catch it before it ascends. When Brandon tilts his head to see who is accosting him, my steps slow to a snail pace. Anger is bouncing off him in invisible waves. Not wanting to intrude on his private conversation, I linger to the side.

A short time later, Brandon joins me. He's frowning, his

mood still low. "Are you aware no one can gain access to your floor without it first being approved by Isaac?"

"No, I wasn't aware of that." *But it does sound like something Isaac would do.*

"Not even an agent, for fuck's sake."

His surly mood is off-putting. He's usually the cheerful, friendly one who doesn't let anything get him down.

"What's going on, Brandon? You seem a bit... *stressed*? Is it because I bailed on you at Parkerville? I'm sorry about that, I just wasn't—"

"Don't apologize, Izzy. You have nothing to be sorry for." His tone is lower and sincerer than previously.

After clasping my hand in his, he guides me to a bank of chairs on the far side of the lobby. The security officer he was grappling with watches our every move, but he doesn't encroach enough for me to feel threatened by him.

Brandon plops into a chair before scrubbing a hand over his tired eyes. His unnerving composure has my knees shaking so much, I have no choice but to sit next to him. "What's going on?"

He licks his dry lips before forcing out, "Carlyle Shroud's death came back as a homicide."

I swallow bitterly, my eyes widening. "But he was... *hanging.*"

"I know, but the coroner determined he died before then." He leans across to secure my hand in his. His wish to be close to me makes sense when he says, "They found poison in the food scraps in the kitchen. It looks like whoever killed him did it slowly in the hope it wouldn't be noticed by the authorities."

My stomach lurches as my chest grows heavy.

"It gets worse..." My eyes snap to his, certain things can't get any worse. I'm proven wrong when he adds on, "Megan Shroud is in Ravenshoe. She has been for the past week."

"How? We had protocols in place to ensure we knew her whereabouts."

"We did. Every database in the country was fixated on her. She must not have used public transportation or hired a car."

"Where is she?" My hammering heart is heard in my tone.

"She's paying cash for a motel on the outskirts of town." He nudges his head like the motel he is referring to is outside the revolving door of my building.

"Does Isaac know?"

Brandon shakes his head. "Not yet, but he soon will."

I eye him curiously, seeking more information. He said his statement with too much confidence for it to be hearsay.

He exhales deeply as the vein in his neck works overtime. "The hospital Nick's fiancée is staying at requested a police presence this afternoon. I hacked the hospital's mainframe. Jenni's blood workup showed she had a high dosage of Misoprostol in her system when she gave birth. It's an illegal abortion drug only sold on the black market."

Oh, god. I think I'm going to be sick.

I talk through the hand clamped over my mouth. "Do you believe Megan drugged her?"

Brandon sucks in a sharp breath before nodding. "The drug is found stateside in New York City. Small minority groups use it for terminations when they can't afford a doctor."

"Isaac will... he won't handle this, Brandon... he loves his brother," I murmur through panicked breaths.

"I know. That's why I haven't passed on any of the information to Hugo or Hunter yet. I wanted to get your opinion first." He stares intensely into my eyes, his admiration unexpected but highly craved. "You're the only person I trust, Izzy."

I jump in fright when someone unexpectedly touches my shoulder. Once I've gathered my heart from the floor, I swing my eyes to the person who just scared me half to death. It's the security officer who's been watching our exchange for the past ten minutes. "I'm sorry, Ms. Brahn, but there's a gentleman by the name of Hugo requesting to be informed if you're in the lobby."

I nearly nod until the entirety of my exchange with Brandon trickles through my tired brain. Isaac won't even let my work colleagues see me, so what are the chances he'll let me investigate Megan's reappearance in Ravenshoe?

With my heart in my throat, I shoot my eyes to Brandon. "Do you have your car here?"

Suspicion crosses his face, but he nods all the same.

"I need one final favor—"

"Anything, Izzy," he assures without a snippet of hesitation.

After exhaling a big breath, I devote my attention back to the security officer. "Please inform Hugo that you have not seen me this afternoon."

Ignoring his shocked expression, I clasp Brandon's hand in mine before dashing toward the glass revolving door of my building. With my mind shut down and my heart wildly beating, I can only pray this won't be the last time I break through the doors of this building.

30

ISAAC

Due to traffic, I pull into the lot of my nightclub a little after five o'clock. The drive from my cabin took longer than predicted. I took the scenic route so I could enjoy the vision of Isabelle in the passenger seat of my car. She was dressed in her regular jeans and a beige jacket, but her smile made her dazzle like a diamond in the sun.

Last night was starkly contradicting.

We hardly slept a wink. It wasn't Isabelle's sexual prowess keeping us awake. It was her nightmares. Usually, her dreams are filled with sweet little moans and sighs that make my cock as hard as stone, but last night, she whimpered in her sleep. The ghastly image she witnessed yesterday morning must be playing havoc with her mind. I'll give it a few nights to see if I can settle her dreams by reverting them back to pleasurable fantasies. If not, I'll seek professional advice on helping her through this traumatic time. A shiver runs down my spine when I recall the visual of yesterday morning, so I can imagine how much it plagues Isabelle's thoughts.

After pulling into the manager's spot, I grab the framed photo of Isabelle from my cabin out of the glove compartment. I'm no longer willing to hide my relationship, so I plan to place her photo on my desk for the world to see. She's mine, and I want everyone to be acutely aware of that—including Col Petretti. I'm ready if he makes a move. He won't know what hit him if he threatens Isabelle again.

Tina stops replenishing the glassware under the counter when she hears the back door of the club opening. "Hey, you're back. How did the negotiations go in New York?"

I smirk, pleased my ruse worked. "Good. Everything is great."

As I stride into my office, I shrug off my suit jacket before slinging it over the coat rack. When I glance at my desk, I catch sight of the documents Isabelle presented to me at the dingy hotel. I still can't fathom how Nick was so foolish he didn't read the document his lawyer supplied him. I paid his bill, assuming he had read the full report. I shouldn't be surprised. Nick has always been the goofball who cruises through life, happy to see where things take him. He was the very definition of a 'player.' Which isn't surprising, considering he learned most of his traits from me. That's all changed now, though. His fiancée, Jenni, was his game-changer. Just like Isabelle is mine.

After gathering the documents off my desk, I place them into the top drawer. I've just stored them away when a cell phone rings. My heart gallops when I realize it's my burner phone. I quickly pace across the room to dig it out of the breast pocket of my jacket. There's no name attached to the call—that's not unusual, we like to keep things simple—but I know who is calling me.

"I found Megan," Hunter informs before I can greet him. "I got her on a CTV image at a local deli this morning. I'm back-tracking the video footage so I can follow her through town."

"How long will it take to find her?"

A keyboard being tapped sounds down the line. "Ten, twenty minutes, max."

I'm about to reply, but a figure outside of my office steals my attention. Nick is standing in the middle of the nearly empty dance floor. My club won't fill with patrons for a few more hours. Even being a Monday won't stop hundreds of people from milling through my doors before midnight.

I divert my attention back to my phone. "Let me know as soon as you've found her."

"Will do."

Snapping the phone shut, I stride toward my office door to prop my shoulder on the doorframe. "You know how to fucking pick them." My tone is harsh, still pissed at Nick's stupidity on how he handled the entire Megan incident. He's only twenty-two, but he's an adult, and now a father, so he needs to take care of his responsibilities.

Nick's head shoots sideways as his eyes widen. "Do you know where she is?"

"I'm taking care of it."

When I walk back into my office, Nick quickly follows after me. "What do you mean you're taking care of it?"

I sink into my leather chair before requesting for him to sit in the chair across from me. When he denies my request with a brisk shake of his head, I gesture more firmly. If I know my brother as well as I think I do, he will want to be seated when I show him the information Isabelle unearthed.

Nick sits across from me, his knee bobbing up and down as his nerves get the better of him. I wait for him to hide his nervous twitch before asking, "Why didn't you read the documents your lawyer gave you?"

"What are you talking about?" His high tone exposes his bewilderment. He's genuinely shocked.

I snatch up the original envelope from his lawyer to throw it into his chest. When he realizes what it is, his lips furl. "She told me everything I needed to know—"

"No, she fucking didn't!"

When he continues glaring at me in confusion, I snatch the envelope out of his hand to pull out the documents inside. I flick through the pages until I reach the page Isabelle displayed to me at the motel before returning it to Nick's chest with a shove. "Read it!"

His throat works hard to swallow as he absorbs the information in front of him. "She was never pregnant?"

"She's a fucking virgin."

He stares up at me, disbelief etched all over his pale face.

"When the gynecologist's scan didn't find a fetus, he did a little more research. Her hymen was still intact. You went and got yourself a fucking psycho." My angry roar bounces around my office. "She's been in and out of the psychiatric ward the past year. She fled a few months ago after knocking the orderly out cold."

Nick's face goes white before he jumps out of his chair to pace back and forth in my office. "I fucking knew she wasn't quite right."

His bugged eyes lift to me when my outdated cell phone skates across my desk. I answer it while gathering photos out of my drawer to hand to Nick.

"Yes," I snap down the phone, my mood surly.

"She's staying in a rundown motel on the outskirts of town," Hunter informs me.

My heart rate kicks into overdrive. "Get one of my men to that motel immediately."

"What do you want him to do once he arrives?"

My eyes shift to the photo of Isabelle I just placed on my desk. Several seconds pass in silence as I recall what she said in my town car when we arrived at Megan's family residence. I want to be the man she believes I am, but I also need to protect the people I love.

"Tell him to await further instructions." I'm trying to bide some time so I can properly assess the situation, so careless mistakes aren't made.

"Okay."

When Hunter disconnects our call, heaving echoes through my office. The graphic images on how to complete an illegal cesarean were obviously too much for Nick's stomach to handle. As he wipes away vomit from his bottom lip with the sleeve of his shirt, his pale, sweat-drenched face rises from the waste bin to me.

"How are you taking care of this?" His voice is hoarse from being sick, but there's no denying it's plea. He's begging for me to ensure Megan will never have the chance to hurt him or his family again.

I'm going to uphold my pledge.

"You don't want to know." *And neither do I.*

When I help him off the floor, I stiffen when he mutters, "She could have killed them both."

My eyes seek his gaze, demanding additional details. What does he mean she could have killed them?

My question is answered in the most sickening way. "We found out today that Jenni ingested an abortion drug. That's why she bled out during delivery. It made her placenta erupt... or something like that."

Fury overwhelms me. "Jesus Christ."

I'm about to demand further information, but Nick shuts down my interrogation by stumbling out of my office. "I have to go, I have to get back to Jenni. Ryan is coming to interview her later today."

Just before he breaks through my office door, I call his name. It feels like I've been sucker-punched when his eyes lock with mine. They're brimming with unshed tears, but they're the same pair of eyes that looked up at me in awe when he gave me the gift of life. The same pair of eyes I promised to protect no matter what.

"I'll take care of this. You don't have to worry. Megan will never hurt them again."

The strain tainting Nick's face eases from my statement. After dipping his chin, he walks out of my office.

I suck in much-needed air before pressing my cell to my ear.

"Boss."

My palms slick with sweat when I say seven words I never thought I'd speak. "Take her to my warehouse in Hopeton."

Hunter's deep timbre is rickety when he replies, "My guy is still en route to the motel. I'll let you know when he gets there."

"Good."

I snap my phone shut, not waiting for his response. As my eyes drift to the photo of Isabelle I placed on my desk, I gather my jacket from the coat rack. Once the final button is done up, my cell phone rings. Mercifully, this time around, it's my sleek black iPhone.

The screen displays it's a call from Hugo, so I answer it promptly. "Yes, Hugo."

"Hey, are you guys taking the long route home?"

My brows furrow, but I remain quiet, unsure what he means.

He endeavors to soothe the groove scoured between my brows. "It's nearly five-thirty, and you haven't shown up yet. I thought maybe you went parking."

I freeze as sick fear melds through my veins. "I dropped Isabelle off at her apartment over forty-five minutes ago."

I hear his throat work hard to swallow. "She never arrived at her floor. I've been waiting by the elevator."

A small stint of silence crosses between us as dread over-whelms me. "Find her, Hugo," I demand. "Find her now!"

My hand shakes when I lower my phone from my ear to dial another number. Hunter answers as quickly as he has the past two weeks. "He's still en route."

"I need your help on another task. I need you to find

Isabelle. I dropped her off at her apartment over forty-five minutes ago, and she hasn't been seen since." Nothing but sheer panic resonates in my tone.

"Hold on, I'll log into the security system of her apartment building."

When I pick up the framed photo of Isabelle on my desk, my grip is so staunch, it nearly shatters the glass. My stomach is twisted up in knots, my body's way of advising me something isn't right.

My attention diverts back to my phone when Hunter asks, "What time did you drop her off?"

"Around a quarter to five."

He doesn't respond, but I hear him tapping on a keyboard. "Okay, I have her entering the elevator at the underground garage at 4:43 p.m." He sucks in a breath, killing me with the delay. "She exited at the lobby a minute later."

"She was supposed to go straight to her floor. Why would she stop in the lobby?"

"Hold on, I have to switch from the elevator camera to the lobby." His hearty breaths whistle down the line. "Brandon was in the lobby. She left with him five minutes later."

I lose focus on the last half of his comment when a commotion outside of my office gains my attention. Anger thickens my blood when I see Brandon yanking himself out of my front-door bouncer's firm grip.

"She's here. I found her," I advise into the phone before shutting it down.

My quick strides have me crossing the nightclub floor faster than a heartbeat, only slowing when I fail to find any signs of Isabelle. I thought she was with Brandon.

"Where is she?"

When he spins around to face me, my heart drums my ribcage. His pupils are wide as if he's just seen a ghost, and his lower lip is quivering. His rattled composure sets me on edge, which adds to the crippling weight on my chest.

"Where is she?"

With my panic as high as my anger, I slam Brandon against the wall before securing a firm clutch on his throat. His hands shoot up to my wrist, trying in vain to loosen my grip, but I don't back down. If anything, his wish to fight me has me firming my clutch even more.

I don't restrict his airways enough to kill him, but enough to ensure he'll answer all my questions.

"You have five seconds to tell me where she is, before I—"

"She's at the police station." His words are squeaked through the firm hold I have on his throat. "If you let me go, I'll tell you everything I know."

My nostrils flare as my jaw tenses. I hate being strong-armed, but this is different, isn't it? Nothing is forced when you're protecting the ones you love.

Brandon drops to his knees to suck in numerous big breaths when I release him from my hold. As he replenishes his lungs with oxygen, I clench and unclench my fists, struggling to rein in the anger that's spiraling me out of control.

Once he's satisfied he has normal oxygen levels, Brandon locks his eyes with me. "They arrested Isabelle."

Blood roars through my veins like an out-of-control wild-fire. "IA?"

He shakes his head, his eyes filling with tears. "She was arrested for the murder of Megan Shroud."

To be continued...

Book three—Enigma: The Mystery Unmasked is already available for purchase! Find it here: Enigma: The Mystery Unmasked

Facebook: facebook.com/authorshandi

Instagram: instagram.com/authorshandi

Email: authorshandi@gmail.com

Reader's Group: bit.ly/ShandiBookBabes

Website: authorshandi.com

Newsletter: https://www.subscribepage.com/AuthorShandi

ALSO BY SHANDI BOYES

** Denotes Standalone Books*

<u>Perception Series</u>

<u>Saving Noah</u> *

<u>Fighting Jacob</u> *

<u>Taming Nick</u> *

<u>Redeeming Slater</u> *

<u>Saving Emily</u>

<u>Wrapped Up with Rise Up</u>

<u>Protecting Nicole</u> *

Enigma

Enigma

<u>Unraveling an Enigma</u>

<u>Enigma The Mystery Unmasked</u>

<u>Enigma: The Final Chapter</u>

<u>Beneath The Secrets</u>

<u>Beneath The Sheets</u>

<u>Spy Thy Neighbor</u> *

<u>The Opposite Effect</u> *

I Married a Mob Boss *

Second Shot *

The Way We Are

The Way We Were

Sugar and Spice *

Lady In Waiting

Man in Queue

Couple on Hold

Enigma: The Wedding

Silent Vigilante

Hushed Guardian

Quiet Protector

Enigma: An Isaac Retelling

Twisted Lies *

Bound Series

Chains

Links

Bound

Restrain

The Misfits *

Nanny Dispute *

Russian Mob Chronicles

<u>Nikolai: A Mafia Prince Romance</u>

<u>Nikolai: Taking Back What's Mine</u>

<u>Nikolai: What's Left of Me</u>

<u>Nikolai: Mine to Protect</u>

<u>Asher: My Russian Revenge</u> *

<u>Nikolai: Through the Devil's Eyes</u>

<u>Trey</u> *

The Italian Cartel

Dimitri

Roxanne

Reign

Mafia Ties (Novella)

Maddox

Demi

Ox

Rocco *

Clover *

Smith *

RomCom Standalones

Just Playin' *

<u>Ain't Happenin'</u> *

<u>The Drop Zone</u> *

Very Unlikely *

False Start *

Short Stories - Newsletter Downloads

Christmas Trio *

Falling For A Stranger *

One Night Only Series

Hotshot Boss *

Hotshot Neighbor *

The Bobrov Bratva Series

Wicked Intentions *

Sinful Intentions *

Devious Intentions *

Deadly Intentions *

Coming Soon

Nanny Dispute *

Protecting Nicole (December 26) *